W9-AWK-782

SPQR VIII

THE RIVER GOD'S VENGEANCE

SPQR

Senatus Populusque Romanus

The Senate and the People of Rome

Also by

JOHN MADDOX ROBERTS

SPQR Series

SPQR I: The King's Gambit

SPQR II: The Catiline Conspiracy

SPQR III: The Sacrilege

SPQR IV: The Temple of the Muses

SPQR V: Saturnalia

SPQR VI: Nobody Loves a Centurion

SPQR VII: The Tribune's Curse

The Gabe Treloar Series

The Ghosts of Saigon

Desperate Highways

A Typical American Town

SPQR VIII

THE RIVER GOD'S VENGEANCE

JOHN MADDOX ROBERTS

THOMAS DUNNE BOOKS
ST. MARTIN'S MINOTAUR
NEW YORK

THOMAS DUNNE BOOKS.
An imprint of St. Martin's Press.

For information, address St. Martin's Press, 175 Fifth Avenue,
New York, N.Y. 10010.

Library of Congress Cataloging-in-Publication Data

Roberts, John Maddox.
SPQR VIII : the river god's vengeance / John Maddox Roberts.—1st ed.
p. cm.
ISBN 0-312-32319-0
1. Metellus, Decius Caecilius (Fictitious character)—Fiction. 2. Rome—History—Republic, 265–30 B.C.—Fiction. 3. Private investigators—Rome—Fiction. 4. Tenement houses—Fiction. I. Title: SPQR 8. II. Title: River god's vengeance. III. Title.

PS3568.O23874S676 2004
813'.54—dc22

2003058560

First Edition: January 2004

10 9 8 7 6 5 4 3 2 1

For Barbie Light

Thirty years was too long to be out of touch.

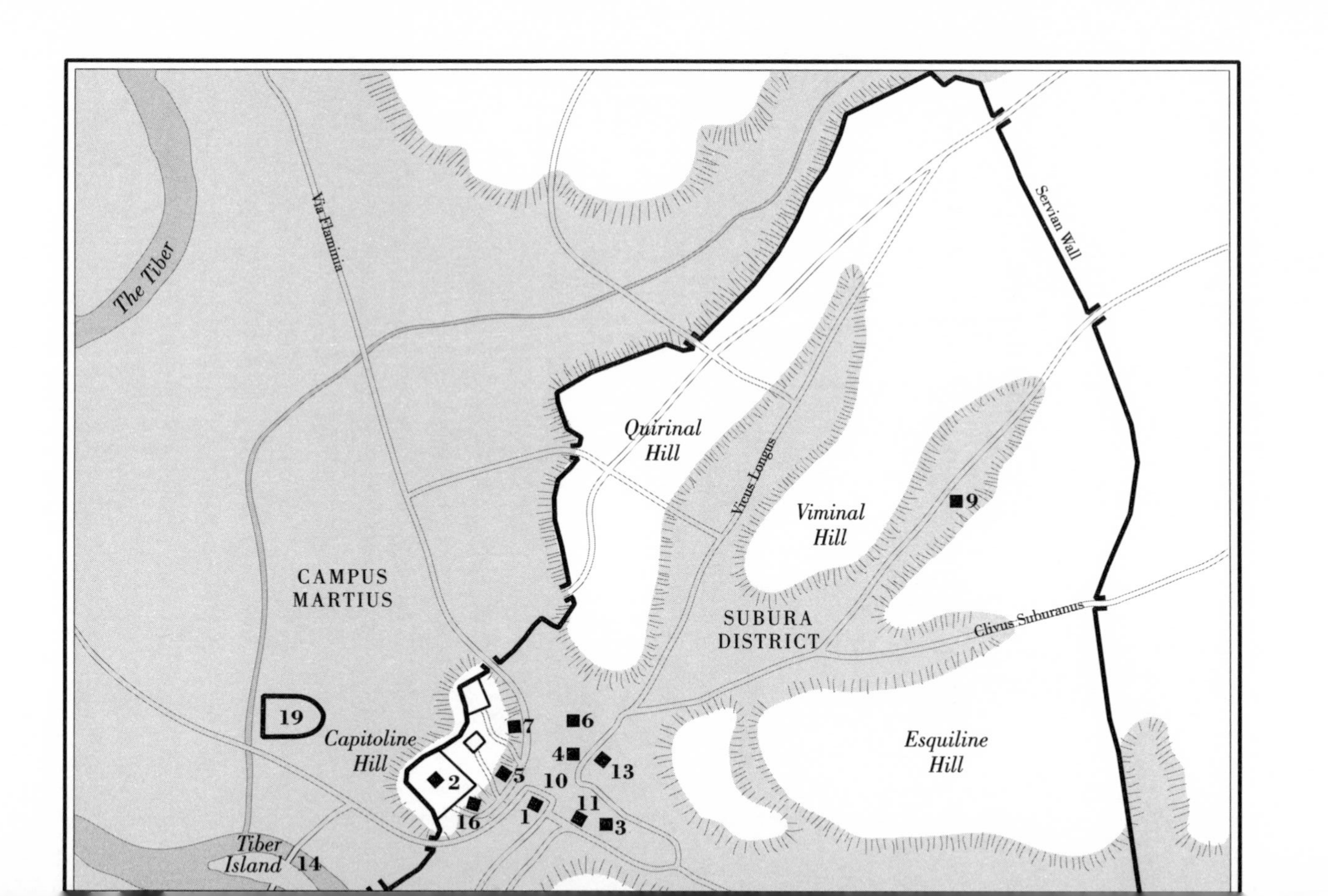

The Tiber
Via Flaminia
Servian Wall
Quirinal Hill
Vicus Longus
Viminal Hill
9
CAMPUS MARTIUS
SUBURA DISTRICT
Clivus Suburanus
19
Capitoline Hill
7
6
4
13
5
10
2
11
16
1
3
Esquiline Hill
Tiber Island
14

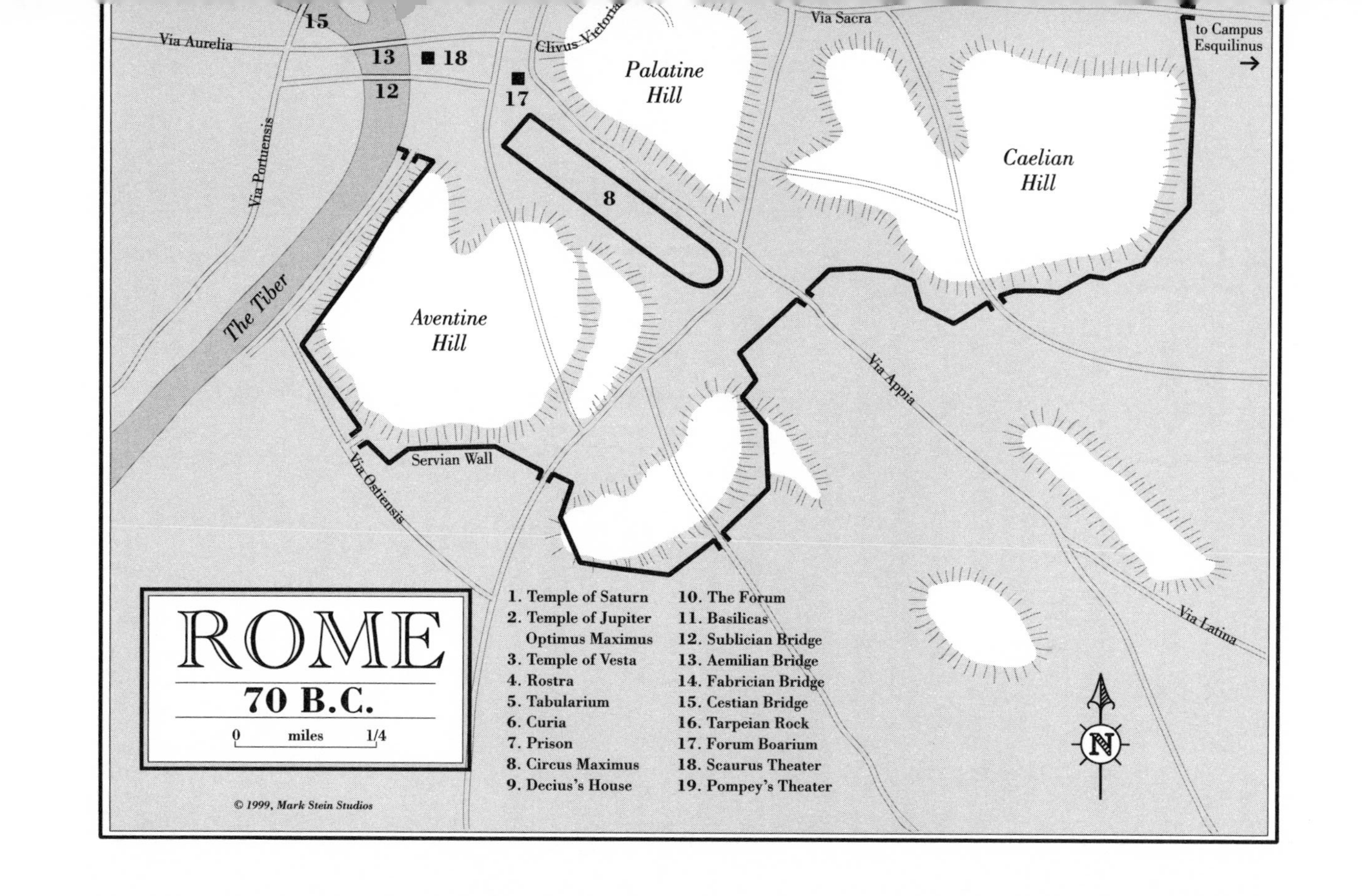
ROME
70 B.C.
0 miles 1/4
© 1999, Mark Stein Studios
1. Temple of Saturn
2. Temple of Jupiter Optimus Maximus
3. Temple of Vesta
4. Rostra
5. Tabularium
6. Curia
7. Prison
8. Circus Maximus
9. Decius's House
10. The Forum
11. Basilicas
12. Sublician Bridge
13. Aemilian Bridge
14. Fabrician Bridge
15. Cestian Bridge
16. Tarpeian Rock
17. Forum Boarium
18. Scaurus Theater
19. Pompey's Theater
Via Aurelia
Via Portuensis
The Tiber
Via Sacra
Clivus Victoria
Palatine Hill
Caelian Hill
Aventine Hill
to Campus Esquilinus →
Servian Wall
Via Ostiensis
Via Appia
Via Latina
N
15
13
18
12
17
8

SPQR VIII

THE RIVER GOD'S VENGEANCE

SPQR

Senatus Populusque Romanus

The Senate and the People of Rome

1

IT WAS THE WORST YEAR IN the history of Rome. Well, perhaps it wasn't quite that bad. There was, for instance, the year that Hannibal defeated our legions at Lake Trasimene, and the year Hannibal obliterated our legions at Cannae. We learned a great deal from Hannibal. Perhaps the worst was the year Brennus and his Gauls overran the City, put it to the sack, and levied an extravagant tribute. In return he gave us one of our best epigrams. When the tribute was weighed out and the consuls protested that the weights were dishonest, the Gaul tossed his sword onto the balance tray and said, "Woe to the vanquished!" He had an excellent grasp of Latin for a Gaul. We took this lesson to heart and applied it ruthlessly to everyone who fell afoul of us in subsequent years.

But those things had happened centuries before. This

was by far the worst year the City had endured in my lifetime. The year of Catilina's conspiracy was a festival by comparison.

In the streets, the gangs of Clodius and Milo, of Plautius Hypsaeus, and several others clashed and rioted daily, abetted by a corrupt Senate whose members clucked collectively over the disorder while, privately and individually, they all supported one gang or another. The political situation was so chaotic that no one was certain, from one day to the next, who held the consulship. If Rome's enemies could have seen how things were in the City, they would have stood amazed.

We did not lack for enemies that year. In the East, Crassus waged desultory war against a series of mostly unoffending nations, gathering strength and treasure for his projected war against Parthia. In the North, Caesar seemed determined to exterminate the entire Gaulish race. Not only that, but he had even made an assault upon the misty, myth-shrouded island of Britannia. The commons praised Caesar's martial efforts because it is always pleasant to contemplate the slaughter of foreigners at a great distance. But the treasures flowing Romeward from Gaul were more than offset by the hordes of cheap Gaulish slaves flooding Italy, further depressing the value of everything, driving the few remaining southern Italian peasants off their land to make way for the ever-expanding, slave-worked *latifundia.*

As you may well imagine, this was the ideal time for me, Decius Caecilius Metellus the Younger, to rise up and fulfill my destiny as the savior of the State, but I couldn't because I was too busy. This was the year of my aedileship.

Of all the offices of the Roman State, that of aedile is the most onerous, disagreeable, demanding, and, by a huge margin, the most expensive. The aediles have oversight of the markets, streets, and buildings of the cities. They have to prosecute usury, assure the honesty of building contractors, drive forbidden cults from the City, keep the sewers and drains clean and in working order, and inspect the brothels.

Worst of all are the Games.

The *ludi* are the official Games of the State, and they include plays in the theaters, chariot races, public feasts, and all the special celebrations in honor of the gods. The State provides only a stingy allotment for these activities, the sums set in a day when Rome and the Games were far smaller than they are now. Any cost beyond the allotment, which is to say about 90 percent of the expense by that time, have to be paid for by the aediles themselves.

And then there were the *munera*. For *munera* you needed wild beasts and gladiators, and a single *munera* could easily cost more than all the other Games of the year put together. Foreigners often think that the *munera* are State Games, but they are not. They are funeral games put on entirely at the expense of individuals. In the past, certain aediles, courting popularity, put on *munera* along with their required *ludi*. Soon, the populace expected and demanded them.

The ironic thing was that the aedileship was not strictly required for election to higher office. Theoretically, one was allowed to stand for the praetorship after a successful quaestorship, assuming that the age requirement was met. In reality, any such ambition was laughably futile. Your only hope of being elected praetor lay with the voters, who would elect you only if you had provided them with memorable Games. Hence, election to the highest offices was possible only if you had incurred the ruinous expenses of the aedileship.

Unless you were Pompey, of course. He was always the exception to the rules that applied to everyone else, even Caesar and Crassus. Pompey was elected consul without ever holding a single one of the lower offices. But then, much may be forgiven a hugely successful general whose unbelievably loyal legions lay encamped outside the gates.

The result was that the aedileship loaded the office holder with debts that would take years to pay off. It may be wondered that the officials in charge of ferreting out corruption were precisely the ones in debt and constantly in need of money. It was just one of the anomalies of our creaky, outdated, old republican system, a system that was soon to end, although we didn't know that at the time.

Needless to say, my mind at the time was not upon the forthcoming death of the Republic, nor even upon my debts, which I knew to be inevitable. My thoughts were fully occupied by my multitude of duties, by the incredible burden of office. By the time I was no more than one-quarter of the way through the year of my aedileship, I was certain that things could not get worse. As usual, I was wrong.

It all began when a building collapsed.

"ANOTHER BODY HERE!" THE public slave yelled, already bored with his task. It was perhaps the fiftieth corpse to be discovered in the ruins. The building was, or rather had been, to keep my tenses straight, a five-story *insula* of a sort becoming distressingly common in Rome at that time—a hulking block of low-grade timber and masonry, jammed with as many impoverished families as could be crammed into its upper stories, with a few decent quality flats occupied by the well-to-do and modestly wealthy on the two lowest floors, the ones with running water. Shops were usually at street level, but this one had been strictly residential. Sometimes a single *insula* covered an entire city block. They were crowded, dark, verminous, and as flammable as an oil-soaked funeral pyre.

Oh, well, I suppose the poor had to live someplace. The occasional earthquake would bring down scores of them, and no small number collapsed from the ravages of neglect and inferior construction.

What made the one where we were working now so distressing was that it was all but new, its mortar scarcely dry, its wood still smelling sweetly of resin. This was not supposed to happen. Which is not to say that it did not happen anyway and with some frequency. The laws concerning building materials and standards of construction were rigid, specific, and flouted quite openly. It was much cheaper to bribe an official than to build according to the law.

"Bring out the body," I ordered the team of slaves who stood by with their tools and stretchers. These slaves were a degraded lot, the ones who tended the Puticuli, the public burial pits outside the City. They had this job because they had no qualms about handling corpses. In a disaster like this one, there was no way to perform the purification rites until the bodies were taken from the wreckage and laid out where the Libitinarii, the undertakers, could attend to them.

By this time, there was a long row of such corpses lying in the little plaza before the collapsed *insula,* many of them terribly mangled, others scarcely marked and probably victims of suffocation. There were infants and old people, young men and women, slave and free. A great throng of people milled around them, trying to identify relatives and loved ones, sobbing and apprehensive. There was a general, low-level moaning to be heard, interrupted from time to time by a loud, wailing outcry as some woman recognized a husband, father, or child among the dead.

There had been few survivors, and those had been carried off to the Tiber Island, where such aid as could be provided would be given them and their screams and groans would not add to the uproar.

"Way!" came a lictor's bellow. "Way for the *Interrex!*" A double line of lictors pushed their way into the plaza, shoving the mourners and gawkers aside with their *fasces*. Behind them came the man who had all the power and prestige of a consul but not the title or the proconsular appointment. There had been such scandals and riots and lawsuits over the previous year's elections that the consuls had not been allowed to take office yet, so an *interrex* had been appointed to preside in their place. This one happened to be a kinsman of mine, the resoundingly named Quintus Caecilius Metellus Pius Scipio Nasica.

"How many dead?" he asked me.

"About fifty so far," I told him, "but we've only cleared away the upper stories. There'll be more. Do you think this rates a day of mourning?" Metellus Scipio was a *pontifex* as well and could declare one.

"If the list of dead is outrageously high, or if someone of note is found in there, I'll call for one in the Senate. It seems rather pointless, though. This year has been so bloody already that the whole City should be wearing black togas and growing beards."

"All too true," I said, "but I'm going to bring charges against whoever built this atrocity. A brand-new *insula* has no business collapsing without an earthquake. There hasn't even been time for termites to get at it."

"At least there wasn't a fire," he observed. When such a building collapsed upon cooking and heating fires, the resulting flames could spread all over the City.

"A little blessing from Jupiter," I said. "It happened just before dawn. No fires lit yet, and the night-lights all burned out."

"Tragic," he mused, "but it could have been worse. Find out who's responsible, and bring me his name. You're going to be too busy to prosecute, but we can find one of the rising young family members to hand it to. My younger son can use the experience." Naturally, he would try to use the catastrophe for family political advantage; we did that sort of thing all the time. It was his next revelation that stunned me.

"By the way, speaking of my children"—he looked around to be sure that no one was eavesdropping—"keep this to yourself for a while, but the family has agreed that my daughter is to marry Pompey."

"Are you serious? We've been fighting Pompey for years!" I was more than a bit put out that I hadn't been let in on the deliberations. Despite my age, dignity, and experience, the elders of my family still thought me too young and unreliable to attend their councils.

"It's been decided that it is time to renegotiate some alliances."

He didn't have to spell it out for me. The family had decided that Caesar was now the more dangerous man.

"But Pompey's supporters have been calling for a dictatorship! We're not going to support them, are we? I'll go into voluntary exile first."

He sighed. "Decius, if you only knew how many of the older men have been calling for your exile anyway. No, don't go all dramatic on us; we're going to work something out that will satisfy everyone."

"I've heard that sort of talk before. I believe in the principle of compromise, but if you've figured out an office between consul and dictator, I'd love to hear about it."

"Give it time," he said. "Just find out who's responsible for this," he made a broad gesture toward the heap of rubble, "and let the higher councils deal with Pompey."

Pompey was proconsul of both Spanish provinces that year, but they were peaceful so he let his legates run them while he stayed in Italy to oversee the chaotic grain supply—and, it seemed, to negotiate an advantageous marriage.

I should have expected it. A similar bout of fence-mending a few years before had resulted in my betrothal and eventual marriage to Julia, Caesar's niece. I shuddered to contemplate how Julia would react to this change in the family position.

All through the day the public slaves labored over the wreckage, loading the rubble onto carts to be hauled out to one of the City's refuse dumps, most of them landfills to create level ground for the ever-expanding suburbs beyond the ancient walls. These slaves were not actually owned by the State, which owned relatively few slaves at this time. They were owned by the *publicanus*, who held the contract for this sort of work. The carts and oxen were his as well.

The man himself stood by one of the carts, making notes with a stylus on a wax tablet, apparently keeping a talley of the carts and their loads. He was a big, tough-looking specimen, as unskilled labor contractors often are. Their slaves are the dregs of the market, sometimes criminals or insurrectionists sold off in gangs by foreign kings. He nodded curtly as I approached him.

"Good day, Aedile. Some mess, eh?"

"Very much so, and I find myself wondering why." I rapped a flat facing brick. "Everything is new and seemingly sound."

"Looks so, doesn't it?" He handed the tablet to a secretary and took one of the bricks from the cart. Pinching off a bit of mortar, he squeezed it between a thick finger and thumb, where it crumbled to powder. "Cheap mortar, for one thing, but that's not why it fell. See, they always make the part above ground look good, else how are they going to get tenants to move in? But I'll wager that when we get to the basement, we'll find rotten timber and not enough of it. The upright supports are supposed to be spaced no more than an Egyptian cubit apart, but I've seen them spaced so you can lie down comfortably between them. The foundations won't be dug deep enough, and they'll be resting on river mud instead of a man's height in gravel, as the code requires. Where you can't see it readily, the builders cut every cost they can."

"Disgraceful," I said, disgusted but far from shocked. "How do they get away with it? Why don't all the buildings collapse?"

He gave me a smile of genial cynicism. "Usually they don't last long enough. How often does an *insula* like this last as long as ten years before a fire gets it? And who's going to notice the code violations then?"

"Every builder in Rome should be flogged in the Circus," I said.

"Well, that's the aediles' job, isn't it?" His implication was clear: Every one of my predecessors in office had been bribed to look the other way when these death traps had been erected.

"I may need you to testify in court," I told him.

"Always at the service of Senate and People," he said with that marvelous, toadying humility that only large, brutal men can display when dealing with superiors.

"Your name?"

"Marcus Caninus, sir."

"And you received your contract from?"

"The Censor Valerius, sir." This was Marcus Valerius Messala Niger, the consul of some seven years previous and still censor the year before I took this burdensome office.

I looked around for Hermes, my personal slave, who carried all my writing materials and was supposed to be standing by to take notes. As usual, he was nowhere to be seen. I began to stalk around the site, plotting his punishment.

Eventually I found him standing by one of the rubble carts, this one piled with wooden beams. He was amusing himself with an ancient Roman pastime, carving his name on the timbers. Every wall, monument, and tree in Rome bear these blessings of widespread literacy. The graffito is the only art form we did not steal from the Greeks or the Etruscans.

"Improving your skills as a scribe, Hermes?" I asked.

He refolded his knife, stuck it beneath his tunic belt, and affected not to notice my ominous tone. "This is fresh wood," he said, tapping the newly carved letters of his name. I had to admit he had carved the letters with some precision. Beads of sap oozed from the incised lines.

"Is that so? I was wondering how a building constructed of new materials could fall, but I was learning that there are many foul little secrets to the builders' trade."

"You aren't supposed to build with wood this fresh," he went on.

"Really?" In truth, the only experience I had with construction was the army sort: putting up bridges and siege works. For that you used whatever timber was readily available, usually cutting it on the spot.

"It's supposed to age and dry out. Wood this new will warp and rot quickly, not to mention all that sap will make it burn hot as a potter's kiln."

"You don't say. Someone is going to have all sorts of fun prosecuting these people." I wasn't really that dense, just preoccupied. My mind was still reeling from the implications of Metellus Scipio's daughter marrying Pompey. If there should come a break between Caesar and Pompey, the family could demand that I divorce Julia. What would I do then? I noticed that Hermes had been carving his name all over the timbers heaped on the cart.

"I knew it was a mistake giving you that knife." It had been a Saturnalia gift a couple of years before, a fine Gallic blade cunningly jointed to fold back into its handle. The blade was no longer than the width of a man's palm, so I couldn't be accused of arming a slave. "I suppose it gives you some satisfaction knowing that your name is destined to be immortalized at the bottom of a landfill."

He smiled. "I have to practice somewhere. You never give me enough time."

"You've never done an honest day's work in your life, imp." Hermes was a handsome, strapping young man at this time, in his early twenties, brown and fit from his time campaigning with me in Gaul and exercising in the *ludus* almost every day in Rome. Always an eager student of arms, this enthusiasm for writing was new. He had a lively, quick intelligence, which nicely complemented his many criminal proclivities. An uncle gave him to me as a present several years previously, when I set up my own household. He was Roman-born, despite his Greek slave-name.

"More bodies here!" shouted the slave.

"They're getting down to the rich people's quarters," Hermes noted.

"Then let's see who we have." I walked with him over to the rubble, which was beginning to take on a pitlike appearance as the debris of the roof and upper stories were carried away. The ground floor had collapsed into the basement. As in most such houses only the ground floor had water piped in. This had been shut off soon after the building fell, but enough had flowed in to leave a foot or two in the basement and already bits of rubble could be seen sloshing around in it.

The slaves were handing up bodies to workers above. Most, of course, would be slaves. A rich man's household would contain far more slaves than family members. The corpses were mostly naked or nearly so, since the disaster had occurred when everyone was asleep. It can be difficult to distinguish between a slave and a poor freeman when both are naked, but there is seldom much problem in telling the servile and the wealthy apart, with or without clothes.

Hermes paused by a row of bodies that had the look of

household slaves, lacking both the marks of hard labor and the jewelry of the wealthy.

"Whoever the master was, he wasn't loved," Hermes observed.

"I noticed." Many of the slaves had the collars of runaways riveted around their necks. I paused by a dead girl of no more than sixteen. Covered by plaster dust though she was, it was plain she had been extraordinarily pretty. She wore one of the neck rings. On an impulse, I beckoned to a pair of the public slaves. "Turn this one over."

The burly men stooped, took her by the shoulders and ankles, and rolled her onto her face. The girl's back, buttocks, and thighs were crisscrossed with a net of deep, ugly whip marks. This had not been somebody playing games with a ceremonial *flagellum;* that stings but doesn't cut. These were the marks of a bronze-clawed *flagrum,* laid on with a will. A hundred lashes from one of those can kill a grown man. Many of the wounds were so fresh that they had bled only hours before, and these were laid atop older, partially healed slashes.

"What could a child like this have done to deserve such punishment?" I mused.

"We haven't seen the mistress of the household yet," Hermes said. "If she was some ugly old bag, just being that young and pretty was reason enough." His face and voice were as impassive as any well-schooled slave's. We had grown close over the years, but I knew that I would never know what he felt looking upon such a sight.

I had some of the other bodies turned over. Many of them were marked as the girl had been, even some who did not wear runaway collars. One was different. She was a plump, middle-aged woman wearing a few cheap bangles, unmarked by punishment. Her hands had never washed clothes or dishes, and she was well fed.

"This is the one who told on the others," Hermes said, "the housekeeper."

"Ah, well, my office doesn't regulate the happiness of households. It does, however, have supervision over buildings. I want a look at these foundations as soon as the wreckage is cleared away."

Not long after this, two more bodies were brought up and laid out. "I think we have the master and mistress now," I noted.

The man was portly, baldheaded, with a fringe of gray above the ears. He wore a citizen's ring but no other jewelry, no marks of military service either. Even minimal soldiering usually leaves a few scars.

The woman, likewise, had considerable heft. Her hair was hennaed and had once been elaborately dressed. She wore an abundance of rings, bracelets, necklaces, and earrings, which she apparently slept in. Even in death her face, with its piggy eyes and small, downturned mouth, was that of a vile-tempered shrew.

"Look there," Hermes said, pointing to a smashed chest from which had spilled some white tunics, one of them now floating in the shallow water. The tunics bore the narrow red stripe of an *eques*, Rome's wealthy but not noble class, those who made their fortunes through business rather than land.

"Now we know his rank, anyway," I said. The bodies were laid out side by side, but their heads were turned away from one another, as if they disliked each other as much in death as in life. The angle was unnatural though.

"Their necks were broken," I commented. "Must have happened when they fell through into the basement."

"Most likely," Hermes said, probably wishing they had died of something more lingering.

"Find me somebody who might be able to confirm the identity of these two," I told him. "I'm surprised no relatives have come to inquire about them yet. News of this must have been all over Rome before noon."

A few minutes later, Hermes returned with a shopkeeper in tow. "I couldn't find any neighbors who knew about them," he reported, "but this man says he dealt with some of their slaves."

"Is this possible?" I said. "This is Rome. Everybody knows all their neighbors' business. Did none of the neighbors know these people?"

"They only moved in less than a month ago, Aedile," the shopkeeper said. "I don't think they were from this district, maybe not from Rome at all. Never called on their neighbors that I ever knew about." He was a stooped little man, smelling pungently of rancid oil. There was no need for me to inquire as to the nature of his business. "Fact is, sir, nobody wanted to have much to do with them."

"Why would that be?"

"Well, sir, there was sometimes a lot of noise from that place, disagreeable noise, screams and such. I think they were pretty rough with their slaves. Some people complained, and there wasn't quite so much noise after that; but maybe they just gagged 'em before they started whipping. I know you have to discipline slaves from time to time, but there's got to be a limit. There were times it sounded like they had Spartacus and all his rebels getting crucified in there." The man clearly had a Roman's love for hyperbole.

"Did you ever have contact with anyone from the household?" I asked.

"That woman"—he pointed to the slave Hermes had identified as the housekeeper—"did their marketing. She was always with a big slave"—he trailed off and scanned the line of bodies—"well, I don't see him here. Probably still down there in the rubble. He carried the purchases. She bought oil a few times at my shop. I never saw any of the other household slaves."

It didn't surprise me that they hadn't let the slaves get out much. "How is it that you can identify the owners?"

"My shop is right there." He pointed to a stall directly across the plaza from the main entrance to the ruined house. It had one of those mildly risqué signs Roman shopkeepers love: Eros pouring oil on the outsized phallus of Priapus. "I saw them just about any time they went out. She was always carried in a chair, usually one without hangings. He mostly walked."

"Names?"

"The housekeeper said he was Lucius Folius, and he was some sort of shipper—not foreign trade, I think. Owned a lot of river barges. I never heard her name. The woman just called her 'Mistress.' "

"That's enough to establish identity," I said, as Hermes scratched the names onto a tablet. "Do you know who owned this building? Even the people in the flanking houses don't seem to know."

"Well, the building that used to stand there burned down awhile back. Crassus bought the lot, but he sold it when he was raising money for his foreign war. I heard the buyer was a speculator from Bovillae, but whether he built the *insula,* I don't know."

"Might the owner have been Folius himself?" I asked.

He shrugged. "If I were rich and could build a whole *insula* to live in, I'd build it better than that."

"That makes sense. Well, we—" I stopped short at a bellow from one of the slaves clearing wreckage from the basement.

"There's a survivor here!"

"Under all that!" Hermes exclaimed in wonderment.

"This should be a prodigy worth seeing," I said. "Let's go."

I took off my toga, folded it, and handed it to Hermes. "Don't drop it in the water, or I'll buy a *flagrum* myself." Since I was a plebeian aedile, it was an ordinary citizen's toga without a purple border, but it was a good one and I had no desire to see it ruined. Hermes was used to this duty by now. My office took me into all the filthiest cellars, drains, and sewers in Rome. Most aediles delegated these chores to their slaves; but in my experience, slaves are even more amenable to bribery than aediles, so I always took a personal hand in serious inspections.

We descended the ladder into what now resembled a crater made by one of Jupiter's thunderbolts. The contractor's slaves had carted away the wreckage with antlike efficiency. The chain of bucket men had reduced the water level to no more than an inch or two, and we splashed our way to a heap of slanting timbers where some slaves were levering up a beam. Beneath it could be seen a large foot, bloody but undeniably twitching.

"Surviving the collapse is remarkable enough," I said. "How did he avoid drowning?"

As the beams were cleared away, we saw why. The man had apparently landed in the basement on his feet and was pinned against a wall in a slanting but near-standing position. The water had never risen higher than his waist. As he was pulled free, we saw that he wore a tunic that covered one shoulder.

"This one was dressed," I remarked.

"Probably on night watch against fires," said Hermes. "Look, he's big, and no scars on his back. What do you want to bet that this was the one who went marketing with the housekeeper?"

"Right. If he was awake when it happened and was favored enough by the master to escape flogging, he may be able to give us some answers, if he lives." The man was badly bloodied, able to make only tormented, incoherent noises.

I shouted up to the slaves from the Temple of Aesculapius, who hovered over the pit with their stretchers: "I want this man taken to the Island and given special care. Until a legal heir of the owner comes to claim him, he is the property of the State. I declare this as plebeian aedile!" Actually, I was not at all sure that I had authority to do any such thing, but in those days you could accomplish a lot just by sheer assertiveness. The man made a sound almost like a word, and I leaned close.

"Gala—gala—" He sounded like a man gargling a handful of nails. His throat was full of plaster dust.

"Hermes, give him a drink. Perhaps the poor wretch can talk after all." Hermes always carried a small skin of watered wine, just in case I should come across someone who needed a drink. Carefully, he trickled some into the man's mouth. There was a long period while the half-dead slave choked, drooled, and tried to vomit, but Hermes patiently sloshed out his throat after each spasm. Soon he was at least breathing easier. He began to mutter something, and I leaned close; but the man was barely whispering.

"Hermes, your ears are younger. See if you can make out what he's saying."

Now Hermes leaned close, frowning with concentration. Finally he straightened. "I can't hear much, and he's got an accent. Sounded to me like he was saying, 'Accursed, accursed,' over and over again."

A moment later the man's eyelids sprang open, staring with round-eyed terror; then, the eyeballs rolled up to show whites alone.

"Is he dead?" Hermes asked.

"Unconscious again," I told him. Then, to the slaves who stood by, "You heard what I want. Take him away."

"Now," I said to Hermes, "let's have a look at this place."

We went to one of the cellar walls where the support timbers were plainly visible, only a thin layer of plaster covering the wooden wall between them. I set my elbow against one and laid my forearm horizontally. The next beam was three or four inches past my fingertips.

"That's a bit wider than an Egyptian cubit," I remarked, "but not all that much. Somebody was stretching the code without violating it flagrantly."

Hermes took out his knife again and made a long scratch in one of the timbers. Immediately, sap began to flow. "Green wood again," he said. "But it's strong enough. It hasn't had time to rot or warp."

"What's underfoot?" I asked. Hermes stooped and came

up with a handful of gravel. "I don't know good gravel from bad," I said, "but that is undisputably gravel. As soon as this wreckage has been cleared away, I want workmen to dig here and find out how deep the gravel extends. What's all this stuff?"

The falling water level had revealed a litter of tools of all sorts: hammers, mallets, chisels, saws, boxes of nails, masons' squares, and things the function of which I could not even guess.

"A lot of builders in this quarter," Hermes said. "They often take their tools home with them after work."

"Maybe this was Vulcan's punishment," I said, "for being such sloppy workmen."

"I'll bet it was these," Hermes said, walking to one of the big horizontal beams that had once supported the ground floor. "There must be rotten timber here someplace, some squirrel or woodpecker den that made a weak place."

"I see your little time in the forests of Gaul made you an expert on arboreal matters."

"Do you have a better idea?" He stooped once again and came up with a couple of pale cylinders about the length and thickness of a man's thumb.

"What are those?"

He held them out to me on his palm. "Candle stubs. They must be from the ground-floor apartment. Poor people don't use them much."

I took one and examined it. Its base was dark from whatever it had been stuck to when it was in use. "Rich people don't use them much either," I commented. Most people prefer lamps because, not only are candles expensive, but they drip. They do burn more brightly than lamps, though. For some reason candles are a traditional Saturnalia gift, so most people use them for only a week or two after that holiday.

"It's getting dark." I looked up and yelled, "Marcus Caninus!"

Moments later the man looked down into the cellar. "Aedile?"

"I want these big support timbers, these joists or whatever you call them, taken to the Temple of Ceres and placed in the courtyard as evidence. I want to examine them tomorrow in daylight."

He made a sour face. "Whatever you say, Aedile."

Hermes was poking at one of the timbers with his knife. "Look at this." He scratched an *X* with his knife so I could see where to look in the fading light. Where the lines crossed was a hole in the wood big enough to stick my middle finger in without fear of splinters. "I'll bet this timber is full of boreholes like this."

"Somebody," I said, "allowed all these citizens to die just to save a few wretched sesterces. Our laws have become entirely too lenient of late. I am going to search the law codes and find absolutely the most savage, primitive, vicious punishment ever laid down for such a man, and then I am going to see it applied to whoever is responsible for this atrocity."

2

WHEN I ENTERED MY HOUSE, Julia began to make a comment on my dirty, disheveled appearance, caught the expression on my face, and thought better of it. She clapped her hands and sent a couple of slaves scurrying for my dinner. We had agreed that, for the year of my aedileship, we would give up any thought of regular meal hours.

"A bad day, I see," she said, taking my hand and leading me to the *triclinium*. "Was there fighting?"

"No fighting this time," I told her as I collapsed onto a couch. "An *insula* fell. Two hundred thirty-three dead at the final count. A lot of injured, and some of them won't live."

She gasped. "Infamous! As plebeian aedile can't you condemn those rickety old buildings and have them pulled down? They cause more deaths in a year than a foreign war."

"I could if I had the time and the staff and the manpower, which I don't. This was a new one anyway. A crooked contractor, inferior materials, no doubt a fat bribe to one of last year's aediles, all the usual factors."

She sat beside me and stroked my brow while ancient Cassandra, who guarded her *triclinium* serving duties like a dragon, laid out bread, oil, smoked fish, and sliced fruit. Hermes brought in wine with the water added according to my standing instructions—by holding it out a window during a heavy fog.

"Eat before you drink any of that," Julia instructed. "Are you going to prosecute?"

"If at all possible. Metellus Scipio wants to give it to his son." I wiped a hand across my face. "How much good will it do anyway? One wretched contractor more or less will mean nothing in the long run."

"Then," she said seriously, "perhaps it's time for you to stand for the tribuneship. As tribune of the people you can introduce legislation to drive all the criminal contractors from the City, demolish all the substandard *insulae* as a menace to the public good, and institute strict enforcement of the building codes. It would do us all a world of good and set a high tone for your political career."

I thought about it. "It's a good idea. The family has wanted me to stand for tribune for years."

"Then it's time to lay the groundwork," Julia said, decisive as only a Julian could be. "There is plenty of time between now and the elections. Take a tribuneship for next year, while people still remember this disaster."

Then I remembered, and a pall fell over my brief enthusiasm. "Pompey may be dictator next year. A tribune means nothing during a dictatorship."

"Surely not!" Julia protested. "Caesar will come back from Gaul and Crassus from Asia before they'll allow Pompey to be dictator!" Like everyone else, she had begun referring to Caesar by the family name as if he alone bore it. This was an archaic, monarchical practice regarded by many of us with deep suspicion.

"Something must be done," I said. "As much as I hate to say it, the chaotic state of the City calls for the most stringent measures. Another year of the usual partisan bickering and we will be ruined. Scipio says we are working for some sort of compromise, but I can't imagine what it might be. Oh, by the way, it looks as if Scipio's daughter is to wed Pompey." I tried to add something, but she stuck a piece of fish in my mouth to keep me quiet while she thought. Political calculation was as natural to her as to me. In fact, she was far more swift and acute than I.

"I see," she said at last. "Well, since my cousin died, he has been in need of a wife. It is natural that he would want to forge an alliance with the Metelli." She spoke of Caesar's daughter, the other Julia, who had married Pompey and died giving birth to his child.

"And he truly loved his Julia," I said. "His grief at her death was not false. His marriage to Caecilia may help to strengthen all our bonds. Pompey just gave Caesar another of his legions for the war in Gaul," which, I did not add, was a far more sincere pledge of friendship than any number of political marriages.

"And if it should come to a break between Caesar and Pompey?"

I placed a hand atop hers. "When Sulla ordered Caesar to divorce his wife, Caesar fled to Spain rather than give her up. I will do no less should it come to that." She smiled and seemed to be reassured, but I knew what she was thinking: Caesar had been ordered to divorce his wife by a political enemy, not his own family.

I WAS AT THE SITE OF THE RUined *insula* at first light the next morning. Nothing remained but the empty basement, the slave gang having labored through the night to haul away the wreckage. Three men remained, digging through the gravel foundation to ascertain its depth.

"Three feet of gravel, then river mud!" shouted one of them when the last bucket of rock was handed up.

"Below code," I said, "but once again not outrageously so. This may complicate the prosecution, when we have someone to prosecute. If you are going to be a greedy villain, why not go ahead and be egregious about it? Why these half measures?"

"Maybe they're like slaves and soldiers," Hermes suggested. "They know how to push authority just so far without being severely punished."

"You may have a point." I always let Hermes speak to me freely when I was not discussing matters with my peers. In public, certain proprieties had to be observed. As it happened, we were alone in that place. "Let's go to the Island and see if that slave porter can talk."

The walk was not a long one. We crossed the fine, still new Fabrician Bridge to the Island and its complex of buildings that combine temple and hospital. The temple itself rejoiced in a new facade, provided by some ambitious politician to celebrate his own glory. I didn't even glance up to see whose name now decorated the pediment. We were barely off the bridge when we heard the groaning.

"Sounds like a battlefield after a fight," Hermes said.

"It means there are more survivors than I'd expected. Maybe some of them can give us some answers."

We climbed the steps, newly resurfaced with gleaming white marble, and passed between a pair of splendid braziers of shining bronze wrought in the shape of the god's serpent-wound staff, topped with a bronze basket in which fire would burn on special occasions. These were also new.

We found the big fellow in a recovery room attended by a temple slave. The priests had taken my instructions for special treatment to heart, it seemed.

"How is he?" I asked.

"He hasn't come around since I've been attending him," the slave said. "He mumbles a little, but mostly he's like this, completely unconscious." The attendant was a young man wearing the livery of the temple, a white tunic embroidered on front and back with the caduceus. He rose. "I will fetch the attending priest."

The comatose slave was as big as any Gaul or German; but washed free of dust and plaster, he proved to have the common features and coloration of southern Italy. He was olive skinned and black bearded, and I thought I detected something of Bruttium in the cast of his features. His eyes were open but unfocussed, and he mumbled continuously, although I could make out no words.

"I don't think this one is going to be with us much

longer," Hermes opined. "Should I go get Asklepiodes?"

"I doubt he could do much. In any case, his specialty is wounds caused by weapons."

Moments later the priest arrived. He was one I knew from previous visits to the temple, a slave named Harmodias. By ancient tradition, one-third of the priests of this temple are freeborn, one-third freedmen, and one-third slaves. The freedmen and slaves are the best consultants on injuries and treatable diseases. The freeborn priests confine themselves mainly to interpreting the dreams of ailing people brought in to sleep in the nave before the statue of Aesculapius.

"Will he be able to speak?" I asked him.

"He has suffered severe injuries to the skull and spine, Aedile. I've seen a good many cases like this, and I've never seen a complete recovery. Even partial recovery is rare."

"I just want him to recover enough to talk," I said.

"He may babble incoherently for a while, although periods of lucidity are not out of the question."

"I can't wait around for that. Have you a secretary who can take down any coherent statements he might make?"

"I could do it myself, but what sort of statement might be of interest?"

"This one seems to have been awake when the disaster occurred. He was dressed at any rate, and it looks as if he was on his feet when the floor collapsed under him. Anything he can say about the events of last night could be of help. Also, we are having difficulty learning anything about the equestrian family to whom he belonged. The name Lucius Folius is all I've been able to find out. I want to know anything he can tell me, even if it's just scurrilous slave gossip. I'd prefer, of course, to hear it personally. If he seems to come around, send a messenger to fetch me."

"I shall do it without fail," he promised. "Of course, this will detain me from other duties—" I snapped my fingers and Hermes passed me my money pouch. I gave Harmodias a couple of silver denarii, and he tucked them away, bowing. "I shall send for you the moment he begins to talk coherently, recording diligently anything he might say before you get here. If he dies, you shall likewise be notified."

"Good. Tell him he'll have a decent funeral. That may put him in a cooperative frame of mind." Slaves usually were thrown into the Puticuli if nobody claimed them for burial.

I tried to question some of the other survivors, but, as I feared, they had nothing to tell me. All had been sound asleep at the time of the disaster. They had awakened to noise, pain, terror, and confusion. Many remembered nothing at all of that night, the shock having disordered their minds.

We left the temple and made our way back across the bridge, thence south along the river to the Temple of Ceres, where I had a cramped cubicle laughably termed an office. For centuries the temple had been the headquarters of the aediles, but in the early days the duties of that office had been far less comprehensive. Office space was as inadequate as everything else attached to the title.

Ceres is an imported Greek goddess, and therefore her worship is in the Greek fashion, overseen by patrician women, unlike the native Roman deities whose priests are all male. The high priestess at that time was a formidable Cornelia, a close kinswoman of the Dictator Sulla and as high-handed as most members of that family. She was waiting for me when I arrived.

"Aedile!" She stalked down the steps of the lovely temple and I could almost see thunderclouds gathering around her head. "Explain this outrage!" She pointed to the great heap of timber piled helter-skelter upon the pavement of the courtyard.

"And good morning to you, revered Cornelia," I said. "Allow me to note that you are especially lovely today."

"Don't try to distract me. The aediles have their offices in the basement of the temple, not in the courtyard! Remove this trash at once!"

"Lovely, gracious Cornelia, this is evidence in an investigation into gross negligence in the building trades. If Rome had such a thing as a municipal wood yard, I would certainly send this evidence there. Alas, there is none. Someone must be prosecuted for using unfit timber for these—these—I think they are called 'joists.' And to do this, I must have the evidence, and this is the only place I have to store it. I promise it will only be for a few more days." I gave her a conciliatory smile, to which she replied with a most unconciliatory glare. Cornelians were notoriously averse to being crossed in any way.

"In ten days," she said, "we begin rehearsing for the *Cerialia*. If the wood is not gone by that time, it will make you an excellent funeral pyre."

"You are too kind, splendid Cornelia," I assured her.

"Too kind by half. I want every termite-chewed splinter of that heap off the courtyard and the flagstones swept before we begin rehearsal or I will speak to the wife of the *Pontifex Maximus* and have you impeached before the Senate the minute you step down from office, do you understand?"

"Perfectly, glorious and pulchritudinous—" but she had already whirled about and stalked back up the steps, surrounded by a cloud of twittery eunuchs. Impeach me, would she? By law, the eunuchs were one part of the Ceres cult forbidden in Rome, and part of my job was to purge the City of degenerate, foreign religious practices. We'd just see about that. The *Cerialia*, the great annual festival of Ceres, would be just the occasion to confront her with it, too.

"Termite-chewed?" Hermes said. "I didn't see any termite damage in the basement."

"We never got a good look at the timber. Perhaps she spoke metaphorically. Go get some of the office slaves and go over every piece of wood in the pile. Mark the ones that look especially unfit. I have other duties to attend to for a while."

He went off in search of some help as I walked toward the little terrace where the plebeian aediles conducted business in good weather. Other duties indeed. The *insula* disaster had cost me a full day I could ill afford to spare in the busiest of all Roman magistracies. Even as I drew near the terrace, I saw the mob of citizens, each of them with a demand that fell beneath the purview of my office.

Besides supervising compliance with the building codes, the aediles were in charge of the streets, drains, and sewers; upkeep of the City streets and public buildings; putting on the public Games; and the aforementioned oversight of foreign cults. Since the State funds allowed for these activities hadn't changed since the days of Tarquin the Proud, the aediles had to pay for much of this work out of their own purses. No wonder so many men spent the rest of their careers using the higher offices to enrich themselves after the expenses they had incurred as aediles.

"Aedile!" chorused a small crowd of men, detaching

themselves from the larger crowd of petitioners. These were my clients, who on most days called on me at my home at first light. They now had standing instructions to meet me at the temple except on days when official business was forbidden. This was the year when my clients earned their keep. Ordinarily I sent them home with gifts and thanks except when I needed a cheering section in the Forum, but not this year. This year I needed assistants, and the State wasn't going to give me any.

Burrus strode importantly forward. He was my senior client, a retired soldier from my old legion in Spain. "Aedile, the supervisor of drains and sewers wants your attention, and he says this won't wait."

"They all say that." I sighed, knowing full well what the complaint would be. "Let's hear him."

The man came forward, a freedman named Acilius, followed by a small group of freedmen who likewise served the City. All wore the harried look of such functionaries. It is a thing practiced even by those with no work to do at all. Perhaps those wear the most harried looks.

"Aedile," Acilius began, "the drains must be cleaned, and you can delay no longer. For the last five years, the aediles have ignored them, and now all of them are utterly choked with mud and trash and unmentionable filth. It is a disgrace!"

"Well, they've gone for five years, why not another?" I did not want to face this problem. The voters remembered your aedileship for the splendor of the Games you put on, not for doing the necessary but disagreeable tasks that kept the City a functioning entity.

"Because," he said, with malevolent satisfaction, "the

river is rising, and the rivermen predict a flood before the next full moon."

"Sir," Burrus said, "those men know the river better than you know politics."

"You don't need to remind me," I told him, "but I don't see how they can be so sure. The rains haven't been heavy of late."

"There was unusually heavy snow in the mountains," Acilius said gloatingly. "It's melting."

"Bring me an assessment of the labor and funds necessary to clean and repair the drains," I said. "I will consult with the other aediles, and we will get the job done." I said this with more hope than confidence. My colleagues were more interested in putting on their career-boosting Games than in doing anything constructive for the City.

The sad fact was that the important office of aedile had become little more than a stepping-stone to higher office, and most ambitious men undertook it solely for that purpose. When one of them bothered to undertake the construction or restoration of a public building, it was usually a temple located in a prominent place, and then only because it entitled him to put his name on its pediment in letters two feet high.

Very few of us had the wealth to build a truly useful structure such as a bridge, basilica, or highway. Centuries before, an Appius Claudius had built the great Rome-Capua highway, the Appian Way, and his name will live forever. Quintus Fabricius built the bridge I had crossed twice that morning; and while it might not last as long as the Appian Way, it will ensure his memory for generations to come.

But it was the Games that had come more and more to dominate the office, and my own upcoming *munera* distracted me from my other duties as would an invading army bearing down upon the City. Quite aside from the plays, banquets, and chariot races of the regular *ludi,* which are costly enough, the exotic beasts and gladiators of the *munera* are staggeringly expensive.

I shook off the daunting prospect and turned to the crowd of petitioners, each of whom had a complaint that demanded the attention of a plebeian aedile. One would complain of the shocking state of the street in front of his place of business, another of the disorderliness of the whorehouse next door. Malicious citizens accused neighbors of infractions that would prove nonexistent, but an aedile could turn no citizen away, just as a tribune of the people was forbidden even to close the doors of his house during his year in office. I had to deal with them all.

While I endured this daily tedium and assigned each case to one of my clients for investigation and report, I allowed myself to envy the curule aedile. He got to wear a purple border on his toga, and all he had to do was sit around all day in his folding chair and supervise the markets, levying fines for infractions. The office that year had been held by Marcus Aemilius Lepidus, a man who had never amounted to much but who became famous anyway years later because he had a lot of soldiers behind him just when two more capable men needed them. They made him a *triumvir.*

I disposed of the last of the petitioners just before midday and went to see what Hermes had been able to discover. I found him going over the timbers, now laid out parallel to one another. He squatted by one, poking at it with his knife.

"Well?" I asked, walking up to him.

"Termites, all right." He held up a handful of dusty

wood pulp. His knife had pried up a slab of wood, revealing a honeycomb of tunnels beneath.

My mind pondered the legal ramifications of these malicious little insects. "Unfit wood, no doubt about it. The builder, when we find him, will, of course, claim that the infestation occurred after he built the *insula*. I am not intimately familiar with the nature of these loathsome little creatures and therefore will have to consult with one of the natural philosophers to find out if there was adequate time between the construction of the *insula* and its collapse for such an infestation to occur. Hermes, I want you to find out who might know about—"

"Trouble is," he interrupted, "this isn't the same wood we looked at before."

I was caught in midthought preparing my denunciation, and this took a moment to penetrate. "What's that?"

"I've been all over this timber. I've looked at every surface. Remember that first borehole I found? I marked it with a big *X*. It's not here."

"Maybe they missed one timber."

He shook his head. "Look at this wood. Forget the termites. Look at how dry it is. The timbers in that cellar were still oozing sap. I'm no expert on wood either, but this stuff has to be older than I am, and it's probably older than Titus Saufeius." This last being a senator some ninety-seven years old and famous only for his longevity, having never held an office higher than quaestor.

"Well, well," I said. "First we have a felonious but rather common instance of violation of building codes. Now we have what looks like conspiracy and tampering with evidence."

"There's always the chance some fool just sent the wrong lumber cart here," Hermes said, playing advocate for the other side, just as I had taught him.

"Such negligence is always more than suspicious when an investigation is involved. Besides, there wasn't a stick of seasoned wood in that house, unless it was part of the furniture. Every splinter of structural wood we saw was green. Somebody went to all the trouble to find this plausibly unsound wood and bring it here."

"Looks that way," he admitted.

"I think we're going to have some fun with this."

He grinned. "I thought you'd see it that way."

3

THE FORUM WAS STILL crowded, even though it was the hour for the midday meal. Many bought food from street vendors and ate standing while conducting business or making political deals or just idling about. True denizens of the City often prefer hunger to leaving the Forum. After all, what could be better than standing at the center of the world? I couldn't think of anything. It certainly beat fighting and freezing in Gaul.

Before the Basilica Julia, a group of candidates for the next year's offices stood about, making sure that they were seen. It was too early yet to don the *candidus* and make a show of it, but they were letting no one forget who would be in a position to do them a favor in the coming year.

I wanted to get to the Tabularium, but family policy dictated that I stride up to one young man, take him by the hand, slap him on the shoulder, and greet him loudly. This was a young kinsman just beginning his political career, Lucius Caecilius Metellus.

"Good to have you back in Rome!" I shouted, as though the boy were deaf. "I hear great things about your service in Gaul!"

"Just basic military work, Aedile," he said, with becoming modesty. At his age it might have been genuine.

"Nonsense!" I bellowed. "I've heard you won the Civic Crown! I've never won that one and neither," here I scanned the other faces ostentatiously, "has anyone else here!" The older men grinned at this shamelessness; but the younger ones, also standing for quaestor, reddened.

"It was just a piddling earth fort," he demurred. "Anyone with legs could get atop that wall."

"But," I yelled, "it takes the balls of a hero to be first, especially when the other side is packed with painted, savage Gauls!"

After many more fulsome compliments, some of them actually deserved, I felt I had done my duty and left him to the crowd of well-wishers who had assembled to see who this prodigy might be. I scanned the clot of candidates for Milo, who wanted the consulship for the next year, and Clodius, who was standing for praetor, but saw neither of them; and a good thing that was. They were both so prominent that they would probably not don the *candidus* until a day or two before the election. In recent months, any time they or their supporters met in public, blood on the pavement soon followed.

I did see one of my least favorite Romans though.

"Greetings, Aedile," called Sallustius Crispus, his swarthy, greasy face split by an ugly smile. "That performance was outrageous, even for a Metellus. I know you are busy, but might you spare me a few minutes? We could retire to a stall for some lunch."

I did some quick political calculations. Sallustius liked me no more than I liked him. He was an enemy of Cicero and Milo, my good friends. On the other hand, the weasely little bastard had insinuated himself into the confidence of everyone of importance, and his knowledge of Roman lowlife was comprehensive. His fund of political and civic gossip was unmatched, if you could sort out the nuggets of truth from the bulk ore of lies. Being a Caecilius Metellus, these calculations took me approximately half a second.

"I would be most pleased to." I turned to Hermes. "Run along to the Tabularium and get those records we spoke about. I shall be there presently." I caught Sallustius's look of annoyance that I had not said which records I wanted. It could be of no interest to him, but he wanted to know everything.

We found a stall in a side street just off the Forum and sat at a table beneath an awning.

"You're holding up well beneath the burdens of office," he said, as a server poured us watered wine. "But the year is young yet. I hate to think what you'll look like by December."

"Don't remind me. I haven't had a good night's sleep or a regular meal since the first of the year. It beats Gaul, though."

"You'll be able to brag that Rome was a better city after your year in office."

"If it's still standing."

"The whorehouses can't be that disorderly," he said,

referring to the common belief that the aediles spent most of their time supervising the *lupanaria*. Some of them, in fact, were known to.

"The whorehouses don't concern me. They haven't changed in a thousand years. The streets are in bad shape but not desperate yet. The public buildings are fine, since Caesar and Pompey got into a contest to see who could restore the most and get their names slathered all over the City. Foreign cults don't interest me at all."

I leaned across the table. "Rome has two great problems right now that concern my office: buildings that won't stay up, and drains that won't stand another flood. You may end up standing atop the Capitol with your *candidus* fluttering in the breeze as you cadge votes."

"That bad, eh?" he said, fingering his acne-pocked chin.

"The watermen say so, and they're seldom wrong about the river."

"Talk of that *insula* crash is all over the City. Five hundred dead, I hear."

"Cut that in half, but it's still bad enough. It's flagrant corruption in the building trades, and I intend to root it out."

"Most commendable," he murmured.

"I believe I detect a note of doubt in your voice."

"It is certainly not that I am dubious of your sincerity, my friend. Your devotion to duty is such that even Cato remarks upon it. It rivals your tactlessness and capacity for making dangerous enemies, but it strikes me that you know little about the building trades."

"Admittedly so," I said, a bit surprised at the turn this conversation was taking.

"Have you Metelli no business at all besides politics, war, and farming?"

"What else is there? For people of our class, virtually everything else is forbidden. The *gens* Caecilia isn't patrician, but we've been consulars for centuries. If I engaged in trade, I could get booted out of the Senate come the next censorship." I pondered a moment. "Of course, there is always Crassus, but he is a law unto himself. He made his fortune in land and slaves. Since the law defines even City land as agricultural and even the most highly educated slaves as livestock, he was staying within the law. It didn't hurt that he could buy the goodwill of almost any censor. He was a censor himself, for that matter."

Sallustius spat out an olive pit. "Ah, yes, the noble practice of agriculture, which these days means sitting on the terrace of your country estate and watching your slaves toil, by law dating back to—oh, I don't know, Numa Pompilius maybe. The only sources of wealth lawful for a senator are plunder from war and the fruits of the land. That last one, more specifically, can be stretched to mean all products of the land, including those to be found beneath it."

"True. A good many senatorial families own mines. Marius got rich that way."

"And what else comes out of the ground?" he asked, coaxingly, apparently getting to his point.

"Oh, well, there's timber, stone, clay for pottery and tiles, and—brick—" These last words trailed off aimlessly as the light began to dawn. Sallustius really did have a clever way of bringing these things out.

He grinned and nodded, dipping a crust into the bowl of oil. "Exactly. Building materials. It's even marginally acceptable to manufacture bricks yourself, since they're of pure clay fired with wood, which is to say, molded and cooked rather than manufactured in the strict sense of the word."

"You're saying that I may not be investigating just crooked building contractors, but highborn, influential people?"

"Perhaps your neighbors of the *curia*."

"But, surely, such senators would merely be engaged in selling raw materials to the contractors. They would not necessarily have anything to do with the contractors, selectively choosing faulty and inferior materials to maximize profit." My lawyer's mentality was asserting itself unbidden.

He nodded solemnly. "One would certainly hope so."

"And what might your interest be in this matter?"

"Like you, I am a member of the Senate. While the Sallustii may not be as noble a family as the Caecilii, we are of respectable antiquity." This was putting it mildly, at least the first part. Sallustius was a Sabine from the mountains of the central peninsula, about as remote from the City as you could get and still be a Roman citizen. He had come to Rome a few years previously to ingratiate himself with powerful men and launch a political career. He had settled on Clodius and his patron, Caesar, as the men of the hour.

I suppose I should not have held the man's alien and obscure origins against him. After all, many of the best men of the day were from outside, Cicero and Milo to name the most famous. And there is no doubt at all that most of the very worst were native Romans who could trace their bloodlines back to Aeneas. It is just that Sallustius embodied all the most scurrilous caricatures of the newly arrived parvenu: vulgar, unscrupulous, ill-mannered, thick-skinned, poorly educated, unaccomplished, and generally unpleasant.

"Forgive me for being obtuse, but I still don't quite understand what you wish to convey." Of course, I was fairly certain that he had already delivered his message; but I wanted him to set it forth plainly, for the sake of later court testimony if need be, but he was not to be so easily led.

"I merely wished to point out a likely pitfall in your investigation, one you may wish to avoid."

I was about to gag on all this ambiguity. "As always, I will go wherever the evidence takes me. And now," I finished off my cup and stood, "it takes me to the Tabularium."

"Good fortune, then. I shall follow your progress with interest."

I felt no need for his interest, but diplomatically forebore to mention the fact. Instead, I wondered how he had learned so quickly of my investigation. But in the small, involuted world of Roman politics, it seemed that everybody got wind of everything at once. I'd spent most of the previous day at the disaster site; I'd spoken to the *Interrex,* I'd sent that heap of timber to the Temple of Ceres. Word had gotten around.

I have spent most of my long life in Rome, and I have dedicated much of that time to the City and its peculiar ways. Few things in Roman life are so intriguing as the spread of news and rumor. As near as I can figure it, slaves are the prime conduits. They are everywhere, from the lowest dives to the chambers of the noblest and most powerful. They hear everything, although people tend to speak as if slaves had no ears. They accompany us everywhere, and they talk to each other. Once I tried to trace a particular report and found that it had been transmitted rather the way a pernicious disease is spread from one sufferer to another.

A certain *eques* named Lollius, whose house was on the Esquiline near the city wall, had returned unexpectedly early from a trip and caught his wife in bed with none other than the Dictator Caius Julius Caesar, who was much given to activities of this sort. It seems that Lollius was more old fashioned and touchy than most men of the day, and there ensued an unseemly farce in which Caesar ended up bleeding copiously from his great Julian beak.

It happened that a party of revelers, returning from a wedding, passed by Lollius's door just in time to see Caesar, laurel wreath askew and blood staining his tunic, stagger forth and collapse into his sedan chair. Moments later, the woman ran screaming from the house, naked and closely pursued by her aggrieved husband, who was slashing away at her with great, whistling strokes of a *flagrum*.

While the half-drunken party collapsed with laughter, certain of their slaves got the story from the *janitor* chained to the doorpost of Lollius's house. Assisting their tipsy masters homeward, they spread the word. Among the first recipients were the chair slaves of the Vestal Servilia, who were bearing her from a service at the Temple of Juno Lucina. From there, they bore the news down the great Suburan Way the whole distance to the Forum, where they deposited their mistress in the House of the Vestals and rushed out to gossip with the slaves lounging around in the Forum, which is what most slaves do when they can get away with it.

From the Forum, the story spread outward like an explosion of noxious gas from an eruption of Aetna. It reached me in the Temple of Jupiter Optimus Maximus atop the Capitol, where Caesar had summoned the Senate for a meeting. I believe the subject was to be the confirmation of Cleopatra as queen of Egypt, but we never got around to discussing the matter. Word of the incident made its way up the Capitol faster than water could have run down it.

When Caesar arrived, his gilded chaplet restored to order atop his bald pate, wearing a snowy tunic and the purple triumphal robe that he had taken to wearing on all public occasions, its color matched that of his nose. Even as he strode importantly into the temple, a senator named Sextus Mummius, a satirical poet of some reputation, was declaiming an extempore ode upon the vengeance of Vulcan on the occasion of surprising his wife, Venus, abed with Mars. It was full of scurillous references and bawdy allusions, and Caesar turned purple from hairline to toes as the whole Senate erupted with laughter at his expense. In those days there were some subjects about which any Roman, even a dictator, could be laughed at to his face.

Having traced the origin and path of the story, I later calculated that, from the passing of the wedding party to the door of Lollius to the tale reaching the Temple of Jupiter, no more than three-quarters of an hour had elapsed. Such is the passion of Romans for spreading gossip.

In any case, I found myself climbing that selfsame hill, although not all the way to the top. The Tabularium, where the censors' records are kept, is located somewhat less than halfway up. I went up the long stairway past the Temple of Concord, a deified virtue much needed in Rome that year, and entered the archive through a basement entrance. The long, beautiful facade of the building, as seen from the Forum, is actually the second story of the eastern side.

It was to that splendid colonnade that I climbed, and there I found Hermes, lording it over the archival slaves as personal assistant to the Aedile. They had scrolls and tablets spread out on the long tables.

"As you requested, Aedile," intoned the freedman in charge of the censors' records, "these are the documents pertaining to the recent censorship of Valerius Messala Niger and Servilius Vatia Isauricus."

The two men were among the most distinguished Romans of their day, as censors usually were. It was also traditional that they be hidebound conservatives, and these two certainly qualified on that account. Vatia Isauricus was also among the oldest members of the Senate, having served as consul during Sulla's dictatorship.

Messala Niger was a much younger man, but just as much a die-hard adherent of the aristocratic party and a patrician of the Valerian family to boot. That put him in the same camp as my own family, and of the anti-Clodian and anti-Caesarean faction as well.

Censors at that time were elected every five years, and their duties were strictly defined. They conducted the five-yearly census of the citizens, carried out the *lustrum* to ritually purify the army, reviewed the list of junior office holders for admission to the Senate, and purged that body of unfit members. Most important for the purpose of my investigation, they handed out the public contracts for such things as tax collection, road repair, supplying military equipment, and so forth. Men were willing to offer heavy bribes to secure those contracts. Other men took to bribery to get into the Senate or to be readmitted after expulsion by previous censors. It was for this reason that the censors were mostly old, distinguished, and rich. It was thought that such men were less amenable to bribery.

I have never understood the logic of this line of reasoning. Men are often rich *because* they are greedy. And a man who was greedy when young is rarely less so in old age. As for good breeding, I never noticed that a long pedigree reduced anyone's share of evil qualities. In fact, high social position often as not bestows greater power and scope to exercise those very qualities. Such was the traditional belief nonetheless, and who was I to question tradition?

"May I know what we are looking for?" the freedman asked.

"At the moment I am interested solely in the public contracts. But not tax farming. Specifically, the work of civic construction and demolition, and I would very much like to see the name of one Marcus Caninus in there."

The freedman sighed. "All right, let's get to it." To the slaves: "Break them down by subject first before looking for specific names. Place all relevant documents here," he rapped on the center of the table. "All others are to be returned to their proper bins. When all the irrelevant documents have been eliminated, we shall divide the remainder and each search for the things the honored aedile needs to know." This seemed like an eminently sensible system to me. I don't know what we would do without the State freedmen. They keep the Empire going while we enjoy the loot.

"Splendid," I commended him. While this first stage of the labor was underway, I paced along the colonnade enjoying the fine view of the Forum, which, due to the aforementioned rivalry between Caesar and Pompey, looked better than it had in years. The rivalry was still friendly at that time, and all Rome profited from it. Each man sought to refurbish buildings and monuments to the glory of his own family.

Pompey had repaired all his father's monuments and had renovated the Temple of Castor and Pollux in his own name, but he had saved the really spectacular work for his immense theater and its adjacent complex of public buildings out on the Campus Martius.

Caesar, whose family was far more ancient and extended, had done more in the Forum. As *Pontifex Maximus* he had restored the house of the *Pontifex Maximus* and the adjacent House of the Vestals, along with a restoration of the Temple of Vesta, which he had had the good taste to leave in its simple, primitive form. He had restored the trophies of Marius, a gesture much appreciated by the commons, who still worshipped the crazy old butcher. Marius had been Caesar's uncle by marriage, and the old Marians were still his main power base.

As aedile he had completely repaved the Forum and its adjacent markets and renovated every building associated with his family. It was one of the most ancient, so that was a lot of buildings.

I pondered this profusion of white marble and brilliant gilding admiringly, comforted in the knowledge that these two great men were willing to squander such immense sums to buy the goodwill of their fellow citizens. There was only one grating fact to mar my pleasure. I couldn't see the front of any new or renovated building without reading their names.

Looking out over the roof of the Temple of Saturn, I saw a group of men round the corner of the Basilica Sempronia.

All wore green tunics, and something in the swagger of their walk said they were up to no good.

"Hermes," I said, "come here." He put down the scroll he had been studying and leaned on the waist-high railing, his sharp gaze following the path of my pointing finger. "Please tell me those are slaves from the stables of the Green Faction."

"I suppose I could," he allowed, "if you didn't mind me lying to you. Those are Plautius Hypsaeus's men. There are so many gangs these days that they've taken to wearing different colors to keep each other sorted out during the street brawls."

"So that's why the last dead Clodians I saw in the streets had orange stripes on their tunics," I said.

"And why Milo just gave all his men new white tunics, although he claims it's just so they'll look smart when they follow him around in public. Aufidius's boys have red borders on their tunics, Scaevola's wear sky blue—" He went on, reciting a list of lesser mobs, each now with its own insignia.

The Plautius Hypsaeus he mentioned was yet another of our political gangsters. Like Milo, he was a candidate for consul for the coming year. It says much of Roman politics of the time that three candidates for the highest offices were gang leaders.

"Uh-oh," Hermes said. "Look over there." He was pointing to another group of men crossing the Via Sacra near the Temple of Venus Cloacina to the north. These had the same swagger, and their tunics were red bordered. Aufidius was a lesser gangster, but he supported Milo, Hypsaeus's rival. "A silver denarius says they're fighting before the redstripers are past the urban praetor's platform." Bloodthirsty little wretch.

"Not a chance," I said. "They're outnumbered, so they'll run over there to Sulla's Numidian War monument and put their backs against it, if they've got the sense of a goose."

"Done," Hermes said. "If first blood falls between the platform and the monument, the bet's off."

As I had anticipated, the two little mobs caught sight of one another across the Forum and stopped in their tracks like two dog packs with their necks bristling. I could almost see their fingers moving as they counted; then the men in green charged forward as those with the red stripes sidled toward the old monument, one Caesar had never bothered to restore since Sulla had been his enemy and had stolen the glory of that campaign from Marius. The red-striped Aufidians just managed to reach the monument and turn at bay as the Hypsaeans caught up with the hindmost man and brought him down with a brick. Hermes slid the denarius along the railing toward my hand. I picked it up and tucked it beneath my belt.

Down below, some women started screaming, and people mounted the steps of temples and basilicas to enjoy the show. The bullies of these gangs were often ex-gladiators who had served their time, so there was sometimes skilled fighting to be seen.

When neither side could make the other run with sticks and bricks, the forbidden blades appeared and the blood began to flow in earnest.

"New bunch!" Hermes cried, as a little gang of men wearing yellow headbands ran in from the direction of the Temple of Vesta and attacked the green-wearers from behind.

"Who are these?" I asked Hermes.

He shrugged. "Never saw them before. They're good."

A general engagement now prevailed in the Forum. A few veteran brawlers wearing no discernible colors had joined in, apparently just for the fun of it. The state freedman who, along with his staff, had been ignoring all the noise, turned from his records at a renewed outburst of screaming and looked at the fighting mob disdainfully.

"Rome should have a decent police force. I am from Pergamum, and my city has never been disgraced by such a scene."

"We've always done well enough without police," I said. He was right, of course. Rome desperately needed a reliable police force, but you don't just admit such a thing to a foreign-born freedman.

"If this is doing well enough, you can have it," he said, turning back to the stacks of documents.

Foreigners often act as if law and order were the highest of civic virtues, especially those from the civilized and monarch-ridden eastern part of the world. Romans were disorderly in those days, but at least they didn't spend their lives kissing the backside of a king. Unlike now.

Hermes and I enjoyed the show in the Forum for a while longer. Two well-known swordsmen of the day, Thracian dagger fighters, climbed on the monument and dueled to great applause and encouragement. Hermes won his denarius back on that one. On the whole, although it lacked pomp and solemnity, gilded armor and colorful plumes, it was almost as good as the *munera*.

"Aedile?" said the freedman. "As much as I hate to interrupt your—"

"Think nothing of it," I said, waving aside his apology. "It's all but over. Nothing much left to do except mop up the blood. What progress have we made?"

"*We*," he said, emphasizing the word, "have separated all the documents relating to the public contracts let by authority of that censorship. I have marked two that featured the name you mentioned." The stack he indicated was much reduced but still substantial.

"Excellent. Have these delivered to my house in the Subura. I shall need to peruse them at leisure."

He looked at me as if a malicious god had just transformed me into a sheep. "You want me to allow state documents to leave the Tabularium?" Judging by his tone of voice, I might have asked him to break into the House of the Vestals and bugger all the virgins.

"Exactly. The Tabularium is not a temple or any other sacred place. It is state property dedicated to the storage of state documents. As an official of the State in pursuit of his duties, I require that these documents be taken to my home."

He folded his arms and stared at me down his long, Graeco-Syrian nose, no small feat since I was far taller than he. "Not without the express order of a censor or one of the consuls." There is nothing to match the hauteur of a state flunky.

"The censors stepped down from office last year," I said, "and the consuls have not yet taken office due to irregularities in the election of last year."

"Well, then, you must simply do your perusing here."

Behind him the state slaves grinned. One of them winked at me and made the universal hand sign for a transfer of funds.

I draped an arm over the freedman's shoulder. "My friend, let us take a little walk and speak together." We promenaded along the beautiful colonnade, where scholars and officials studied a multitude of state documents at the long tables, the southern exposure affording them the best possible reading light. As we walked, heads close together, we negotiated.

Luckily for me, the man did not want his bribe in the form of cash, of which I had little to spare; but he knew that I would be a praetor within a very few years, and there was a promotion he very much desired, which, in that office, I would be in a position to grant him. He likewise wanted to name the state slave to be manumitted and placed in his own present post. I knew that it was from that man he would receive his cash bribe, making his transaction with me more like a respectable exchange of favors. By the time we returned to the table, we had come to an agreement, and he directed some of the slaves under his charge to box up the documents and deliver them to my house.

This was a fairly straightforward transaction as such things were practiced at the time. A straight transfer of money was crass and vulgar, but a mutual exchange of favors was much esteemed. It was an unfair, inefficient, and corrupt system; but at least it worked, after a fashion. The First Citizen has spoiled it all by creating a bureaucracy made up of his own freedmen, handpicked by him and educated to their tasks, subject to periodic review and promoted or demoted accordingly. It is awesomely efficient and service is much improved, but the freedmen owe their loyalty only to him.

I prefer the old way.

4

WE WERE WALKING BACK across the Forum when Festus caught up with me.

Now that the fighting was over, a couple of praetors had come out with their lictors to make arrests. A number of men lay about groaning, trying to crawl away, or just lying inert. I couldn't tell if any particular gang had emerged victorious, but that really wasn't the point. It is seldom possible to determine the winner in a brawl. The idea is to disrupt civic life and cow and terrorize the citizenry so that nobody dared stand for office against the gang leaders or the politicians they supported. The elections themselves were usually decided by bribery. I never said the Republic was perfect.

"Patron!" Festus shouted. Then, correcting himself, "I mean, Aedile!" He was an officious little man, son of one of our country stewards, come to the City and prospering as an oil merchant. He was one of the men I had sent to check on the troublesome drains.

"Yes, my friend?" I said, gesturing broadly. One of the rewards of clientage was being recognized publicly by a high official. Festus basked in the attention.

"Aedile, the state freedman Acilius wants you to come at once. He has something he says you must see."

"He does, does he?" I had been looking forward to an hour or two at the baths, free of official worries. "This freedman summons a high official like a household slave?"

Festus smiled obsequiously. "He says it's very important, sir."

"Oh, well. What's an aedile anyway? Just a glorified errand boy at everyone's beck and call." I went on in this fashion for some time. I did a lot of complaining that year. While I lamented the woes of the aedileship, we walked to the Forum access to the Cloaca Maxima, first and biggest of Rome's sewers.

This access was covered with a shrine in the form of a miniature temple dedicated to Venus Cloacina, she who oversees the purity of Rome's water. Inside this diminutive sanctuary, a steep staircase led down to the great drain. The distance was not far, for the tunnel lies just beneath the surface of the streets, angling downhill to the river. The stairwell was lined with tiny niches in which burned oil lamps. By the time we reached bottom, my eyes were almost accustomed to the dimness. The air was cold after the unseasonable warmth of the open air.

I was always uneasy intruding in this subterranean realm. There seemed something unnatural about this aqueous city beneath the City. It took an effort to maintain my air of official *dignitas* as we entered the small landing, its walls painted with ancient murals depicting half-forgotten gods and demons; snake-haired harpies with bulging eyes; long-nosed, donkey-eared, Etruscan death guides; and creatures that had no names in the whole vast nomenclature of Roman religion. Most prominent among them was the ferryman common to most religions, the one who takes the shades of the dead across the river Styx.

His near-double was waiting for us. Tied up to the miniature landing was a barge built like a small riverboat, painted black but decorated with the serpents, ox skulls, and red dogs traditionally associated with underground deities carved in low relief all around the sides, twined with painted myrtle and cornel shoots. Chained in the stern of the barge was an old slave whose white hair reached his elbows, bearded to the waist, clutching a long pole in hands like twisted claws. In the lamplight, his deep-shadowed eyes glittered like obsidian. In the subterranean gloom, he was as sure sighted as an owl, but he would have been struck blind by sunlight.

This ancient apparition was, naturally, known as Charon, and he had been a sewer bargeman since my father was a boy, condemned for some long-forgotten crime to ply the dark waters and never return to the surface.

"Welcome, Aedile," said Acilius, who stood on the landing with a couple of his assistants. "If you will accompany me in the barge, I will show you a few things that demand your immediate attention."

"Splendid," I said, stepping into the craft and seating myself on one of its benches. "There's nothing to liven up a fine afternoon like a boating expedition in a sewer."

Actually, that stretch of the Cloaca Maxima was not at all objectionable, Many people never realize that the Forum was once a swamp, and the original cloaca was a simple canal dug to drain it. In time, the channel had been lined with stone to make it permanent; then it was roofed and paved over back when Rome had kings. Those old kings had built well; and after four hundred years, the stonework was as solid as ever, needing no upkeep at all.

"Roman engineering at its best!" I exclaimed, admiring the great, beautifully fitted tufa blocks overhead and to both sides. Here the water was relatively fresh, but that did not last long. Soon we came to the first of the public latrines situated directly over the sewer. Luckily for us, Charon, with his long pole, was adept at avoiding these conveniences, so we were spared being the targets of descending missiles. At intervals we passed lower arches, where smaller sewers contributed their outflow to the greater stream.

The air began to grow dense as the water grew thicker. Soon we were plowing through a horrid scum through which unpleasant bubbles rose and burst, like the bubbles of fermentation in a wine vat. I withstood the stench manfully. It was little worse than some of the fouler alleys of the Subura where the inhabitants dumped their slop jars and kitchen refuse into the streets and where the muck would suppurate through a hot, rainless summer until just passing by such an alley could be lethal to one not native to the district. The Cloaca Maxima had a long way to go before it would be that bad.

"Fine prospect, eh?" Acilius said exultantly, as if this were his own, personal triumph.

"It's not exactly boating on the Bay of Baiae," I said,

not to be intimidated, "but it smells better than a Gallic town that's been under siege for a month or two." This put him in his place nicely. Being a freedman, he had never served with the legions, whereas soldiering was the primary duty of my own class. Like the rest of them, I often pretended that I enjoyed the horrid business.

"Six years ago," he went on, "this water was nearly clean all the way to the Tiber."

"So what has happened in the last six years?" I asked, with a sigh. Some men cannot simply state what is on their minds. First, they have to unburden themselves of a whole philosophical system.

"Nothing," he said.

"Nothing?" *Here it comes,* I thought.

"Exactly! Nothing has been done by the last censors or the last five sets of aediles to care for these drains and sewers, the very lifeblood of the City!"

"I would have used a more suitable anatomical metaphor, but I get your point. Is the structure in danger?"

"Aedile, as far as I can tell, this system has not required repair to the structure since it was built. Even the smaller, later sewers that drain the lesser valleys are perfectly sound and will last another thousand years, barring a truly terrible earthquake."

"Well," I hazarded, "there are rather more people in the City than there used to be. Pompey's veterans who couldn't get land settlements, for instance, and they've brought in countless slaves that were a part of their loot. And all the manumitted slaves who—"

"Still not enough to strain the system," he said, impatiently. "And most of the new population have taken up residence in the new districts outside the walls, the Trans-Tiber and the Campus Martius. No, Aedile, what we have here is plain neglect." He turned to our boatman. "This one," he said, pointing to a low arch from which black fluid flowed sluggishly.

"Hold your breath," Hermes muttered.

"Don't worry," Acilius said, "we won't be going far."

The light of our torches barely pierced the foul haze within the sewer. Drain openings overhead shot occasional beams downward, but the water was too clogged and murky to reflect anything. We heard occasional slithers and splashes, for there are creatures that prefer such an environment. Eventually the prow of the boat nudged something and would go no farther.

I squinted ahead but saw nothing but a shapeless mass before us. "Give me a torch." Hermes passed me one, and I held it out over the prow. It wasn't much improvement. I could make out nothing but a hulking mass of indescribable rubbish. I thought I could make out a few broken pots, a bone or two, but the great mass had crumbled, melted, rotted, or otherwise metamorphosed into a form of matter unknown to the philosophers of Alexandria. The stench that emanated from it was as palpable as a brick in the face.

"Careful," Acilius warned. "Even here, you could set it afire."

"That could only improve things," I said. I removed the torch from dangerous proximity though. "How did this come about, and how extensive is it?"

"It came about through long neglect of the sewers, coupled with widespread violation of the ordinances against dumping trash in the drains. Everything people are too lazy to carry to the dumps outside the walls gets thrown down the nearest drain. The objects that will not float build up in the channel until they form veritable reefs, then *everything* piles up against them, and high water from the heavy rains just heaps it up higher. You asked how extensive this problem is?"

"I did," I said, as if either of us needed reminding.

"Every last sewer in Rome is like this, Aedile. Only the main channels of the largest sewers are clear: the Maxima, the Petronia, and the Nodina. Those follow the courses of old creeks and have a relatively steady flow, and even their bottoms are getting full of nonbuoyant refuse. The smaller, tributary sewers are clotted just like this one, all of them. And it's not just broken furniture and kitchen trash, Aedile. There are a great many corpses down here."

"Corpses?" I knew that something more potent than garbage had to account for that smell.

"Oh, yes. The poor use the drains to dispose of aborted or unwanted infants. And people often want to be spared the expense of burying their dead slaves or the inconvenience of hauling them to the pits outside the Esquiline Gate. And these are not just the slaves of contractors and factory owners, either. Slaves of the wealthy sometimes find their way down here, and, of course, the occasional murder victim."

"Infamous!" I said, meaning it. Not that murder was so great a crime, and the exposure of unwanted infants was lawful if distasteful, but to deny proper burial even to the lowliest was impious and could draw down the wrath of the gods. "The whole City could suffer for this!"

"I'd say it was suffering right now," Hermes said, gagging.

"We've seen enough, let's get away from here," I told the boatman. He began to pole us back toward the main channel. Soon we were breathing what seemed to be, by contrast, almost clean air. I ordered Charon to take us to the river.

"Who is responsible for scouring out these channels?" I asked.

"Like most such work," Acilius said, "it is done on a basis of public contracts let every five years by the censors, then overseen by the aediles. A thorough cleaning of the whole system should have been undertaken, at latest, two years ago, during the censorship of—"

"Don't tell me," I interrupted. "It was Messala Niger and Servilius Vatia. Didn't those two do *anything* while they were in office?"

"Not much," Festus commented. "But what's new about that? You were back from Gaul while they were in office, weren't you, Patron?"

"They'd been sitting for about six months when I returned. They were supposed to get the public contracts settled in their first month or two, then conduct the census and purge the senatorial lists, and wind up with the *lustrum*. When my father and Hortalus were censors, they got the whole task done in their first six months."

"Not every Roman magistrate is as energetic and conscientious as your father, Patron," Festus observed. "And Vatia Isauricus was awfully old, you'll recall."

"Messala was lively enough," I said. "And still is, for that matter. I may have to speak with him." One more thing to look for in those documents I'd bribed away from the Tabularium.

Ahead of us, the half circle of the river portal seemed as bright as the rising sun. Charon nudged the boat alongside the raised walkway that formed an elongated landing. The old boatman squinted, dazzled by the clear light. We disembarked and walked toward the light. The tour of the sewer had been so oppressive that I had to restrain myself from breaking into a run.

Moments later we were standing by the river, filling our lungs with clean air, blowing like so many porpoises to clear our heads of the nauseous miasma. The daylight seemed incredibly clean and clear.

"You will do something about this, Aedile?" Acilius asked.

"Decidedly. What we just saw is a menace to the health of all Romans and an affront to the gods. Why"—I gestured toward the river before us—"Father Tiber himself must be insulted that the unburied dead are committed to him."

"He doesn't look too happy as it is," Hermes said. "Look, he's risen since we crossed this morning."

He was right. The waterline was noticeably higher than that morning. "Come along, Hermes. We need to speak with the rivermen." I dismissed the rest of the party with further assurances that I would do something about the condition of the sewers, although just what was unclear even as I promised it.

We had emerged into daylight with the Aemilian Bridge to our right. Turning left, we passed under the Sublician Bridge, walking along the great westward bend of the river. Beyond the Sublician lay the river wharves, where the barges up from Ostia unloaded their cargoes then reloaded them with the products of Rome and the inland farm country to be taken down to the harbor for export.

This was one of the liveliest, most active districts of the City, most of it outside the walls. The natives spoke a river dialect all their own, and a score of foreign languages could be heard. Sailors from every nation touched by the sea coming upriver to trade or see the sights are among our most numerous visitors. The factors of many foreign companies had their offices along the wharves.

Foreign tongues were not the only alien sounds to be heard. The cries, roars, bellows, and squawks of exotic beasts and birds were everywhere, as cages from Africa, Egypt, Spain, Syria, Phrygia, and places even more remote were brought in for the gardens and estates of the rich and, more often, for the hunts in the Circus. There were lions and leopards, peacocks, ostriches, bears, bulls, racing horses, zebras, camels, and even stranger creatures.

About as many slaves were being unloaded for the markets, but they walked off the barges under their own power and were far quieter than the beasts. This was a sight I found far less agreeable than that of odd animals. I am quite aware that civilization cannot exist without slaves, but some limits should be observed. There were far too many slaves in Rome already, and the recent wars had flooded the markets with even more, so cheap that even poor households could afford a few.

The great bulk of the slaves were sold to the vast *latifundia* of Sicily and southern Italy before they ever saw Rome. The others were, for the most part, the better looking and more skilled captives destined for household service. There were beautiful young women and boys for the houses of the wealthy and the brothels, trained masseurs for the baths, artists, cooks, and so forth, plus a few stalwart young warriors to be trained as gladiators. These last seldom had to be chained or coerced and usually faced their fate cheerfully. Raised as tribal warriors, the prospect of being given their keep and no duties except to train and fight suited them well enough. Being set to labor would have been an unthinkable disgrace.

But I was not there to enjoy the sights. We walked along the wharves until we came to a stretch of the river walk paved with colorful mosaic, where a stout, baldheaded man sat at ease behind a stone table, shaded by a yellow awning and attended by a secretary. He rose when he caught sight of me and raised an arm.

"Good day, Aedile! What brings you to the wharves this fine afternoon?"

"Good day, Marcus Ogulnius!" I called to the wharf master. He was a *publicanus* charged with collecting import duties, docking fees, and so forth. A bit of each transaction stuck, lawfully, to his fingers, so he was a rich man. I didn't see much of him because, strictly speaking, his office came under the purview of the curule aedile as regulator of markets. "I've come to confer with knowledgeable men about the state of the river."

"If you'd come a day later there might have been none for you to confer with," he said. "When this lot of barges is finished unloading, they'll be headed back to Ostia; and we'll see no more for a while. I'm amazed they made it here today with this current. This evening I'll pack up my office and move to higher ground for the duration."

"That bad?" I said. "I saw that the river was rising, but we're still far from flood stage."

"Cast your eyes up there, Aedile. Look at the Janiculum." I gazed toward the hilltop where the red flag flew as it had for centuries, to be lowered only if an enemy approached the City. The long strip of scarlet cloth stood almost straight out, its tip snapping back and forth in a blurring motion. "That wind's from due south, straight out of Africa. Here in Rome it just makes for some nice, warm days in a season when it's usually still cold. But it's blowing full blast on the mountaintops, and it's melting the snow."

"I heard something of the sort earlier today," I allowed.

"Well, you can believe it. You'll soon be getting word of mountain towns destroyed by floods and wiped out by avalanches. The snows this winter were the worst in living memory, so I'm told. Those snows and this sirocco make for a bad combination, sir. The river's about to rise faster than anyone's seen it rise, and this bend of the river right here's going to catch the worst of it. It always does."

"Have any precautions been taken?" I asked him.

He shrugged, surprised. "What can be done about a flood? When Father Tiber decides to get out of bed and move about, you'd best get out of his way."

"Sound advice."

He thought for a while. "There were some engineering works supposed to be undertaken awhile back to keep the river in its banks, but they never got past the planning stage. Of course, that was under the censors—"

"Servilius Vatia and Valerius Messala!" Hermes and I chorused together.

The wharf master looked at us strangely. "That's right."

A thought occurred to me. "You obtained your public contract from them, did you not?"

"Renewed it, actually. I've held this post for more than twenty years, and my father had it before me."

"It is done by open bidding, is it not?"

"Assuredly. It's all in knowing the job. There's others would like to have it, but my family's done it for so long that I know to the last sestertius what it's worth to the State and what it's worth to me. Anyone who tries to underbid me is a fool who doesn't know the work and will bollix it up, costing everyone. The censors know that, sir, and they renew my contract every five years accordingly."

More likely, I thought, *he has grown so rich that no one who wants the office could bribe the censors half so well as he.* I didn't hold it against him. He was an honest man by most men's standards and collecting revenues for the river traffic was too important to the State to be left to a fool or an amateur.

"How long do we have, do you think, before the low parts of the City are flooded?"

He rubbed his chin. "Some predict the river walk will be ankle deep by morning, and that's why I'm clearing out tonight. It could be up into the Forum Boarium and in the Circus by next morning. Personally, I don't think it's going to be all that quick, but I'm not taking any chances."

"Wise move. What about the warehouses and the boats?"

"The river people have known this flood was coming for more than a year. They've taken precautions. Goods have been stored up higher than usual. Anything made of wood's likely to be lost though." He shrugged again. "Nothing that can't be replaced. Inside the City"—he jerked a thumb back over his shoulder toward the city wall that rose behind him—"that, I'm not responsible for. But I hope your house is on high ground."

"High enough," I told him. Something was tickling away at the back of my mind, some business that I had previously had planned for the wharf area. That was my greatest problem—I had too many things crowding my mind, each demanding my attention. Then I remembered.

"Do you know of a barge owner named Lucius Folius?"

"Certainly. He owns at least a hundred barges on the river. I heard he was killed in that *insula* collapse yesterday."

"He was, along with his wife and his whole household. Has anyone been acting for him here, a factor or a business partner? Someone is going to have to take over his operations."

"No one's showed up yet, but it'll take awhile in any case. I know he had a factor downriver at Ostia to handle the overseas part of the trade. All the river trades have their headquarters at Ostia. Like I said, nothing's going to come up from Ostia for a while."

"He can come by road," I told him. "I'm going to send a summons. I have questions about Lucius Folius that need answering. What sort of trade did he engage in?"

"At this end, it was mostly general cargoes: slaves, worked metal, oil, some livestock, and paying passengers. Light loads for the most part. A lot more comes into Rome than goes out of it."

"And what did he bring in?"

"He had some fish barges, Rome being a great consumer of sea fish. The usual wines and exotic slaves for the great households. That was at the Ostia end. He also brought in a good deal of cargo from along the river. I'd estimate that at least half of his imports were picked up at the wharves between here and Ostia."

"Agricultural products, I take it?"

"For the most part. And building materials."

My neck prickled in that old, familiar fashion, and I felt a little smile tugging at the corners of my mouth. "Building materials, you say?"

"Absolutely. I won't say that he had a monopoly on the stuff—a lot comes in through the landward gates—but I'd wager that more than half of the timber and brick and roofing tile, sand and mortar and so forth, that came up by river arrived in his hulls."

"Stone? Marble? Lead and bronze for roofs?"

Ogulnius shook his bald head. "No, those things are used mainly for the big public projects—the temples and porticoes and the restoration works. In the last ten years, 90 percent of that material's gone into Pompey's big theater and its complex out on the Campus Martius. The great men like Pompey mostly contract independently for work like that, use their own slaves and freedmen, and buy directly from the quarrymen. I heard Pompey just bought his own quarries and workers outright to spare himself the trouble of going through middlemen. He bypassed the wharves here and built his own up past the Island, where he could unload near his project.

"No, Aedile, men like that would not deal with the likes of Lucius Folius, unless they were putting up housing for the workers. Even then they'd deal directly with the building contractors, not with a man who hauled brick and mortar."

"You've been of great help, Marcus Ogulnius," I commended him.

"Always happy to be of service to Senate and People," he said, beaming. They had certainly been a source of profit to him.

We reentered the City near the Sublician Bridge, just off the Forum Boarium of which Ogulnius had just spoken. It, along with the nearby Circus Maximus, lay on the lowest ground within the walls and was thereby the area most vulnerable to flooding.

Here, just a few hundred paces from the rising Tiber, nobody seemed to be taking any action. All the gossip I overheard was about the brawl in the Forum earlier that day. On a whim I went over to one of the stall keepers, an old fellow from across the river who sold kids and smelled very much like his merchandise. When I asked whether he and the other market people were preparing for a flood, he merely looked amused.

"The river's always rising, sir. Sometimes it floods; sometimes it don't. Not much we can do about it either way."

I found this to be the general attitude. Several people pointed out to me that it hadn't rained recently. Mountain snow meant nothing to them.

"I hope they've got the horses out of the City," Hermes said, pointing to the huge establishments of the racing factions situated near the Circus. Like most Romans, he didn't care if the rest of the City washed away or burned down as long as it didn't interfere with the races. A few hundred drowned citizens was a prospect he could face with equanimity. A loss of several hundred fine chariot horses was a tragedy beyond imagining.

"They're all out in the pastures this time of year," I assured him. "The season doesn't start until the Megalensian

Games next month." As if I needed to remind him when the racing season started. I didn't need to be reminded either since I would be in charge of a major portion of this year's Games. There were days when I thought of little else.

"That's a relief," he said. "What now?"

I contemplated the geography of the City. My own house, while not far up the slopes like the more fashionable mansions, lay high enough to have escaped the last couple of floods. "Are any of the baths on high ground?" I mused.

"None I can think of," Hermes answered.

"Then I'd better get a bath now. They may be out of commission tomorrow."

"Good idea," he said. "I'll run and get your bath things."

"First go up there," I pointed up the slope of the Aventine to the Temple of Ceres no more than a hundred paces away. "Find a messenger, tell him to get a horse and whatever else he needs for a dash to Ostia, and report to me at my usual bathhouse. Then to my house. Tell Julia I'll be late again, and find out if the documents from the Tabularium have been delivered. Bring back a skin of decent Falernian, and don't drink any on the way. I'll know if you've diluted it." He looked offended and trotted off. Julia's dowry had provided me with a better quality of wine than I had been used to maintaining. Keeping the boy's hands off it was a full-time job.

I made my way slowly to my favorite *balneum,* located near the Temple of Saturn. Really large bathhouses were just beginning to be seen in Rome, but this was an older establishment and rather modest. It was handy to the Forum and was frequented by many senators. It charged a bit more than others of the same quality, making it more exclusive. Besides providing a decent bath, it was a good place to pick up political gossip.

I did a bit of meeting and greeting in the Forum; and by the time I got to the *balneum,* Hermes was there with the skin, towels, scented oil, and my scraper.

"Julia was concerned," he reported, as he relieved me of toga, tunic, and sandals. "She had heard about the riot in the Forum and was worried that you might have been involved. I assured her that we watched the whole thing from the Tabularium, and she was relieved."

"Did she know about the coming flood?"

"Hadn't heard a word of it. Cassandra told her that flood water has never reached the place as long as she's been a slave there."

"Why is it," I said, bracing myself for the torture of the cold pool, "that everyone in Rome finds out about the most foolish rumors instantly while staying blissfully oblivious of momentous news?"

"Must be a trick the gods played on us," he said. "Like when they gave what's-her-name the gift of prophecy but made it so that nobody would ever believe her."

"Cassandra," I informed him, "daughter of Priam. Yes, that may be it. Gods do things like that sometimes. They have a sense of humor, you know."

I decided that since this might be my last chance for some time, to go for the full treatment. So I went out into the exercise yard, and while Hermes helped me oil up I sought out a suitable training partner. A number of the younger senators were wrestling, some of them with considerable brutality, in the sand pit. Older ones contented themselves with rolling in the sand to get a good coating. The smell of overheated bodies coated with cheap olive oil was pungent, but after those sewers I scarcely noticed.

"Decius Caecilius!" shouted a loud voice. I turned and saw a handsome, ox-muscled young man swaggering his way toward me. "I'll try a few falls with you." It was Marcus Antonius. He had recently returned from a stint with the army of Aulus Gabinius in Syria and Egypt, where Antonius had won great distinction as a soldier. He had come back to Rome to stand for quaestor that year, not bothering to campaign for the office because Caesar wanted him for his staff in Gaul and the Centuriate Assembly would simply name him and send him off without a ballot. Things always came easy to young Antonius.

"You won't break my nose again?"

"As long as you don't grab me by the balls like last time."

Within a few seconds, he had me pinned to the ground with an arm twisted behind me and his knee against my spine.

"You've been away from the legions too long, Decius," he said, letting me up. "When you were first back from Gaul, it took me twice that long to pin you." Then he yelped as I grabbed his heel in both hands and heaved upward with my whole body. He landed on his back, and the breath went out of him in a great whoosh.

"Never underestimate age and treachery," I warned him. "Youth and strength are no match for them."

"I'll remember," he said, launching himself from the sand like a Hyrkanian tiger, catching me around the waist and making me fly.

Some time later we limped from the pit, completely

covered with sweat, oily sand, and clotting blood, most of the latter still pouring from my nose. True to his word, he hadn't quite broken it. Hermes began efficiently stripping the mixture from my skin with the bronze scraper, snapping the accumulation with a practiced flick of the wrist into the box provided for the purpose. Antonius's slave was doing the same for him.

After all the violent activity, the cold bath felt almost good. The tepid bath was better yet, and the hot bath was like ascending to Olympus. The Falernian helped, too. It was considered bad form to drink at the baths, but I was never terribly conventional and compared to Antonius I was the soul of decorum. The young man was swiftly living up to his family's reputation as a pack of violent criminals. He was enormous fun, though, and consequently very popular.

"When do you depart for Gaul?" I asked him.

"Not for another nine months," he said unhappily. "Everyone insists I have to wait until after the elections. I don't see why. It's not as if there's any question about my getting the quaestorship."

"It's because there's been too much flouting of the rules already, and it makes people uneasy. First Pompey gets all his commands without working his way up the *cursus honorum,* then Caesar gets an unprecedented five-year command, which it looks like he's going to have extended. It looks bad. If a mere quaestor just starting out his career can ignore the rules, people will start thinking it means a return to the bad old days with Romans fighting Romans for position and power."

"I suppose you're right," he said. "We have to keep up appearances for the sake of the mob, as if the Senate and its old-fashioned rules still had any use in the real world." He downed another slug of unwatered wine.

I sighed. How typical of an Antonine. They were as bad as Claudians. Worse, even.

A patter of sandaled feet announced the arrival of my messenger. Bare feet are the rule in the *balneum,* but a messenger is exempted from most of the rules of protocol. This one wore the livery of the guild: a brief, white tunic that left one shoulder bare; a round, brimmed hat with little silver wings attached; high-strapped sandals with silver wings on the heels; and a white wand. At this time the messengers were an independent company working on a State contract, much like the lictors.

While he waited I dictated a letter to the quaestor at Ostia, requiring him to find Lucius Folius's factor in that city and deliver him a summons to report to Rome for questioning. Hermes copied the message on a wax tablet and held it out for me to stamp with my signet ring. Then he closed the wooden leaves and tied them together.

"Ride hard and you will be in Ostia well before dark," I said, as the messenger tucked the tablet into his satchel made of waterproof sealskin. He knew perfectly well how long it took to make the fourteen miles from Rome to Ostia, but he was accustomed to people giving him unneeded advice. He saluted and ran off, silver flashing from his winged heels.

"What's this about?" Antonius asked, so I told him about the late Lucius Folius and the trouble his near-anonymity was causing me.

"Folius? I think I've met that bastard. He's from Bovillae, I think. Was, I should say. If it's the one I'm thinking of, he was a client of my uncle's. The fellow was more than my uncle could stomach, and he let him know that he was unwelcome."

"Antonius Hybrida found someone too vicious for his taste?" I said, aghast.

Young Antonius laughed heartily. "Hard to imagine, isn't it?" His uncle, Antonius Hybrida, was as depraved a rogue and bandit as ever left high office in Rome to go on to do even worse things in the provinces. Cruel and corrupt, he was the epitome of all things Antonian.

"Actually, it wasn't Folius so much as that iron-plated bitch of a wife he had. Rome's a better place today for her passing. Once, when they had Hybrida in their house for dinner, she said the duck was overdone, or something of the sort, and she had the cook dragged in. The poor fool was a Greek, trained in Sybaris, cost a fortune. She had a big slave jam the whole duck down the man's throat, then she had him trussed up to a *triclinium* wall and flogged to death in front of the guests. Spattered blood on everyone's best clothes."

My jaw dropped. "Was this in *Rome?*"

"In a house Folius rented on the Quirinal. It was too rich even for Hybrida, but typical of those climbers who come here to weasel themselves in with the better people. Folius's wife thought it would impress the great Romans that she would kill an expensive slave just because he'd spoiled dinner. Hybrida let them know that here in Rome we punish our slaves decently, in private. I think he sent them the laundryman's bill the next day."

It was a shocking story, to be sure. Behavior such as he had described was the sort we ascribed to Orientals and other barbarians. The punishment of slaves was, of course, left to their masters, and legally this included the right to inflict death; but for a master to do this capriciously or over a trifling fault was depraved behavior. To do it publicly, in front of guests, was the very final word in poor taste.

I took my leave of Antonius and dried off. I passed on the massage tables. I still had much to do while the sun shone. My wrestling bout with Antonius had, for some reason, set me pondering upon the way Lucius Folius and his unpleasant wife had died.

5

"WHERE TO?" HERMES ASKED, slinging his satchel of bath equipment over one shoulder.

"Across the river. We're going to visit the *ludus*."

"Have some new boys arrived to fight in your Games?" he asked brightly, the bloodthirsty little wretch.

"No, I need to consult with Asklepiodes."

We went back across the Forum Boarium and crossed the Sublician Bridge into the Trans-Tiber district. I was beginning to wonder if my sandals would last the day. On a typical day during my aedileship, I could cover more ground than a legionary on a forced march. I tried to tot up how many miles I'd walked since leaving my house that morning, then shrugged it off. Anything was better than Gaul.

When we arrived, the Statilian School resounded with the clash of practice weapons. The school itself, which consisted of exercise yard, barracks, and business offices, with attached mess hall, hospital, baths, and practice arena, was far more spacious and better designed than the old school, which had stood on the Campus Martius and had been displaced by the erection of Pompey's Theater. The owner and operator, Statilius Taurus, was the son of a freedman once belonging to the great family of that name.

I found my old friend Asklepiodes in the infirmary, setting the broken finger of a hulking brute who had the bull neck and massive shoulders of a Samnite gladiator—the sort who fought with no armor except for the usual helmet, bronze belt, and arm wrapping, with the addition of a small greave strapped to his left shin. By way of compensation, his shield covered him from chin to knee and curved halfway around his body.

"Good day, Aedile," Asklepiodes said with a smile. "I'm afraid the new men from Capua haven't arrived yet."

"That's not what I'm here about," I said, admiring the Samnite's calm during what had to be an excruciating procedure. These men were schooled to accept immense pain without flinching. "I need to talk with you concerning some recent deaths."

"Murders?" he asked, his smile even brighter. He loved this sort of thing.

"I didn't think so, but now I'm not so sure."

He gave the finger a final wrap and tied off the bandage. "Off with you now, and henceforth oblige me by wearing the padded glove during practice."

"Can't get the feel of the hilt with one of those on," the man said, in a thick Bruttian accent.

"It is when you are fighting with the real sword on the

sand that proper feel of the hilt really counts," Asklepiodes reminded him. "You won't be wearing a padded glove then. Wounds absorbed in training earn you nothing, neither honor nor money."

The fellow went away grumbling, apparently more distressed at the unmanliness of wearing protective gear than by the prospect of any number of wounds, which were an expected part of his profession.

"Now," Asklepiodes said, "who has died?"

I told him about the fallen *insula* and its inhabitants. "It didn't occur to me at the time that I might require your expert advice," I told him, "but something has been preying on my mind since yesterday morning. The two of them had their necks broken. I've just been wrestling with young Antonius, and several times he tried to remove my head, which I resisted. It struck me that it is not an easy job to break a neck, yet these two died that way, side by side. Some of the dead were horribly mangled, but most looked as if they'd died of suffocation."

"Were there head injuries?" he asked. "If the two were dumped into the cellar and landed on their heads, the weight of their falling bodies could easily have snapped their necks. Recall, you had your neck muscles braced when you were wrestling. A neck breaks much more easily if the victim is unprepared or, better yet, unconscious."

"Of course I didn't handle the bodies, but the heads didn't seem deformed; and there was no blood soaking their hair."

"There need not be an obvious injury. I would have to palpate the skulls to be sure. Where are the bodies?"

"Since nobody stepped forward to claim them, I had

them taken to the Libitinarii by the Temple of Venus Libitina. I'd be most grateful if you would examine them and send me a report."

"I will be most happy to be of service. You have no idea how boring it gets here with nothing to do save patching up fools who refuse to take care of themselves. I will go right now before someone comes along and reduces them to ashes."

"I cannot express my gratitude."

"You'll think of something." He called for his slaves and his litter and I went back outside, where I found Hermes watching the sparring practice.

"You spend half your time here as it is," I reminded him. "I'd think you get to see enough of this."

"I've hardly been here at all since you took office," he protested. "Anyway, I train here in the mornings. I don't get to see the men who train in the afternoons. And there are at least two hundred here who've arrived since my last visit."

It was true. The swordsmen were coming in from all over Italy and from as far away as Sicily, where some of the best schools of the day were located. It wasn't just for the upcoming festival season, though. Between bouts, most of them hired out to the politicians as bodyguards, although their duties more often involved breaking up the rallies of their political opponents, intimidating voters, disrupting speeches, and the like. It made for the sort of rioting we had witnessed that morning. Worse, it affected the quality of the fights because the men were too busy being hired thugs to train properly.

"Oh, by the way," Hermes said, "Titus Milo is here. He says he'd like to speak with you."

"Why didn't you tell me?" I asked, exasperated.

"I just did." It was no use. "He said wait until you were finished with your business. It's not urgent." He led me to a corner of the yard where a number of men sat around a small fountain. On two folding chairs sat Milo and Statilius, the owner. Several giants stood behind Milo or sat on the edge of the fountain. I recognized them as his personal bodyguard, all of them famed champions of the arena, now retired and riding high on Milo's political fortunes. Milo could have outfought any of them, but his current dignity as ex-praetor and candidate for the consulship made personal combat in the streets unbecoming. These days he left most of the head breaking to his subordinates. He was as splendidly handsome as ever, but I was astonished for no good reason to see that his hair was flecked with gray. I had thought Milo immune to that sort of thing.

"Greetings, Aedile," Milo said, standing to take my hand. In some ways he was the most powerful man in Rome at that time, but he was as punctilious as Cato about observing the proprieties of office. "We've just been discussing some matters that concern you."

"How is that?" I asked. It seemed that everything concerned me since I had taken office.

"First off, these men of mine," he indicated the thugs, who nodded curtly, "have all volunteered to fight in your *munera* at a nominal rate. I'll send their contracts to your office in the next few days, but you may go ahead and publish their names in your announcements."

"That is most generous," I said to them. "Metellus Celer was a very great Roman, and the people will expect extraordinary magnificence at his funeral games. With such famous names on the bill, their success is all but assured." They grinned and said they were glad to honor the memory of so great a man. Of course, they weren't doing it for Celer or for me. They were doing it for Milo, who was my friend.

In truth, the risk they took was not as great as many people imagine. They would fight only with champions of equal rank, where it was no disgrace to be defeated. They had so many fans, they would all but certainly be spared in defeat. It was the tyros on their first bouts and the men who had not been fighting long enough to gain a following who suffered the high mortality rates.

Still, men who had been spared, and even men who won, sometimes bled to death from a bad cut; and a trifling wound could mortify and bring death as surely as a severed artery, only after weeks of suffering. So it was no small thing for men like these to leave a prosperous retirement to reenter the arena. Usually, a single pair of retired champions to top off a day's combats was the most an aedile could afford. They could cost as much as all the rest of the day's combatants together. But the people would rather see two such fight than any number of half-trained tyros. To have so many, and at a low price, was the best news I had had in months.

"We've been discussing another matter, Aedile," said Statilius. "Rome needs an amphitheater; and not just a wooden one, but a permanent, stone structure."

"It's true," said a fighter named Crescens. He was tall but lean and sinewy, belonging to the new category of net-and-trident fighter. "I've fought in the amphitheaters of Capua and Messana. Even Pompeii has a fine one. Yet here in Rome we have to fight in the Forum, where the monuments get in the way, or in the Circus, where half the audience can't see us on account of the spina."

"You aren't telling me anything I don't know," I said.

"Since my father founded this school," Statilius said, "the City has doubled in population, and the typical *munera* has more than tripled in size. If politicians insist on outdoing each other in the magnitude of their Games, then we must have a proper venue for celebrating them."

"I'm familiar with the problem," I told them, "but towns like Pompeii and Capua have advantages over Rome in this regard. They are rich, and they are small. I've attended *munera* in both those amphitheaters; and at full attendance, with people coming in from the nearby villages, they need to hold no more than four or five thousand spectators. Rome would need one big enough to hold at least thirty thousand, even if we restrict attendance to adult, male, freeborn, native citizens as, I remind you, ancient law dictates."

"That's a law I've never seen enforced," Milo said ruefully. "If my wife were denied her front-row seat at the fights, Rome would suffer for it." His men laughed, but uneasily. Milo's wife was Fausta, daughter of the Dictator Sulla, and high-handed even by patrician standards.

"There you are," I said. "Include the women, the resident aliens, and the freedmen of limited citizenship rights, and you need an amphitheater that will seat at least a hundred thousand. Who could undertake such an expense? Only Crassus, and he's sunk everything into his foreign war, from which few expect him to return save in an urn. Pompey might have, but he spent everything on his theater. Lucullus has retired to private life and spends only on himself. Who is left?"

"Caesar," Milo said, "may return from Gaul very wealthy."

Now I saw which way this conversation was leading. "That is quite likely. He's been amassing something of a fortune. Even the wild Gauls, the ones who wear trousers, are not quite the impoverished savages we thought. There's been a great deal of gold and silver, not to mention all the slaves he's taken."

"I can't approach him about this," Milo said. "Nothing personal, of course, but everyone knows I support Cicero, while Clodius is Caesar's man. You, however, are married to his niece."

"That is so," I said. This may not have been as strong a tie as he imagined, but I was not one to belittle my influence with an important man. This was definitely not the time to tell him about my family's shift of support toward Pompey. "I could bring up the subject when I write him next. I do so almost every week."

"After all," Milo said, "there hasn't been a great public building erected in Rome to the honor of his family since the Basilica Julia centuries ago." He rose from his chair, nodded slightly to the others. "Aedile, would you walk with me for a bit? I have some other matters to discuss." This was more like it. Rome's lack of a decent amphitheater was not the sort of thing to which Titus Milo dedicated much concern.

The last thing I needed was more walking, but we made a private progress around the portico surrounding the exercise yard.

"Decius," Milo began, "word has reached me that you are looking into the doings of the *publicani*, specifically those in the construction business."

"Word does get around," I said.

"Then it's true? I feared so. Decius, perhaps you don't

understand this, but you could end up attacking some of the most important men in Rome."

"People have been dropping heavy hints to me all day," I told him, "most notably Sallustius Crispus."

"That little rat. Well, even a rat can be right upon occasion, and this is one of them."

"Why so?" An unwelcome suspicion dawned on me. "My old friend, I do hope that you are not involved in this murderous trade?"

"Not personally, but I have clients who are, and some of them have already approached me about this matter. They do not want an aedilician investigation."

I stopped and faced him. "They do not, eh? Well, I've never hauled a felon into court who *wanted* to be put on trial for his life or freedom. I will prosecute those who violate the laws enforced by my office, however highly placed they may be. And for every client in the building trades, you have a hundred who live in those *insulae* that keep falling at such an alarming rate."

"Have you consulted with your family?" he asked.

"Not yet. What do you mean?"

"Talk this over with old Cut Nose and Scipio and Nepos. They may have some cautious advice for you."

This made no sense. "Just yesterday Scipio was ready to give the case to his son for prosecution."

"See if he feels the same way today."

He was making me angry, but I felt a chill from my scalp to my toes. "Titus, what is going on?"

"Our political situation, you may have noticed, has been fluid."

"Chaotic is the word I would have used, but I suppose

'fluid' is a reasonable euphemism. What of it?"

He flexed his big hands. "Just what is it that keeps us functioning at all, lacking as we do the institutions of monarchy?"

"We have our ancient customs," I said, "our republican tradition, the citizen's respect for office—" I trailed off. It was a good question. Just what *did* keep us going? "And I suppose the gods help out from time to time."

He nodded solemnly. "In other words, we have absolutely nothing we can count on."

"I'll grant you it doesn't work very well, but it works, after a fashion. What would you have us do, go back to kings?"

"Not me. A man of my birth would have little chance to rise in a monarchy. But it's not all that easy to do it here, either. Look, Decius, for centuries the Senate has drawn its members from a few families, families like your own. You are the landed gentry. Any citizen may stand for office, but there's little point in it for most people."

"Certainly," I said, wondering where this was leading. "Public office is notoriously expensive. We spend years serving the State, and we aren't paid for it. On the contrary. Only in the propraetorian and proconsular positions do you ever have a chance of enriching yourself. Maybe one senator in ten ever makes it to praetor. Even then riches are not assured, unless you draw a rich province to govern or a profitable war. And you'd better win your wars. It's foolish to aspire to office unless you have landed wealth."

There were exceptions to this, of course. Caius Marius had soldiered hard as a young man, making himself a popular hero as well as attracting the patronage of wealthy men.

When the time came to stand for higher office, the money and the votes were there for him. Cicero, from the same obscure town as Marius, had made his reputation as a lawyer beyond peer. It was, of course, unlawful for a lawyer to accept fees, but his grateful clients always gave him lavish Saturnalia gifts. It didn't hurt that grateful provincials remembered his honest administration fondly and sent him plenty of business.

But even acknowledging these exceptions, the general rule held that it was futile to aspire to office without the resources of a wealthy family. Thus the Senate was full of *equites* who had been willing to undertake the onerous but relatively cheap office of quaestor in order to enter the Senate and share in its prestige. This, under the constitution Sulla had given us, was the minimum necessary for admission to that august body.

"The connection with falling buildings still eludes me."

"There was a time when only patricians could be senators. They lost that privilege long ago, but they set the fashion. They were the nobles, they derived their incomes from the land, and they decreed that income from any other source was dishonorable."

"It seems to me I had this same conversation just a little while ago with Sallustius."

"Then the little toad, as usual, was talking in hints and innuendoes. Let me give it to you straight. The patricians are nearly extinct. The old families have been dying out generation by generation. How many are left? The Cornelians, the Scipios, the Claudians, the Caesars, maybe ten others at most, and the bulk of them are so obscure that you never hear of them anymore. In another generation they'll be all but gone. Yet we follow their ancient customs as if they were decreed by the gods."

This was an incredibly long speech for the usually reticent Milo. Clearly, this was something he felt deeply about, but he still hadn't made his point. I followed an equally uncharacteristic path and kept my mouth shut.

"Who owns all that land now? A handful of great magnates, most of them living down in the southern part of the peninsula, who take little interest in State politics. The land the patrician families still cling to doesn't produce a third of what it used to now that it's worked by slaves instead of industrious peasants. And yet, as you've pointed out, public office is expensive. Where does our money come from, Decius?" He did not wait for me to answer. "It comes from the *equites* and the resident alien merchants. From the businessmen!"

This last word was a legitimate one, but it seemed somehow foreign and distasteful. In polite society, words such as "merchant" and "businessman" have always been pejorative. Buying and selling for profit have always been activities perceived as fit only for foreigners and freedmen: enormously profitable, perhaps, but dishonorable. Lowest of all were bankers and auctioneers, who made money without actually producing anything—activities that, to right-thinking people, had the aspect of a species of magic.

"I follow you so far," I told him.

"There are three major businesses, Decius: import-export, the slave trade, and construction. Import-export is mainly owned by foreigners, usually operating here with Roman citizen partners; the slave trade is greatly depressed because of all the foreign wars; but the City is booming.

Construction is the most profitable business here by a huge margin."

"So," I said, "there can be very few men in public life who are not beholden to these builders?"

"And none more so than the aediles and, every five years, the censors."

"They haven't approached me with bribes," I protested. "I'm sure I would remember."

He smiled wryly. "You've acquired a reputation for—I won't say incorruptibility. It is more that you have an eccentric interpretation of what constitutes corruption along with your unswerving adherence to duty."

"I suppose there are worse reputations to have. I'd hate to be thought another Cato."

He laughed aloud this time. His men laughed too, although they couldn't hear what we were saying. "Nobody thinks that, never fear. But most of your colleagues in the Senate have far fewer scruples."

"I've always known that. Are you saying they'll unite against me if I prosecute the crooked contractors?"

"When do they ever unite for anything? No, but there will be a few who see their own fortunes threatened. It doesn't take many of them."

"Clodius?" I asked.

He shook his head. "Much as I hate to absolve him of anything, the influence of the builders is not enough to move him. He has plenty of other sources of wealth, and Caesar has instructed him to leave you alone. He won't endanger his alliance with your uncle-by-marriage."

"Who am I to watch out for?" I asked him.

"I'll compile a list of names and send them to you. Keep

in mind that I don't know all of them. I think you should leave this matter alone."

"This isn't just theft, Milo, it's murder. I can't overlook it."

He sighed. "When did you ever accept good advice?" He clapped me on the shoulder. "Come on, let's go discuss the upcoming fights."

An hour later, Hermes and I were on our way back into the City proper. The messenger from the Temple of Aesculapius caught us crossing the bridge. "Aedile," he said, "the physician Harmodias sends me to tell you that the slave from the *insula* of Lucius Folius has died."

I performed a colorful, multilingual curse for the edification of all within earshot. "Did he speak?"

"Harmodias has charged me to tell you that he made no coherent statement before he expired."

That seemed an odd way to put it. "Where is the body?"

"I am instructed to tell you that the temple will take care of its disposal."

It all sounded very wrong, but I wasn't going to discuss it with a temple slave. "Come on, Hermes, let's go back to the Island."

"What is it?" he asked. "He was the only survivor from the ground floor. It's no surprise that he croaked as well."

"I'm more interested in why they are so anxious to take charge of the body," I said.

We hurried to the Island. It was getting late, but I was in no mood to quit for the evening. The eyes of Harmodias widened to see me back.

"Aedile, you honor us again. Is anything wrong?"

"A number of things. For one, I was looking forward to what that slave had to say."

"Alas," he said, spreading his hands, "some things are beyond our power. The man died without regaining consciousness. He spoke no understandable words, merely mumbling in terminal delirium. He died perhaps two hours ago."

"I want to see the body," I said.

"The body of a slave dead in an accident? Why?"

"That is my business. Where is it?"

"I am afraid it has already been taken away for burial."

I knew it. Something was wrong here. "Isn't it customary to wait long enough for someone to claim the body?"

He assumed the prissy, fastidious air we expect from physicians. "Sometimes, but not when the corpse is that of an inferior slave following a disaster in which mortality has been high. And, as I understand it, Aedile, there has been some difficulty in finding a responsible person to claim the bodies of the owners. Had you wished to retain the corpse, you should have issued orders to that effect before you left."

I felt the blood mounting to my face. "I gave instructions to exactly that effect, you fool!"

"As I recall your words, Aedile, you said that, should he regain consciousness, I was to assure him that you would give him a decent funeral, that he might be rendered more cooperative. But the occasion never arose."

This was useless. He had been bribed or intimidated. "Who took the body?"

"It was turned over for interment in the usual place to a teamster driving one of the carrion wagons."

As I stalked out, he showed not the least distress that

he was losing the gratuity I would surely have rewarded him for efficient service. That clinched it. He had been bribed.

"Come along, Hermes," I said. "He has been taken to 'the usual place.' I want a look at him. If we hurry, we can get there before it's too dark to see anything."

"Not there!" Hermes said, horrified.

"It's not so bad," I assured him. "You can just hold your nose."

"But it's such a long walk!"

He was right on that point. From the river to the Esquiline Gate, we had to traverse the whole width of the City. No burials were allowed within the City. The better sort were cremated and had their ashes decently interred within the many tombs lining the highways that led from Rome in all directions. For the rest—the paupers, the least valuable slaves, foreigners who had not made other arrangements, dead animals, and all others who were not considered worth the firewood it would take to incinerate them—we had that fine old Roman institution, the euphoniously named Puticuli or "putrid pits."

In the pits, the corpses were tossed into excavations and sprinkled with quicklime to hurry the process of dissolution. On a hot summer day, an unfortunate wind blowing across the City from that direction was staggering. This archaic practice was a disgrace to Rome, and every Roman owes a debt of thanks to Maecenas, who a few years later was to buy up that ground, cover the pits under countless tons of soil, and turn the whole area into a beautiful public garden. Every time I walk there, I praise his name, even if he is one of the First Citizen's closest friends.

The sun was setting as we passed through the Esquiline Gate and turned left. To our right lay the Necropolis, where the modest tombs of the poorer people lay. These humble monuments were mostly erected and maintained by Rome's many funeral clubs. Most free workmen and many slaves belonged to these societies. They all paid a small annual fee into the general fund, which paid for a monument and the hire of professional mourners. When a member died, they all attended the funeral, so even a poor man could have a decent send-off.

Not everyone was so fortunate, and soon we passed the Necropolis and came to the final resting place of the others, although I, for one, could not find much rest among the corpses of, not only my social inferiors, but animals of nearly every sort. These included dead horses; animals rendered inedible because of disease or because they had been sacrificed and their livers or other organs had carried ill auspices; work oxen too old, tough, and stringy to be used as food; and dogs. We had few cats in Rome in those days.

The slaves who toiled in this place were little better off than old Charon in his sewer barge. It was decidedly unpleasant work; but by way of compensation, they got to keep whatever they could scavenge from the corpses. Usually this consisted of whatever rags of clothing they were wearing, but coins and even jewels were sometimes discovered in various bodily orifices, and there was a thriving if illegal trade in body parts, mostly sold to practitioners of magic.

I accosted one such slave, a dull-eyed lout dressed in a black tunic, his arms and legs smeared with some sort of indescribable filth. I stood well back from him as I asked him where the latest batch of carrion from the City had been deposited. He pointed a blackened claw toward the northeast.

"The new pit's that way, sir. Been maybe forty wagons unloaded there today. There'll be a lot of workmen around it. Can't miss it."

It was incredibly true that the new pit couldn't be missed. Apparently the designation "new" meant that it had been collecting corpses only for the past year or so. The excavation was a circular crater that would have done a volcano proud. The slaves around its perimeter were shoveling corrosive lime onto the day's accumulation of corpses, bipedal and quadrupedal. At our approach, the work crew's overseer came to us. He was distinguishable from the others by his relative lack of filth. He was no prettier, though, bearing an oddly deformed head and limping on a clubfoot.

"May I help you, sir?"

"I am the Aedile Metellus. I need to see the body of a slave who was brought here probably in the last two hours."

"There's been quite a few, what with the usual death toll, plus that *insula* collapse yesterday."

"He was a big, black-bearded fellow, brought here from the Temple of Aesculapius on the Island."

"Probably still warm, too," Hermes added helpfully, his voice sounding odd because he was pinching his nostrils shut.

The overseer scratched his shaven, malformed head. "Vulpus usually takes deliveries in that district. His wagon was here just a little while ago. Over here, I think—" We followed him around the rim of the excavation to its northern quadrant. Inside the pit was an unbelievably ghastly mess of putrescence: bodies and pieces of bodies in many stages of bloat and decay. Some were as dessicated as Egyptian mummies, some looked like inflated pig's bladders, while yet others, more recently expired, looked as if they could get up and walk out of the pit. The legs of dead horses thrust upward like ship's masts in a harbor.

What made it all the more horrible, if anything could, was that the weight of the relatively whole corpses on top pressed down on the semiliquid mass of decayed flesh mixed with lime below, forcing a disgusting, bubbling stew of putrefaction to the surface. The resulting mixture of slimy fluid, recognizable human fragments and patches of fur all mixed together looked like the primal soup from which all life had been created.

The air was full of fine, powdered lime. This kept us continually coughing, which made it all but impossible to breathe through our mouths. The hideous stench was unavoidable.

"Is it always as bad as this?" I asked, just to be saying something. My wits were addled with disgust.

"This is just the usual. You get so you don't notice it after a while. You should've been here right after Pompey's triumphal Games. We had dead elephants in the pits, then."

Hermes and I jumped involuntarily when the relative quiet of the ugly scene was disturbed. First came a faint rumble that seemed to come from beneath our feet. Then there was a roar as of a powerful, subterranean wind as, a hundred paces away, a fissure appeared in the ground and a plume of dirt and lime dust shot into the air.

"Demons are escaping from the underworld!" I cried, my nerves already unsteadied by the infernal scene.

"Just gas venting from an old pit," the overseer assured me, as the pall of stench from the fissure beggared all that we had smelled thus far. "They'll keep farting like that for years. Pay no mind."

He called to a little group of pit slaves, and they talked for a while in the shortened, simplified Latin spoken by the lowest of Rome's poor. It sounded like something dogs would use to communicate among themselves and is a foreign language to most of us. Four of them descended into the pit, and the overseer came back to us.

"They think they can reach the ones from Vulpus's last load. They'll drag your man up here. Of course," he grinned crookedly, showing scummy teeth, "they'll expect a little reward."

"Hermes, a sestertius for each man and a denarius for our friend here." Hermes dug into my rapidly shrinking purse, clucking at this extravagance. I didn't think it an opulent reward. I wouldn't have gone into that pit for the loot of Tigranocerta.

Within a few minutes the men returned, carrying a limp body, too recently dead to stiffen. Even in the dimming light I could tell that they had found the right man. They laid the burly body at our feet, and I crouched beside him. He was lightly dusted with lime, so that he resembled a statue carved from rather inferior white marble. Just below his breastbone was a small blotch.

"Well, what have we here?" I mused. I grabbed up a handful of dry grass, absently amazed that anything could grow on this blighted ground. With it I scoured away at the mark, unafraid of contamination. The death rites would have been performed when he died at the temple. At least, I hoped so. With the clotted blood and lime scrubbed away, a neat little incision, less than an inch wide, was revealed.

"Expertly done," I said. "A dagger thrust beneath the breastbone, angled upward into the heart. Instant death and all bleeding internal." I straightened up. "I've seen enough. Thank you, overseer."

He shrugged. "Always glad to be of service to Senate and People." Then, to his men, "Toss this stiff back in."

"Can't you do anything about this place?" Hermes asked, as we hastened back toward the Esquiline Gate.

"Fortunately for me," I told him, "an aedile has no powers or responsibility outside the walls of Rome. At least there is one awful mess that doesn't come under the purview of my office."

6

WE WERE ALL BUT STAGGERING with fatigue by the time we reached my doorway. Inside, Julia rushed forward to greet me, then stood back.

"Decius, where have you been?" Her expression was almost comically horrified.

"The Puticuli," I told her. "Actually, I feel rather lucky. That's usually a one-way trip for those who go out there."

She wrinkled her nose. "I don't think I want to hear about this." She all but snatched my toga off, sending me spinning. She tossed it to a slave and said, "Take this up to the roof and spread it out on the arbor to air. Decius, take that tunic off and put on a clean one. We have guests."

"Guests? I wasn't expecting any." She hustled me into our bedroom, yanked my tunic off over my head, opened a chest, drew out another, gave it a shake, drew it down over my head, settled and belted it, all with amazing speed and talking the whole time.

"How can you expect anything? It's still dark when you leave the house in the morning, and it's dark before I see you again. I've had slaves out looking for you all evening, but they couldn't locate you."

"It's been a busy day, as they've all been lately. Who is here?"

"Your father, for one, and some other distinguished men. They were about to leave in a bad temper, but I refilled their cups and persuaded them to stay just a little while longer."

"Just what I needed," I said. "Father in a good temper is unpleasant enough. Who are the others?"

"You'll see for yourself, won't you?" she said, impatiently. "Now stop wasting time." With a palm at my back, she pushed me into the *triclinium,* where my father and the others sat sipping wine around a brazier of glowing coals, brought in to take the chill off the air. Even if the African breeze was melting the mountain snows, Roman evenings were still cool at that time of year. With him were two other Metelli, Scipio and Nepos, and a man I recognized from the Senate meetings he had presided over a few years previously.

"About time," Father groused. "You haven't been out carousing as usual, have you?" My father, Decius Caecilius Metellus the Elder, who had held every public office including the censorship, still treated me as a child even though I held office. Legally it was his right to do so, since he had never seen fit to go through the manumission ceremony that would have granted me full adult status. By law, I married and held property only at his whim. This was yet another of those quaint old customs that cause me to wonder how we

Romans ever amounted to anything in the world.

"Your son is an incredibly busy man," said Marcus Valerius Messala Niger. "Especially since, unlike too many of our aediles, he is so attentive to the duties of his office." This from a man who, as I was rapidly learning, had used his own offices only to enrich himself at sore cost to the citizens. I hated to think what his provincial administrations must have been like. He was a burly, balding man with a ready smile and blue eyes that twinkled merrily.

"We all remember what it was like to be an aedile," Nepos said. His presence was almost as great a puzzle as that of Messala. He was a lifelong adherent of Pompey's, making him the only prominent member of my family who was not of the anti-Pompeian faction. Here was yet another evidence of the family's new tilt.

I took a cup from the table and tried to get some of the taste of the Puticuli out of my mouth. "What brings such distinguished visitors at this odd hour?" I asked. "Not that you would not be welcome at any hour, of course. And such an oddly assorted company, too."

"A number of things," Father said. "Surely you have not forgotten that the three of us"—he indicated himself, Scipio, and Nepos—"are all contributing substantially to your Games?"

"I could hardly forget. Speaking of which—" and I told them about Milo's pet thugs. They listened carefully to the list of names, nodding with enthusiasm.

"This is splendid news," Scipio said. "I've seen all of those men fight, and they're at the top of the first rank. Celer will have the best funeral games ever."

"And to get them so cheap!" Father gloated.

"Clodius will be enraged," said Messala. "He'll say these are Milo's games."

"Forget Clodius," Nepos advised. "He's just Caesar's dog, and Caesar is kicking in for Decius's *munera,* as his wedding present for his niece. Now, if you would like something really unusual to liven up the proceedings, I know two senators who've fallen out over some mutual accusations of bribery. They're eager to fight it out, and they've told me they'll volunteer to fight in your *munera,* Decius."

I thought this intriguing. Men of high rank sometimes contended as gladiators to get around the laws against dueling. Since the fights were religious observances, voluntary sacrifices, so to speak, they could not be prosecuted for it afterward.

"I forbid it!" Father said, emphasizing his words with a chopping motion of his hand. "It is infamous that senators and *equites* are seen performing in public! There has been too much of that lately, and I will not be a party to such scandalous behavior." What a spoilsport.

"When Scipio Africanus celebrated his funeral games for his father and uncle," Metellus Scipio said complacently, "all the combatants were free men who volunteered to honor the dead and Africanus himself. There were senators, centurions, and other ranking soldiers among them, as well as the sons and other high-born warriors of allied chieftains." He was never slow to remind people of his glorious ancestors.

"That was a hundred and fifty years ago," Father objected, "before the rules of the *munera* were settled as they are now. And those Games were not celebrated at Rome, but at Cartago Nova."

Valerius Messala seemed highly amused. "Besides,

there are no Romans of such distinction to honor in this generation." A subtle jab at both the Scipios and the Metelli. "Anyway, I know the two you mention, and they are both fat and unskilled. It would be laughable, and we can't have the citizens laughing at senators. We give them too much to laugh about as it is."

Father held his silence sullenly. He always hated it when someone agreed with him for the wrong reason. So do I, for that matter. I hadn't expected to find Messala such an agreeable sort. Admittedly, my taste in these matters was not shared by many. I'd liked Catilina, too. I don't consider this to be a lapse of judgment on my part. Often, the very worst men are the most likable, and the upright and incorruptible ones the most repulsive. Marcus Antonius and Cato are two excellent cases in point.

"So much for the Games," Father said. "They shall be celebrated, and they shall be a success. My boy, I understand you have wasted the bulk of two valuable days looking into the collapse of a single, shoddily built *insula*."

"Your boy," I informed him acidly, "spent the morning in a sewer and the evening in a charnel pit. Activities, you will agree, in which I seldom indulge on normal days. My office, however, demands it."

"Your office involves the whole City," Father said, "not the prosecution of a single crooked builder. Assign a client or freedman to investigate the matter and get on with your job!"

"I am not investigating a single builder," I said, trying to rein in my temper. "I am investigating what looks to be vicious corruption suffusing the whole residential building trade in Rome." I did not want to argue openly in front of a nonfamily outsider, but Father was forcing the issue. This was extraordinarily tactless of him. Old age was catching up with him at last, I decided.

"The late Lucius Folius was the builder of that *insula,*" said Valerius Messala. "I know because he was awarded his licenses and contracts during my censorship. It seems he's been killed by his own greed, like a character in a Greek play."

I had been expecting something like this. I said nothing about the murdered slave. "Sometimes the gods dispense justice. But no contractor builds only a single house." I thought of the stack of archival documents in my study and decided that I had better not mention them to these three. Of course, it was likely that Messala already knew all about them. To change the subject, I said, "Does anyone besides me and the rivermen know that Rome is about to be flooded?"

"I've heard some talk of it," Father said. "It happens every few years, and there's nothing much we can do about it."

"It's going to be worse than usual this year," I informed them, "because the drains are going to be all but useless. They haven't been scoured in years, and the water could stand in the lower parts of the City for weeks, and then we'll have pestilence on top of everything else." I looked at Messala as I said this. He looked back blandly.

"You are too easily alarmed. Even if we're inconvenienced for a while, it's no catastrophe," Nepos insisted. "The forums are easily evacuated, the temples and basilicas are built well up on their platforms, and only the poorest people have their homes on low ground. Give them fine Games when it's all over, and they'll forget all about their troubles. Concentrate on that."

There was a small commotion from the direction of my gateway, but I ignored it. *Doubtless some petitioner,* I thought. An aedile's lack of privacy was not as extreme as that of a tribune of the people. At least we were allowed to close our doors. But in an office that concerned the public weal, the public was not shy about expressing its wants.

"The hour grows late," Messala said, "and we should not detain the aedile. He has work to attend to."

"Right, right," Father said, shaken from his grumpy reverie. "Decius, there is something you should know, since it concerns both the family and your tenure of office."

At last they were getting to it. "I confess I was puzzled by the presence of so distinguished a gathering. Two excensors and a *pontifex,* no less. May I assume this has something to do with our family's growing warmth toward Pompey?"

"Don't get ahead of yourself!" Father barked. "We have to get this awful year done with first."

"And the great difficulty with this year," Messala slid in smoothly, "is that the past election scandals have yet to sort themselves out. We've been forced to appoint an *interrex*"—he nodded toward Scipio—"and it looks as if we shall have to continue the *Interregnum* for some time to come."

"Is there a constitutional limit on the period of an *Interregnum?*" I asked. "I confess that I've never looked into it."

"Cicero and Hortensius Hortalus have researched the matter, and there seems to be no limit that's ever been spelled out."

"The real limit," Scipio said, "is that it's such a disagreeable office. There is great prestige, of course, since the

Senate only chooses *interreges* from among the most distinguished members, but"—he threw up his hands in disgust—"you have all the duties and responsibilities of both consuls, only no *imperium* and no province to govern afterward. It's a great burden."

When the Republic was founded, we expelled our kings, and Rome has been very hostile to the concept of monarchy ever since. Only two very ancient offices survive with the title "*rex*" in them: the *interrex*, the "king-between," and the *Rex Sacrorum*, "King of Sacrifices." Neither office is invested with any real power for the very good reason that no Roman would confer power on anyone called a king of any sort.

"For that reason," Scipio went on, "I will step down from this office at the end of next month."

"Will the consuls be able to assume office at that time?" I asked.

"Not without violence," Father said. "Valerius Messala will take up the *Interregnum*. There will, of course, be a pro forma vote in the Senate, but it is foregone. No one else really wants the office in a year as disorderly as this one."

Messala smiled. "One does what one must in the service of the Senate and People."

"The consuls," Father continued, "when they finally do assume office, will have no more than half a term. Forget about them. They are nobodies. It is next year we must be prepared for."

"Scipio hinted at something of the sort yesterday," I said.

"Exactly." Father rubbed at the great scar that all but halved his face. "The City is in chaos, and this disorder must be suppressed before civic life can return to normal. It's tearing the Empire apart. There is only one man with both the military prestige and the popularity to do the job, and that's Pompey."

"You can't be proposing a dictatorship!" I objected. "Not after all our family's opposition to him!"

Father favored us with one of his very rare smiles, the sort he allowed himself only after pulling some superlatively underhanded bit of political chicanery. It was a ghastly sight. "Not precisely. What we are going to do is make Pompey sole consul for next year. Full *imperium* and no colleague to overrule or interfere with him."

I let the political implications sink in, saying nothing. Pompey would be virtual dictator except in one all-important factor: A dictator held an unaccountable office. Not only did he have full *imperium*, but he could not be called to account for his actions when he stepped down from office. As sole consul, Pompey would have a free hand to take whatever corrective measures he pleased, but he could not abuse the office because he would be an ordinary citizen when he stepped down and could be sued for his actions by any other citizen. Pompey would take only the necessary measures because he was a truly gifted administrator, when he wasn't besotted by military glory.

"Excellent," I said at last. "It's an inspired compromise." Barbarians, with their traditions of monarchy or tribal wrangling, never understand that our Republic was powerful, not because of our rigid adherence to principle, but because of our ability to compromise.

Father nodded. "I knew you'd catch on quickly. You are a Caecilius Metellus after all, in spite of all appearances."

"Pompey has agreed to appoint a colleague as soon as

he has restored the peace," Nepos said. "His colleague will be our current *interrex,* Quintus Caecilius Metellus Pius Scipio Nasica." He gestured grandly as the imposing name rolled off his tongue. Scipio bowed modestly.

"It's the perfect choice," Messala pointed out. "Pompey is the most glorious soldier of the age and immensely popular with the masses; but he has no family, and you know how the people are about names. Once Pompey has restored order, he will have a colleague who combines two of the greatest names. The clan of Caecilius Metellus is famed for its moderation and for its opposition to Pompey, thus allaying fears of a tyranny. The name of Scipio is synonymous with 'Savior of the State.' In fact, Pompey will retire to the country and leave Metellus Scipio to preside. I think we can look forward to a much happier and more orderly Rome."

"I approve," I said, nodding brightly, waiting for the axe to fall.

"There will be much to be done once the City is set to rights," Father said. "We've decided to get the Plebeian Assembly to prorogue your office at the end of the year."

Cold talons of horror gripped my heart. "You can't mean you want me to be aedile for *another year!* I've held this office for only three months, and I'm ready to fall on my sword!"

"Oh, it will be much more agreeable than this year's tenure," Messala said, smiling. "You won't have to put on another set of Games; you can leave that to the other aediles. Pompey has promised to put his own freedmen at your disposal. They are extremely capable. They've been sorting out the grain situation for the last two years."

"Think how popular it will make you," Father said. "Everyone will know what a sacrifice you'll be making. You'll have your praetorship for the asking."

"And," Nepos put in, "it will be one more year you won't be spending with Caesar in Gaul."

This caught me up short. I hadn't thought of that. Maybe another year in office wouldn't be so bad after all. Of course, these three clearly wanted me to exercise that office according to their wishes, but we could see about that when the time came.

"This bears thinking about," I said. "I'd have no objection to cooperating with Pompey, so long as his powers are limited and constitutional. I'll have no part of a dictatorship."

"Use your head," Father said disgustedly. "What need would he have of you or anyone else if he was dictator? He could order anything he wanted in that case, and not a thing any of us could do about it. This way, we keep our authority and we help to guide Pompey's actions, and that is important. Fine soldier and governor that he is, Pompey is a political jackass. He needs us more than we need him."

I looked at Valerius Messala. "And what do you get out of this?"

He arched his eyebrows. "Why, the satisfaction of being of some modest service to Rome."

I nodded. "So you're Pompey's middleman in this, eh? Putting together a Caecilius Metellus–Pompey coalition to dominate Roman politics?" I cut a look at Nepos. Messala would have approached the family through its only member in Pompey's camp.

"It is what Rome needs," he said, unapologetically. "Your family forms the single most important bloc in the Senate. You are also vastly influential in the Centuriate Assembly. Pompey is also strong in the Centuriate Assembly, and he is the darling of the Plebeian Assembly. It would be an unbeatable combination."

"Caesar has strong support in all three bodies," I pointed out.

"Caesar will be tied up in Gaul for years to come," Nepos said. "Much can happen to him. He could die there. If he loses just one battle, all his popularity will be gone. In the meantime, we will be preeminent in Rome."

"Please," Messala said, "you speak as if Caesar and Pompey were rivals. They are close friends. Do they not say so themselves, often and publicly?"

"Save that for the *rostra,*" I advised him. "We all know that those two will be at swords' points before much longer. Two such men will crowd Rome intolerably."

"That's for the future," Father said. "Our concern is getting Rome through this year and the next." Abruptly, he stood. "We must be going. Important as you like to fancy yourself, my son, we have many other calls to make. Good evening to you."

I walked them to the door, only to find Julia sitting in the atrium with Asklepiodes, their heads together, deep in conversation. They stood when the great men walked in, both of them bowing formally. The four acknowledged them perfunctorily and walked out, on their doubtless nightlong mission of arm twisting. This was how much of the business of the Senate was done. The loud floor debates were usually just the final stage.

"I wasn't expecting to see you tonight," I said to Asklepiodes when they were gone. "I am sorry to have kept you waiting out here."

"Your gracious lady has been wonderfully attentive," he assured me.

"Let me offer you a late dinner, at least. I, for one, am famished."

"I've already given orders," Julia said. "The *triclinium?*"

"In my study," I told her.

We retired to the little room off the small courtyard with its tiny pool and fountain. A goatskin bag of documents from the Tabularium sat on the floor next to my desk. Moments later, my slaves laid out cold chicken, boiled eggs, sliced fruit, bread, pots of oil and honey, and cups of watered wine, lightly spiced and heated.

"A bit Spartan," I said, by way of apology, "but I eat when I can these days. Never time for a proper dinner."

"This is splendid," he assured me. "I would rather help you and eat on the fly than put in any ordinary day's work followed by a lavish banquet. You've no idea how bored I get." He spoke and ate rapidly, interrupting his words for small bites of food and sips of wine. He was an excitable little man for a philosopher.

"Ah, you've learned something!" I said. "Did the bodies display signs of foul play?"

"I couldn't say," he said, dipping bread in a mixture of oil and *garum.* "I didn't see them."

"Eh?"

"It seems there are no bodies."

"Just a moment," I said. "I distinctly remember bodies. Two of them. Lucius Folius and his wife. I couldn't be mistaken."

"Oh, certainly there *were* bodies; I have no doubt of it." He vastly enjoyed my perplexity, as usual.

"Perhaps you had best describe your mission, in sequence and in detail."

"Excellent idea. Well, from the *ludus* I went to the Libitinarii quarter near the Temple of Libitina. A bit of questioning got me to the establishment of one Sextus Volturnus, where the bodies had been taken from the destroyed *insula.* Upon questioning, the proprietor informed me that the bodies in question had been claimed."

"By whom?" I asked.

"An heir presented himself, a certain Caius Folius, from Bovillae."

"Young Antonius told me Folius was from Bovillae," I said.

"It seems that the heir was in some haste to remove the bodies for burial in their ancestral town. He had them loaded on a cart and taken away."

"Did this heir claim the bodies of any of the household slaves?"

"I didn't think to ask. Excellent wine, by the way. Julia has improved your cellar."

"Did this Caius Folius present any proof as to his identity?"

Asklepiodes's eyebrows went up. "I did not think to ask that either. Is it customary?" He chewed an olive and spat the pit into a bowl that was rapidly filling with fruit peels and cheese rinds. "My old friend, you sent me there to examine the bodies, not to play the role of a State freedman."

"Just so," I said. You had to let Asklepiodes do things his own way. He could be as temperamental as a Greek tragedian. "It's unfortunate that you couldn't get a look at them."

"And yet my visit was not entirely unfruitful."

"How so?" I asked patiently.

"I spoke with the undertaker's assistants. These men had the task of washing the bodies, disguising injuries, dressing hair, applying cosmetics, and so forth, to make them presentable for the funeral. They are highly skilled and, in their own way, are nearly as knowledgeable about wounds as many surgeons and physicians. I asked them about the condition of the bodies of Lucius Folius and his wife."

"And?"

"Those who'd washed the bodies informed me that there were no cuts or severe abrasions. They might almost have died of suffocation like so many of the others, except that there were no signs of struggle."

"Struggle?" I said.

"Yes. Suffocating people, unless unconscious, usually fight frantically, striking and kicking against whatever obstacle is pinning them down. When the medium is a relatively unyielding building material such as wood, stone, or brick, there is often extensive laceration of the hands, feet, elbows, and knees."

"That makes sense." I shuddered even to contemplate so hideous a situation. It makes death on the end of a Gaul's spear seem pleasant by comparison.

"The hairdresser told me that there were no lacerations of the scalps, and he detected no shifting of the skull bones beneath the scalps. Had the bodies been dropped into the basement to land on their heads hard enough to break their necks, strongly depressed skull fractures would certainly have been the result."

"So," I said, "their necks were broken before they dropped into the basement."

"Exactly. This is confirmed by another curious factor." The wine had warmed him, and he was slipping into his enthusiastic teaching mode.

"Tell me about it." Asklepiodes was always interesting, even when he carried on to excessive length.

"You must understand, here I speak of an area that is not within my realm of expertise. As physician to the gladiators, I am accustomed to treating wounds almost immediately after their infliction. However, I have studied the writings of scholars dealing with every aspect of medicine, attended lectures by all the greatest physicians, held long and extensive discussions with many of them, so I am not entirely unacquainted with the subject of postmortem medical study."

"This being?" I inquired.

"The study of the changes that take place in a body after death. There are few experts on the subject."

"I can well imagine," I said. "Most people pay a physician to make them well again, not to keep track of how they rot."

"It is a popular misconception that bodies merely decay immediately after death," he said.

I thought of the Puticuli. "From recent experience, I can assure you that they rot." I poured myself another cup.

"So they do, and we are in the habit of burning corpses within a day or two of death for that reason. But there is a quite regular and predictable sequence of stages through which corpses pass in the progress of bodily dissolution, and much may be inferred from these. The Libitinarii informed me, for instance, that the bodies of Lucius Folius and his wife were discolored on the dorsal surface. That is, there were deep purple, bruiselike discolorations of the back, the buttocks, the rear surface of the thighs, and so forth.

"This postmortem condition is common and is called 'lividity.' The learned Simonides of Antioch has written extensively of this condition, and it seems to come about thus: During life, blood is distributed somewhat evenly throughout the tissues and organs of the body. It is also under a certain amount of pressure. We have all seen how blood oozes from a minor cut, pours freely from a larger blood vessel, and when an artery is severed, will actually spurt for several feet. The exact mechanism by which this occurs is a matter of considerable philosophical dispute.

"Upon cessation of life, this pressure and distribution cease, and the blood settles to the lowest part of the body. In the case of a supine individual, such as the late couple, that would be the rearmost area of the body. Living blood is bright red. When the body is dead, it quickly turns rust colored, then an almost blackish brown, resulting in the bruise color."

"I know what you mean," I said. "I've been in command of details when we had to gather Roman dead from a battlefield a day or two after the fighting. If a man died lying on his side, that side was dark, the other was pale. And once I saw the body of a man who had fallen head down into a well and drowned that way. His head and shoulders had turned almost black."

"Exactly the phenomenon I mean. Simonides has written in some detail of the progression of this condition, with allowances for the time of year, bodily dissolution being far more rapid in hot weather than in cold. Degree of lividity can tell one with an experienced eye how long the deceased has lain in the same posture dead."

"And your conclusion?"

He held up an admonitory finger. "Bear with me yet a little longer. The corpse handlers told me that the necks of both were broken quite cleanly, a severing of the neck vertebrae usually characteristic of a sharp, twisting action. A blow shatters the bones and hanging pulls them apart. It takes a rather freakish accident to wring the neck in such a fashion. I have seen it when, for instance, a charioteer is thrown headfirst into the spokes of a competitor's vehicle. In the absence of any other injury to the head, I can only conclude that someone grasped the chin and the back of the skull of each victim and twisted violently."

"And would this feat require great muscular strength?" I asked him. This was exactly the train of thought my wrestling bout with Antonius had set in motion.

"If the victims were soundly asleep, with all muscles perfectly relaxed, any person of moderate strength could have accomplished it, provided he had been instructed in the proper technique."

"And is there a special technique?"

"Allow me to demonstrate." He rose and flexed his fingers.

"Easy, now," I cautioned him. "You've had a bit to drink and your control may not be all it should be." Asklepiodes loved to demonstrate obscure and exotic means of killing people. More than once he had inflicted minor injuries upon me doing this.

"I shall be delicate," he assured me. "Now, an inexperienced person seeking to break a neck in this fashion will grasp the head thus." He placed his left hand on the back of my head and with his right grasped my lower jaw, my chin in his palm and his thumb and fingers curling around the mandible. "In this way, when pressure is applied—" he began to twist and my jaw slid sideways until it creaked.

"Ow!" I cried, never having mastered that Stoic attitude so admired by my contemporaries.

"You see? Done this way, the lower jaw can dislocate before pressure has been applied sufficient to disjoint the vertebrae. It is much better to grasp the head thus." He left his left hand where it was, and repositioned his right higher, so that the heel of the palm lay athwart the upper jaw, his thumb curling around my cheekbone. This time, when he twisted, my lower jaw moved little and I quickly felt the strain on my neck. I slapped the table in a wrestler's surrender, and he released me.

"You see?"

"Clearly," I admitted. "You think this is how it was done?"

"I could say with certainty if I had been able to examine the bodies myself, but the description I had from the Libitinarii leads me to believe so. Keeping in mind that I have only secondhand descriptions to go on, but acknowledging that these descriptions came from knowledgeable sources, my conclusions are as follows: Lucius Folius and his wife were murdered in their bed, while asleep, by a person accomplished in the technique of snapping a neck swiftly and silently. They lay in that position, dead, for not less than four hours before the house collapsed and they were precipitated into the basement."

"Wonderful!" I commended him. "That is just the sort of information I wanted. Will you swear to this in court?"

"With the disclaimers and hedges I have already specified, of course. But you must realize that there is no evidence now. The bodies, even the house, are all gone."

"Evidence doesn't mean that much in court," I assured him. "A really loud voice helps a lot. A forceful assertion carries more weight than quiet evidence." I told him about the switch pulled on me with the house timbers and the murder of the big slave.

"It sounds as if someone is cleaning up after himself," he said cheerily. "That slave, though, sounds like a fine candidate for the murder of the master and mistress."

I nodded, but there was much doubt in my mind. "That was my own thought, but there is much about that household that gives me pause. Let me tell you something that young Antonius related to me." So I told him about the unfortunate cook and of the neck rings and punishment marks I had seen on the dead slaves at the disaster site.

Asklepiodes shook his head and clucked. "How distasteful. Of course, as a Greek, I am quite prepared to believe Romans capable of any sort of enormity, but this seems the very epitome of bad taste."

"I have a feeling that until I have some idea of who was doing what in that house, and for what reasons, I will never get to the bottom of this. And it is plain that someone is making it his business to ensure that I learn nothing. In any case, your aid has been inestimable, as always."

"Then," he said, rising, patting his belly, and belching all at the same time, "I will take my leave of you now. Please convey my compliments to your lady, together with my apologies that I could be of no greater aid in her difficulty." With that enigmatic utterance, he left my study. I walked him to the gate, where his slaves waited patiently beside his litter.

I longed to go over the documents sent from the Tabularium, but dim lamplight would be too much for my aching eyes, and I was weighed down by a dreadful fatigue. In our bedroom I found Julia waiting up for me. I undressed and lay down beside her.

"What's going on?" she demanded.

So I told her all the events of my long, long day. She laughed when I told her of my boat ride in the sewers, turned her face away in revulsion when I described the Puticuli, and sharpened attentively when I related my conference with the family elders and Messala.

"Then it's true?" she said. "Your family is going over to Pompey?"

"They've struck a reasonable compromise," I said. "No reason to put too extreme an interpretation on it."

"That isn't how it sounds to me. It sounds to me as if there has been a decisive and irreversible shift in policy."

"There is no such thing as an irreversible policy," I insisted. "Not in Roman politics, anyway. And they are right. We need a period of powerful central authority to straighten out the City, and there is no man for the job except Pompey. Even I can see that, and you know better than anyone how much I loathe the man."

"Yes, this is something of a change for you," she said suspiciously. "Why this sudden cessation of hostility toward Pompey?"

I laced my fingers behind my head and marshaled my thoughts. This was something that had been stewing in my mind since Gaul. The faint flicker from the tiny night lamp danced over the new frescoes Julia had commissioned for the walls—the fanciful, elongated architectural and vegetation designs that had lately come into fashion.

"Pompey is through," I said. "I can see that now. For years I worried about him and Crassus. I thought someday it would come to civil war between the two of them. Now Crassus is a senile old fool, headed for his death in Parthia, if he even gets that far. Pompey is getting no younger and neither are his soldiers. They haven't fought a decent war in years. If he calls, they'll rally to him; but they've grown fat and idle on the farms he wrangled for them in Campania and Tuscia. He's no longer the threat I once thought him to be. Since his last consulship, he's overseen the grain supply and accomplished what everyone thought was impossible: rooted out corruption and put the whole business on an efficient basis. He has the right combination of ability, prestige, and popularity to restore order in the City."

"Somehow," she said, "I don't feel that you look forward to a rosy future for Rome and the Empire, with or without Pompey."

"Caesar is now in command of the largest Roman army since Marius and Sulla fought it out more than thirty years ago. If things go well for him in Gaul, he'll come back rich, prestigious, and backed by an experienced army fresh from victory. It is a dangerous combination. The people love Caesar, but the Senate is growing alarmed. If they get frightened enough, they'll back Pompey against Caesar, and they'll be backing a loser, as they've done so often in the past."

"Caesar will never take up arms against Rome!" she said indignantly.

"Nobody ever takes up arms against Rome," I pointed out. "Every would-be Alexander claims to be the savior of the Republic. The other man is the one with ambitions to be tyrant; you know that as well as I. Well, we'll know soon enough."

"If Pompey takes a firm hand," she said, "it could be the end for your friend Milo."

I had thought of that. "Yes, but he'll have to squash Clodius and the others, too. Milo is my friend, but this gang warfare is tearing Rome to pieces, and it must end. I hope Milo will accept honorable exile and not fight it out to the finish."

Her voice softened. "You have been undergoing a change of heart, haven't you? Which way will you go when the time comes?"

"That will depend upon the times," I told her, "and the times are changing rapidly. There is no way to make a decision just yet, but I won't let my family determine it. Nepos has gone his own way and done well enough out of it."

"Right. And just how did Valerius Messala come to be steering the family policy of the Metelli?"

"That has my head spinning just now," I said. "The Valerians are a great and ancient family, patricians as noble as any Cornelian or Julian, but the man's a schemer. I think he senses a weakness in my family, and he is moving in."

"Weakness?" she asked, astonished. "Yours is the most powerful plebeian family in the history of Rome!"

"In sheer numbers, yes. In the Senate and the Assemblies, in officeholders and in clientele, we are powerful. But the leadership is weakening. Celer and Pius are dead, Nepos is Pompey's man, and Scipio is adopted and seems to prefer his old name to the one Pius gave him. And I'm afraid Father is failing."

"How is that?"

"Tonight he wasn't acting like himself. He allowed intrafamily squabbling in there tonight, and we've always maintained unity in front of strangers. I think old age has finally caught up with him."

"It happens to everyone if they live long enough. It's time for you to take your place in the family councils. Make that the price of accepting a second aedileship." Julia was nothing if not practical.

"I'll consider it. Now, what were you talking about with Asklepiodes?"

Caught unawares, she stammered, "I—I—" then, calming, "I asked him about a certain treatment my great-aunt Aurelia recommended: fresh honey and fennel seed mixed with powdered shell of owl's egg."

So that was it. I might have known. We had been married less than two years, but Julia was already tormented by an old family fear. It was the famous infertility of the Caesars. Men and women, they had few children; and of these, perhaps one in three lived to see their fifth year. Julia had already miscarried once and was certain that she shared the family curse. She was her father's only living child. Julius Caesar at that time had only a single daughter from his multiple marriages.

"Julia, Asklepiodes specializes in wounds suffered by men whose profession it is to inflict such wounds. The special conditions of a woman's fertility are the domain of witches and midwives, not physicians and surgeons."

"I know that," she said. "It should tell you how desperate I am. I spoke with him mainly because he is such a sweet and reassuring man, and it is not his profession to be so, as you point out. He told me that time was the best remedy, but he did recommend an Alexandrian woman named Demetria"—I was about to object, but she silenced me—"and no, she is not some country wise woman. He assures me that she is a highly educated physician and philosopher who has studied at the Museum. Alexandrians are much more liberal in these matters than we are. I intend to seek her out tomorrow."

"Well," I said reluctantly, "if Asklepiodes recommends her, she must be acceptable. See her if you will, but I think he was right the first time. You just need to give it some time; you'll see. Remember the family you've married into. We Caecilians became so powerful by outnumbering everybody else."

She turned over and placed her head on my chest. "All right," she said sleepily. "I promise not to worry for a while. But I'm still going to see Demetria tomorrow."

If she said anything more, I do not remember it because I was sound asleep in another instant.

7

I DIDN'T EVEN GET AS FAR AS the Temple of Ceres the next morning.

"Aedile!" The shouter was a man I recognized, a freedman from the staff of Publius Syrus, the famous actor and playwright. "Please come to the theater! My patron says that it is an emergency!" The man was quite excited, but then he was a Greek, and his master was a Greek-Syrian, and all Greeks are excitable people. They invented philosophy just to get themselves under control.

The previous year I had contracted with Syrus to provide the theatricals for my upcoming Games. The first Games of the calendar year were to be the Megalensian Games, celebrated the next month. These were not nearly as lavish as the really big celebrations of the fall, the Roman Games and the Plebeian Games. But I was determined to make the first spectacles as splendid as possible to set the tone for my aedileship.

"What is the problem?" I asked. "I have a great many duties to—"

"It can't wait!" he yelled, cutting me off. "You have to come at once!"

"Don't talk to the Aedile like that, you jumped-up foreign catamite!" Hermes shouted at him.

"No, Hermes, we'd better go," I said. "I can't risk anything spoiling my show."

So we followed the man down toward the Sublician Bridge. Near the bridge towered the giant theater erected a few years before by Aemilius Scaurus during his aedileship. At this time there were two theaters in Rome worth the name: the Aemilian and the Theater of Pompey. Pompey's was built on the Campus Martius and was made of stone. The Aemilian was made of wood.

I had chosen the Aemilian for a number of reasons. Pompey's theater had been damaged during his triumphal games when his elephants stampeded; then he burned a town onstage, and the proscenium caught fire and the damage was not yet repaired. Also, it was far from the City center and seated perhaps forty thousand spectators. The Aemilian was a far shorter walk for most citizens, it held eighty thousand people, and, best of all, it wasn't built by Pompey. I didn't want people watching *my* games and thinking about Pompey.

And just because it was built of wood instead of marble doesn't mean it was not splendid. The vast, semicircular structure shone all over with paint and gilding, which I had had renewed. It was decorated with mosaics in semiprecious stones, amber, and tortoise shell, each arch of its upper galleries displaying a fine statue. It was equipped with huge awnings against the sun and a system of fountains that would spray a fine, perfumed mist over the audience in hot weather. These latter features would not be required for the Megalensian Games, but I would definitely need them for the Apollinarian Games, which were celebrated in the hottest days of summer.

As we entered the cavernous building, we were struck by the powerful smells of fresh paint, turpentine, pitch, and fresh-cut wood. Like all large, wooden structures that are open to the sky, the theater required constant maintenance. And, like all others of its sort, it made constant noise, an almost musical chorus of groans, creaks, and squeaks as changing temperature and every buffet of wind made the whole structure move, timber flexing against timber, boards stretching and pulling against nails, the huge masts that would support the awning whipping back and forth as if they wanted to go to sea like all the other masts.

Publius Syrus was on the stage, rehearsing his cast and chorus, his support crew, and all the rest of the multitude he needed to get a whole set of theatricals presented. Most of us, seeing only the performance, which involves a mere handful of people, are never aware of what a mob is required to present a single play.

"Ah, Aedile," Syrus cried, catching sight of me, "you have come!" As if I needed to be told this. But artists like Syrus had to be handled delicately.

"As always, I am prepared to drop everything to consult with my Master of Theatricals," I said heartily. "Is anything wrong with the plays?"

"The plays? Of course not! They shall be superb!" All

this declaimed with many broad gestures. Then, more calmly, "If, that is, there is a theater to celebrate them in."

"Eh? What are you talking about?"

"Come with me, Aedile." He looked up at the stage. "The rest of you, continue practicing! You have only days to master your roles and your duties!"

"Have the seat cushions arrived yet?" I asked, scanning the nearby seats. "I ordered seat cushions, good ones made of Egyptian linen, stuffed with raw wool. No grass or hay, mind you. Newly sheared raw wool."

"It's far too early for that, Aedile," Syrus insisted. "They'll just get wet. You don't want cushions delivered until a day or two before the festival."

"Well, they'd better be in place by the first performance or heads will fall." I was especially determined to have these cushions because everyone would think I was being terribly extravagant. Actually, one of my clients dealt in wool and cloth, and when the performances were done he would dismantle the cushions and get me back at least three-quarters of my outlay. Best of all, the cushions would outrage Cato. He always went into frothing frenzies anytime an innovation appeared that made people more comfortable.

We walked into a passage beneath the stage, and Syrus praised himself and his work. "Aedile, I have rewritten the scene where King Ptolemy tries to burgle the house of Crassus. Instead of finding Crassus in bed with Caesar's wife, he discovers General Gabinius in bed with the wife of Crassus!"

I nodded. "The news from Egypt has it that Gabinius has been very successful. He really needs to be smeared and lampooned and slandered."

Syrus smiled happily. "My very thought. Too much praise attracts the jealousy of the gods, so we will be doing him a favor." Syrus was the foremost practitioner of this sort of political satire. It was considered scandalous, and various senators had tried having it declared criminal; but it was wildly popular with the plebs, so the tribunes saw to it that no such legislation was passed. Everyone who could hired Syrus to libel and belittle their political rivals and enemies. Sooner or later, someone was going to hire him to give me this treatment, and I was not looking forward to it.

"How are the rehearsals for *Agamemnon* coming along?" I asked him.

Syrus looked as if he had bitten into something sour. "It is not the *Agamemnon* of Aeschylus, Aedile. It is *Antigone,* which is by Sophocles, you will recall."

"Ah, yes, I always confuse those old buggers. They all sound alike to me, but my wife is very fond of them. Rehearsals going well, are they?"

He closed his eyes. "Beautifully, Aedile. Tears and pity and terror shall be the order of the day."

I didn't see that it mattered very much, but I was trying to be polite. Nobody would want to attend the tragedy anyway, except for scholars like Cicero and high-born ladies and whatever protesting husbands they could drag along. What the plebs loved were the comedies and satyr plays, the mimes, and the Atellan farces; and I planned to deliver these in good measure. I wasn't going to be as radical as Pompey, though, and provide large animals and armies clashing in mock battle on stage. It was dangerous, and his innovation had been a failure anyway, spreading panic and dismay. Such activities properly belonged in the arena, not the theater. The Roman public was extremely conservative about this sort of thing.

We came out onto an outside gallery used by the scene shifters and other workmen of the theater. The gallery ran along the straight side of the semicircle, and it was cluttered with heaps of rope, buckets of paint, parts of the crane used for lowering gods into the action, and so forth. It all looked like total chaos to me; but to those whose business it was, it was as orderly as the arrangement of a seagoing vessel.

"Look down there, Aedile," Syrus said, leaning over a railing and pointing downward.

I did likewise, and so did Hermes. The theater backed almost against the riverbank, and the gallery upon which we stood projected out over the mud flat like a balcony. Below us, a crew of workmen were shoring up the building with heavy wooden beams. The muddy, turbid water of the Tiber was already within a few yards of their feet.

"They arrived at first light this morning, sent by the agent of Aemilius Scaurus. It seems we are to be flooded. What am I to do?"

"Why, carry on, of course! This building has survived the high water of the last few years. Maybe it will survive this as well."

"But suppose it doesn't!" he cried excitedly. "All will be ruined! What shall we do then?"

I took him by the arm. "Now, Publius Syrus, you just leave all the petty details to me. If this theater is destroyed, we can always move operations to Pompey's, much as it would pain me to do so." I steered him toward the tunnel that led back to the stage. "Just go back and drill your troops.

Whatever happens in the next few days, the water will have subsided by the Megalensian Games. I will see to everything."

Muttering to himself, shaking his head, wringing his hands, he retreated into the interior. As if I didn't have enough on my hands already, I had to deal with temperamental artists, too.

"Let's go talk to these men," I told Hermes. There was a rickety stairway leading from the gallery to the mud flat. Downriver to our left was the Sublician Bridge. Before us the river itself had achieved alarming breadth and swiftness of current. The bridge, like the upriver Aemilian (built by an ancestor of the Aemilius who built the theater), was lined with gawkers, pointing at the water, gesturing, and doubtless all exclaiming how they, personally, had predicted this very thing. People always do that.

Most of the workmen appeared to be slaves, but these were not unskilled foreigners like the gang we had seen demolishing the wreckage of the *insula*. These men knew their business, and they were constructing a stout brace beneath the overhang of the huge theater, with heavy timbers set horizontally, vertically, and diagonally, resting atop blocks of cut stone. To my unpracticed eye, it all looked very secure. What made me uneasy was that my eye was, indeed, unpracticed.

Bossing the crew was a man whose clothes were of better material than those of the workmen. His hair and complexion were a bit darker than those of a typical Roman, though he wore a citizen's ring.

"I'm the plebeian aedile Metellus," I told him. "What is the likelihood that your work here will save this building in a severe flood?"

He bowed slightly. "I am Manius Florus, freedman of Manius Florus. My patron's firm has been retained by the steward of the proconsul Aemilius Scaurus to try to preserve his theater from the coming high water. To answer your question, Aedile, all will depend upon the flood itself. If the current is terribly swift, the bank here could be eaten away so severely as to drop the whole structure into the river.

"However,"—he swept an arm wide, taking in both bridges—"situated as it is, here between these two fine, strong bridges, I have hopes that it will be spared that. It has been my experience of such floods that the upstream bridge," he pointed toward the Aemilian, "will break much of the force of the current here in the bend and redirect it toward the center of the stream, where it can do little harm. That bridge has survived many, many floods over the centuries."

"I truly hope you are right," I said.

Hermes came up to me. "I think you had better look at this," he murmured. It was unlike Hermes to murmur. I followed him to the heavy framework. "Look at that," he said, pointing. Into the surface of the timber was scratched, in large, crude letters, HERMES.

"You wanted me to see this?" I demanded. "I know you can write your name."

He gave me a look of exasperation. "I didn't put this here this morning."

"Eh?" My mind was not working at full power that morning.

"Look." He poked with a fingernail at a blob of sap that had oozed from the cut. It was soft, but a thin crust had formed over it. "This is one of those timbers I scratched my name on the day before yesterday. They were loaded on the wrecker's carts. Isn't this illegal?"

I swore luridly, something I did well. "This is an outrage! The law states very clearly that condemned wood is not to be used in any aspect of construction or shipbuilding. It is to be employed only as firewood or for funeral pyres!"

"It shouldn't surprise you by now that people are flouting the law," Hermes pointed out.

"No, but this time it involves a building I need for my Games! Manius Florus!" I bellowed.

The man ran up, startled. "Aedile? Is something wrong?"

"Something is very wrong." I pointed at the offending beam. "Where did this timber come from?"

"My patron had me pick up this wood at the salvager's yard out by the Circus Flaminius. It is where we usually get timber for braces, scaffolding, bleachers, and so forth, anything that isn't going to be part of a permanent structure."

"This beam," I said, "until two nights ago, was part of an *insula* that fell down. All of its materials were condemned by my order."

He didn't seem particularly shocked. "Well, it's perfectly sound wood, I can assure you of that. Certainly, it is too green to use in an *insula,* but it is perfectly adequate for this purpose."

"Who owns the salvage yard?" I demanded.

"A man named Justus. He's a freedman, but I don't know who his patron might be."

"Well, get back to your work. I don't want this theater floating away." I went back to the stairs. "Come along, Hermes, we have some people to see."

We went back through the theater and Hermes's importunate words interrupted my thoughts.

"Wouldn't it be funny," he said, "if this whole place"—he rapped his knuckles against the solid-seeming wall of the passage—"was built by whoever built that *insula?*"

A chill gripped my heart as we walked out into the vast *cavea,* and I looked up at the seats that ascended, row upon row, incredibly high, like a staircase in a palace of the gods. Above them the sky-piercing spears of the awning masts stood arrayed in their curving rank, gilded tips gleaming in the morning sunlight. The theater could be seen by travelers miles from the City. Now I looked at it with new eyes, picturing those seats filled to capacity with spectators, picturing them all standing and saluting formally as I entered the theater to take my place as giver of the Games. Picturing them—

"All the gods protect me!" I said. "What if this whole, rickety, wooden basket comes crashing down with eighty thousand Roman citizens in the stands? During *my Games!* The name of Decius Caecilius Metellus the Younger will stink worse than a week-old mackerel as long as Rome stands! I'll be right up there with Tarpeia and Brennus and Hannibal when the people chant execrations upon Rome's greatest enemies and traitors! If I don't manage to open my veins quickly enough, I'll be impaled on a hook and dragged through the streets and be crucified outside the Capena Gate!"

"Senators don't get crucified," Hermes protested. "Slaves and foreigners get crucified."

"They'll pass a new law just for me! The tribunes of the plebs will demand it!"

"Don't worry about it," Hermes said uneasily. "It's stood like this for at least five years. It'll last another. I wish I hadn't said anything."

I wished he hadn't, too.

Marcus Aemilius Scaurus, I recalled, had been an aedile in the mold of Caesar, squandering immense sums on public works, of which the lavish theater was only one, to buy favor with the public. He had also donated a luxurious bathhouse to the City. It was the first of Rome's really large *balnea,* and he provided free admission to all citizens for a year, together with bathing oil and towels. He gave numerous public banquets and paid for regular doles of bread and oil for the poorest citizens, although he never went to Caesar's extreme of paying everyone's home rent for a year.

It was, needless to say, a wildly popular tenure of office, and he had been given the urban praetorship practically without having to stand for it. After stepping down from his curule chair, he was given Sardinia to govern. Sardinia was a proconsular province, so he held the title of proconsul without having to be consul first.

It was the custom for politicians, having ruined themselves and descended far into debt, in order to pay for their public offices, to squeeze their provinces; and Scaurus duly squeezed Sardinia, so much so that he was prosecuted for corruption and extortion immediately upon his return to Rome. Flush with plundered wealth, he had no difficulty in getting a jury to see things in a sympathetic light, and he had recently been acquitted. It was a fairly typical career of the times. It took a prosecutor like Cicero to get a Roman jury to return a verdict of guilty against a Roman magistrate on behalf of provincials.

We tended to wink at these little escapades on the part of our promagistrates. You had to lose a foreign war to get Roman citizens to take an interest in what you did while away from the City. Unfortunately, this attitude rested upon a wholly erroneous assumption: that a man could go to a foreign land and behave like a rapacious, unregenerate criminal, then come home and act like an honest citizen. It never seemed to work that way.

Luckily for me, the house of Aemilius Scaurus was not far from his theater, next to the old city wall near the Flumentana Gate. It was a fairly imposing building, but built back in the days before there was any such thing as a fashionable neighborhood in Rome. Like most such older mansions, it had shops and slum housing crowded right against it, and behind it was a tiny market specializing in fresh and preserved garlic.

The *janitor* admitted me, and a few minutes later a portly individual appeared, his eyes widening slightly at sight of me. He was bald with a bland, doughy face and rings on every finger. The tip of his nose was decorated with a large, purple wart.

"Welcome, Aedile! This is most unexpected. I am Juventius, steward of my patron's City property. I trust all is well at the theater?"

"Well enough so far," I said. I had never met the man, but one of my clients had made arrangements to rent the theater for my Games, so this must have been the man he dealt with. "The workmen are reinforcing the structure right now, but the rest is up to the river."

"I have already sacrificed to Father Tiber," he said. "Let us hope that he finds it acceptable."

"You performed the sacrifice?" I asked. Ordinarily, all religious observances are overseen by the head of the household, not a subordinate.

"Yes, the proconsul left the City yesterday to spend some time at one of his country estates."

"He did, eh? Wanted to be on higher ground, or is he hiding out from Sardinian assassins?"

The man's obsequious smile faltered. "Sir?"

"I need to speak with your master, and I find him fled from the City. Most of us go to our country estates in the hottest days of summer. Why such haste to be away?" Of course I had no authority to demand explanations for the actions of a man of such rank, but if you hold office you can accomplish a lot just by being pushy and obnoxious. Flunkies like this one have an ingrained habit of groveling to authority.

"Why, Aedile, I—I—." He gathered himself and said, "Actually, I believe he went to oversee the planting of a new vineyard. Yes, that was it, a vineyard. Couldn't wait until summer for that." The man had probably never set foot outside the city walls in his life, and I doubted he'd know a vineyard from a fish pond.

"Did Aemilius leave orders to contract with the firm of Manius Florus to shore up the theater against the coming flood?"

"Oh, yes sir. The family of Florus is among my patron's clientele. He has given them a great deal of business in the course of his many public works."

"Then it seems that I need to speak with Manius Florus in your master's absence." I turned to go.

"But, sir, is something wrong?" I had the poor fool badly rattled.

"Nothing you need concern yourself with." Then I thought of something and turned around. "Which estate has he gone to?"

"Why, the one near Bovillae, sir. Shall I dispatch word that you need to speak with him, Aedile?"

"Don't bother."

I walked from the house. Bovillae again. Lucius Folius and his wife had come from Bovillae. A supposed heir had made off with their bodies for interment at Bovillae. I don't believe in coincidence.

We passed through the city wall at the Flumentana Gate and into the sprawling Circus Flaminius district. Like the Trans-Tiber, the Flaminius was far less congested than the City proper. Unconfined by walls, houses and businesses could be located on extensive lots; and in this district, many businesses that required plenty of room had been established, such as the salvage yard we were looking for, as well as those that employed a hazardous level of fire. The kiln yards of several pottery and brick factories were located in the district.

By asking at a few lumberyards, we came to the salvage business run by the freedman named Justus. The premises consisted of nothing more than a small, one-roomed building in a corner of a sprawling yard, where heaps of rough timber, finished beams, and planks rose to twice a man's height, given some protection from the elements by crude roofs set atop high poles. Teams of slaves in dingy brown tunics, their hair pale with sawdust, loaded wood onto the carts of builders or unloaded wood from the carts of wreckers.

I found Justus sweating along with his workmen, loading a wagon with what appeared to be wood so deteriorated that it was useless for any purpose save burning. He was distinguishable from the slaves solely by his citizen's ring, made of plain iron. When he caught sight of me, I crooked a finger and he walked over, brushing debris from his hands.

"You're the Aedile Metellus, aren't you?" he asked.

Unlike the curule aedile, the plebeian aedile rated no insignia of office: no lictor bearing the *fasces,* no curule chair, no purple border on one's toga. "You've seen me before?"

"At the elections. Someone said that crowd around you was the largest assemblage of ex-praetors, ex-consuls, and ex-censors in Rome."

"There is nothing like a distinguished family for that helpful boost at the polls," I said.

"How may I be of service, Aedile?" The man's eyes were bright and direct; he did not seem in the least nervous or guilty, although he was speaking to a man who could have him severely punished for infractions of the civic codes.

"I am tracking several cartloads of condemned timber. They were salvaged yesterday and the day before from an *insula* that collapsed in the night. The contractor who hauled away the wreckage was one Marcus Caninus."

"Oh, yes sir. That was all delivered here." He looked around. "In fact, it looks as if most of it is still here."

"That lumber was condemned," I told him. "It was my impression that all such rubble was to be carried out to the landfills."

"That's true for brick and mortar and tile, but decent wood is always salvaged for other purposes. So is good cut stone, if the building it was part of didn't burn."

"Is that how the building codes read?" I asked him.

He shrugged. "I don't know. I never read them. But the

custom has always been that as long as a building wasn't destroyed by fire, and didn't fall because it was built of inferior materials, we can salvage the stone for reuse. A good earthquake will keep us stocked with cut stone for years. When a really big project comes along, like Pompey's Theater, you can bet that salvaged stone was used everywhere the builder could get away with it. Just the outer facing was cut especially for the project."

For a man like this, ancient custom carried far more weight than any law written down in a book he'd never seen.

"But this building collapsed because it was not built to code," I said, "and I condemned its materials myself, so how does it come to pass that some of that very material is in use this morning, by the contractor Manius Florus, shoring up the river side of the theater of Aemilius Scaurus?"

"Oh, that. Well, you see, that wood's not being used in a permanent structure. For temporary structures, bracing and so forth, it's all right to use such wood. It was perfectly good timber anyway, if a bit green."

I rubbed my forehead, which was beginning to ache. Here was yet another free interpretation of the law. I decided that I was going to have to drag all those laws and building codes out of the Tabularium, have them carved in stone, and set them up in a public place. Another expense I could ill afford.

Justus scratched his own curly head, causing a minor snowfall of sawdust. "How did you know that it was timber from that *insula,* if you don't mind my asking?"

"I take my duties as aedile seriously," I told him. "I put secret markings on the wood to thwart those who would flout the laws of the Republic."

He nodded admiringly. "Smart move."

"Here's more of it!" Hermes shouted. He had been wandering among the piles of timber, and now he was kicking at some heavy beams. I walked over to join him, and Justus hurried along beside me.

"These are those joists we saw in the basement," Hermes said. "See, here's one of those woodpecker holes." He nudged at the heavy beam with a toe.

"Yes, this was taken from the *insula,*" Justus said, frowning. "Caninus brought it by and dumped it here, then said he needed some weak, rotten old timbers, the same size. Usually, those are sold off for funeral pyres. Why pay for good wood if you're just going to burn it? Anyway, nobody important had died recently, so I had what he needed. I asked him what he wanted it for, and he said that men who don't ask stupid questions don't get their tongues cut out. I can take a hint as well as the next man."

"I know where that wood ended up," I said, thinking of the courtyard of the Temple of Ceres.

Justus squatted and looked at the hole Hermes had kicked. He stuck a finger into it, then withdrew the finger and studied its tip. "This isn't any woodpecker hole," he announced.

"Squirrel, then?" Hermes asked.

Justus laughed. "Don't know much about wood, do you?"

"Enlighten us," I said.

"Well, sir, somebody bored this hole with an auger, the way you do when you're going to fasten two timbers together with a heavy spike."

Hermes and I looked at each other. "Remember those tools we saw in the basement?" the boy asked.

"Justus, I want a close look at all these timbers," I ordered.

He stuck two fingers in his mouth and whistled. The slaves came running, and he barked orders. Within minutes, all the timbers were laid out in good light in an orderly fashion, so we could walk around them. The slaves stood by to turn them over at my instruction.

"More holes," Hermes said, pointing at two no more than an inch apart.

"Here, look at this," Justus said. He was squatting by the end of one of the shattered timbers. The ragged end still displayed three parallel furrows. "It was bored through here. That's why it snapped at this point. That *insula* didn't just collapse, Aedile, it was brought down on purpose."

Hermes had his knife out in one hand, brushing with his other hand at the surface of a timber where he had spotted a circular depression. He stuck the tip of his knife into the edge of the depression and, slowly, carefully, pried upward. A long, whitish cylinder appeared and a moment later Hermes had a six-inch candle impaled triumphantly on his blade. Its base had been rubbed with soot or some other dark substance to blend with the wood.

"Remember all those candles we found floating in the water down in that basement?" Hermes said.

"Justus," I said, "you are the expert on wood. What does this tell you about the man who did it?"

"Aside from that he was a cold-blooded murderer, you mean? Well, he didn't know much about timber or about building. This was done pretty haphazardly, drilling holes here and there. If he'd known anything about construction, where the main stress points are and so forth, he could have brought the place down with no more than a dozen holes drilled close together at the right points on the right timbers, three or four holes per timber."

"Could he have escaped in time?" I asked.

"Most likely. Heavy timbers like this make a good deal of noise just before they go. If he'd known what to listen for, and had a good way out prepared, he might have had a few seconds to get clear. The way this looks," he waved a hand over the ruined wood, "it gave way all at once, in six or seven places, just dumped the whole *insula* into the basement."

"Justus," I said, "I want you to hide these timbers. Cover them with trash or something. I am going to want to use them as evidence in court."

A look of alarm crossed his face.

"Don't worry, you have nothing to fear. It is clear to me that you are guilty of no wrongdoing."

"To be honest, sir, it's not you or the courts that worry me."

"I intend to arrest Marcus Caninus immediately," I assured him, "for tampering with my evidence if nothing else."

"I'll do as you order, Aedile."

Something occurred to me. "Was Justus your slave name?"

"Yes, sir. I was manumitted along with fifty others to celebrate the birth of my master's first grandson."

"And you didn't take your former master's name?" I asked, that being the usual custom.

"Well, sir, I did, but I never use it. I suppose it's the name that'll go on my tombstone; but Justus isn't a foreign name, and I've been used to using it all my life. Besides," he lowered his head sheepishly, "I'm just a working man, doing the same work I did when I was a slave. I'd feel foolish going around calling myself Marcus Valerius Messala Niger."

I left the salvage yard with much to think about.

8

NEAR THE GATE WE STOPPED AT a little tavern. The sun was well up, and I needed a pause to think. Also, it was time for a drink and something to eat. Who knew when I'd get a chance again? We found a table against a wall of white stucco beneath an arbor that was all but bare so early in the year. Light fell through the arbor in lozenge-shaped patches, making the table, the floor, and ourselves look like pictures in mosaic. I ordered the wine to be very lightly watered, and we used it to wash down oil-dipped bread and olives for a while.

Hermes spoke first. "It was the big slave, wasn't it?"

"Had to be," I concurred. "That's why he was dressed, and it's why he was trapped there standing. I don't know why I didn't think of it before. It was pretty far-fetched to think he dropped there, landed on his feet, and got pinned there that way. He drilled one hole too many, and the building came down too fast."

"Why did he do it?" Hermes wondered. "Just to kill the master and mistress? I can understand why he'd want to. You saw how they treated their slaves. But why kill more than two hundred people just to get rid of them?"

"I suspect he *did* kill them, personally," I said. "He could have broken their necks easily, then gone down to the basement to bore those last few holes, figuring to disguise the murder as an accident. But he didn't step lively enough."

Hermes shook his head. "It still doesn't make sense."

"No, it doesn't. Revenge was a good enough motivation for the slave, but it doesn't explain how everyone else has been acting since the disaster. He may have had a personal justification for ridding the world of those two, but someone must have put him up to the final deed."

In a bit of spilled wine my fingertip traced a circle, then drew a slash across it. It took me a moment to realize what I had unconsciously drawn: the Greek letter "theta." In the shorthand of the Games, it stands for Thanatos: killed. After the *munera,* this symbol is scratched on the walls, following the names of the gladiators who have been slain.

"Two names keep cropping up," I said. "Marcus Valerius Messala Niger and Marcus Aemilius Scaurus."

"Those are two important names," Hermes pointed out.

"Yes, and Valerius Messala is in the process of weaseling himself into the political affairs of my family. The family has been hinting heavily that I should drop this investigation."

"Maybe you should."

"And let someone get away with murdering a whole *insula* full of people, free and slave?"

Hermes spread his hands. "I'm just a slave; I do as I'm told. But if your family is against your prosecuting the people responsible for this, you are going to have some serious trouble accomplishing anything."

I mused, almost to myself, "They have been doing a number of things I am having trouble countenancing. Hermes, do you know *why* my family is so important?"

He was taken aback. "Well, yours is one of the most ancient of the noble names—"

"Certainly. But the Caesars are even more ancient, and they've amounted to nothing for centuries. Caius Julius is the first to win real distinction since Rome had kings. No, we Metelli have supplied Rome with praetors and consuls and censors since before written records, but we've dominated Roman politics for the last thirty years for one reason: We backed Sulla against Marius. When Sulla was dictator, the men who are now elders of the family, and some who are now dead, were his most forceful supporters: Celer, Pius, Creticus, old Numidicus, and my father."

Hermes shifted uncomfortably. "I don't take much interest in politics or history. It's not a slave's business."

"What a liar you are. And a poor liar, at that. Those big flap ears of yours take in anything that's to your advantage. And as my personal slave, you have to know more about politics than most senators. Well, go ahead, pretend to be stupid. You may live longer that way."

To some it may seem strange that I would speak so openly to a slave. But the fact is that Rome has never been a place where the status of slave was a life sentence. A capable slave, or a lucky one, like Justus, could expect to be manumitted and then rise in the world. After a generation or two, all taint of servitude was forgotten. In the Senate, I sat beside many men whose grandfathers had been slaves. On occasion, even that generational period was waived. Many well-born men who were sonless adopted an especially esteemed freedman to carry on the family name with full privileges, the same as if he had been born into it.

And I fully expected to manumit Hermes, as soon as he showed the faintest sign of a sense of responsibility. As my freedman, he would still be bound to me by bonds of patronage, but he would be a free man, able to vote in the Assemblies, own property, and marry at will. I had been at some pains to educate him for this eventual role. I have mentioned his criminal proclivities, but I had a few of those myself. As Rome was in those days, it was no bad thing for a man to have a bit of the criminal and the thug in his character. It made survival a greater likelihood. Rome has changed, of course. Since the First Citizen's reforms, the desirable qualities are those of the toady, the lickspittle, and the informer.

"It is clear that I am going to have to tread carefully. I may have to go armed again. From now on we can expect to be attacked. In ordinary times, even the gangs have avoided violence against a serving magistrate; but these are not ordinary times, and it isn't as if I were a praetor or consul. A plebeian aedile doesn't rate that high." In the past I had usually carried concealed weapons while in the City, skirting the law for the sake of my own hide. I had fondly hoped that my office conferred some sort of immunity, but that hope was fading fast.

Hermes was fidgeting impatiently.

"You have something to say?" I asked.

"Why must you always think as if you must act alone? You have friends, allies, even political opponents who would be willing to help."

I considered this. "In the past, I've availed myself of Milo's aid, but that would look very bad now. He's responsible for a good deal of the bloodshed in the streets, and he wants to be consul next year. There is too much wrangling among the consular and proconsular persons just now to expect help from that quarter, and it looks as if Messala will be *interrex* soon. It's like trying to separate fighting elephants. I'd be trampled. Besides, he was among the first to warn me against this investigation. Influential clients of his are worried about it."

"What about Cicero? He loves to prosecute, and he's always liked you."

"Liking is a fleeting thing," I pointed out. "I revere and admire Cicero, but he's growing obsessive in his opposition to Caesar. He knows that Caesar, for whatever insane reason, values me. And I'm married to Caesar's niece. Right now those things outweigh any lingering affection he feels for me. If I were to approach Cicero on this, he would suspect that Caesar was playing some subtle game, using me as a cat's-paw."

"Then what about Cato?" Hermes asked, exasperated.

"Cato?" I barked. "I detest Cato!"

"So what? You need help, not love! He was a great

tribune of the plebs. The whole population sings his praises as upright and incorruptible, the enemy of all corruption and impiety, and, best of all, he is absolutely fearless! He's taken on the whole Senate more than once. He took Cicero's part when people called for his exile if not execution. He's turned down bribes that would have tempted a pharaoh, and he doesn't even know how much you loathe him because he's too thick-skinned to notice your insults!"

So much for Hermes's ignorance of political affairs. I didn't like even to contemplate going to Cato for help; then again, I didn't like being in Caesar's camp, either, but there I was. Everything Hermes said about the man was true. A great many Roman politicians made a public show of antique virtue and incorruptibility, contempt for greed and foreign luxury. They were all lying hypocrites, except for Cato. He meant every word, and he practiced as he preached. It didn't make me like him any better. Reasonable laxity of character and a pleasing personality have always been more to my liking.

"Let me consider this," I said. "We have the Libitinarii to question first. Then perhaps I can nerve myself up to talking with the glorious Marcus Porcius Cato."

The Libitinarii of Rome had their district surrounding the Temple of Venus Libitina. We identify Venus with the Greek Aphrodite, but the pretty, mischievous Greek deity has no aspect as a death goddess. Our Libitina is different. We Romans see no contradiction in having one goddess to preside over both copulation and death, since you pretty much have to have the one before you can have the other.

Neither the Libitinarii nor their establishments are especially gloomy, since we are very fond of funerals. We figure that you are only going to get one funeral, and it is the last thing people will remember about you, so it might as well be gaudy. The Libitinarii, with their bizarre Etruscan trappings, are frightening figures; but that is mainly because they deal with corpses that are still in their dangerous, recently dead state. Romans have little fear of death or the dead, but we are horrified of the ritual *contamination* of death. Once the Libitinarii have carried out the *lustrum* that purifies the corpse, we are much easier about the whole business.

The establishments of the Libitinarii in this quarter were built, not like shops nor like factories, but rather like houses, with alterations suitable to their purpose. A little asking brought me to the business of Sextus Volturnus. Libitinarii favor Etruscan names, even if they are not of that ancestry. We have always associated the Etruscans with the underworld deities, since they are so fond of them.

This house looked little different from my own, except that the gate that opened onto the street featured a double door and was far taller. This was so that pallbearers carrying a corpse on a litter could pass through easily. It was almost twice a man's height, since some people still preferred to be carried to the pyre sitting upright in a chair. The atrium was very large for the convenience of those who would lie in state at the funeral house instead of in their own homes. This allowed for more visitors than most houses could comfortably accommodate. All was painted in bright colors, with many floral designs and frescoes of the open countryside, nothing to associate with death or the underworld.

The man who came forward as I entered the spacious atrium of the place wore the only symbol in sight of his profession: a black toga. This was not merely the dingy, brown toga most of us wore when in mourning, but a genuine, midnight black toga. Somehow, in the cheery surroundings, it looked all the more ominous. His expression, when he saw me, was stricken.

"A great Roman has died!" he intoned. "Alas!"

"Eh?" I said. "See here, I am the Aedile Metellus—"

He clasped his hands together, all but squeezing the blood from them. "The gods forbid it! Your father, the great censor, has left us! All Rome will weep! Sir, if you will leave all the arrangements to me, I shall be honored to—"

"Nothing like that!" I said. "Nobody has died. Nobody in my family, anyway. I need to inquire into the disposition of a couple of corpses I sent here yesterday morning."

"Oh." He lowered his hands to his sides, severe disappointment written upon his face. "That would be Lucius Folius and his wife."

"It would." I was beginning to wonder whether the woman had ever had a name. "I sent a physician here to examine them for signs of foul play, and he informed me that they had been taken away."

"They were. Barring any instructions to the contrary, it is customary to surrender the bodies of the dead to whatever heirs or others who wish to remove them for cremation and interment. Since these rites were to be performed in their ancestral town of Bovillae, there was no need to keep them here."

"And this heir was one Caius Folius?"

"So he said."

"Did he provide any proof of identity?" I asked him.

The man was totally mystified. "Is there some sort of law requiring this? I certainly never heard of such a thing.

Proof of identity? What would that be? And who would claim a body without cause? These weren't like the mummies of pharaohs, decked out in gold and jewels. They were just a pair of corpses getting no more fragrant with the passage of time." He was growing quite indignant.

"I get your point," I said, holding out a palm for peace. "Did this Caius Folius claim that he was a son of the late couple?"

"Not likely. He looked older than either of them, and I took him for a brother or cousin or some such relative."

"What did he look like?"

"Balding, plump, wore a lot of rings. He looked rather nondescript altogether"—he thought for a moment—"except for his nose."

"What was singular about his nose?"

"He had a large, wine-colored wart on it. If I'd been getting him ready for the pyre, I'd have dusted it with powder to make it less glaring."

"Thank you, Sextus Volturnus," I said, grasping both his clammy hands in mine. "You've been a great help!"

"If you say so. Please keep me in mind should any of your illustrious relatives depart."

We left the funeral home and turned our steps toward the Forum. So Juventius, the steward of Aemilius Scaurus, had claimed the bodies of the late Folii; and they were, in all likelihood, on their way to Bovillae with Aemilius himself. Why? That, along with a great many other questions, remained to be answered.

Cato wasn't hard to find. He never was.

Marcus Porcius Cato was the enemy of all things modern or foreign. These things included sleeping late, eating well, bathing in hot water, and enjoying anything beautiful. He studied philosophy and even wrote philosophical tracts, but he was naturally attracted to the Stoics since they were the most disagreeable of all the Greeks. He believed that all virtue resided in the practices of our ancestors, and that the only path to greatness lay in narrow adherence to those practices. He revered above all others his ancestor Cato the Censor, the most repulsive man among all Rome's many disgusting personages, most of whom were content to be cruel and vicious on their own behalf. Cato the Censor wanted everyone to be as nasty as he was.

There was a trial that morning in the Basilica Opimia, and I was sure that Cato would attend because it was a capital case and he had been complaining that Roman juries hadn't been demanding harsh enough sentences lately. He would want to be there to press for the most savage punishments decreed by his revered ancestors.

Sure enough, there he was on a bench, surrounded by his cronies, many of whom affected his "antique simplicity." Despite the coolness of the weather, he eschewed a tunic, wearing only a primitive, square-cut toga that draped him awkwardly, leaving half his torso bare. Instead of having his hair cut and styled by a barber, he shaved his head every month or so, so that he sported an uneven stubble over his whole scalp.

When he saw me, he got to his bare feet. He thought sandals to be an effeminate luxury, unworthy of our barefoot ancestors, and wore footgear only when campaigning with the army. He was not a large or imposing man and was not particularly powerful, but he refused to recognize any weakness in himself and so was capable of extraordinary feats of strength and endurance through sheer stubbornness.

"Hail, Aedile!" he cried, like a soldier saluting his general as *Imperator*.

"And a fine morning to you, Marcus Porcius Cato," I said. "Did you get the felon cut in two with a timber saw or torn to bits by Mollosian hounds or whatever the punishment was?"

"It was a woman who poisoned her husband, and the jury voted for exile just because the man had been beating her regularly." I did not know whether his grimace of distaste was for the mild punishment or my own levity, another thing of which he disapproved. He had no sense of humor whatsoever.

"Well, better luck next time. Marcus Porcius, I may soon need your help on a matter pertaining to my activities as aedile."

His perpetual frown deepened. "You have seldom sought my help in the past," he said. "Never, now that I think of it. Why now?"

"Because my usual sources of support have turned their backs on me, and for once I think you will approve of what I am doing."

"That would indeed be a prodigy," he said, with his usual, heavy sarcasm. "I am listening."

So I told him of my investigation and where it had led me. His expression did not change throughout the recital, but I knew that he was absorbing every word and would be able to repeat them verbatim ten years hence. He had a rare fixity of concentration. When I was finished, he gave a curt nod.

"This is most worthy," he said. "You have a genuine

devotion to duty, Decius Caecilius, despite your deplorable frivolity. I especially disapprove of your emphasis on theatrical performances in your upcoming Games. Such alien entertainments render the people weak and passive. You need more combats and animal hunts and executions. Those are the things that strengthen and harden the citizens. And awnings are a totally unnecessary luxury. Let them endure a few hours of sunlight; it will do them good. And another thing—" and so on and on. You had to put up with this sort of thing from Cato if you wanted his aid. *Wait,* I thought, *until he hears about my seat cushions.* Finally, he got back to the business at hand.

"I think it has been far too long since anyone has taken action against the whole pack of greedy, money-grubbing builders. I don't recall a serious campaign against them since Sulla. He fined them, drove them from the City, and executed a few as an example. That is what we need now."

"I couldn't agree more," I said, "but you realize that it means crossing some of the most important men in the Senate as well as the richest of the *equites?*"

"What of that?" he snarled. "Anyone, however highborn or powerful, who puts riches above the public weal should be cast from the Tarpeian Rock, then dragged on a hook through the streets and down the Tiber steps and cast into the river, preferably still breathing through the whole ordeal. That's how we used to deal with traitors! And traitors they are, Decius! It is bad enough that wealthy freedmen have gained so much power, but now they have corrupted their betters as well. Since our earliest days, filthy commerce has been forbidden to the nobility. Using money to make money is an abomination! Some avaricious sophist came up with the dodge that stone, clay, and timber come from the land and therefore owners of estates may traffic in them legitimately as products of virtuous agriculture."

This was a typical rant from Cato. As usual, he blamed all corruption on foreigners and the lower classes. His own class had been pure, pristine, and above it all before they were tempted by those whom the gods adored less.

My own interpretation of our social history differs somewhat from Cato's. Dispensing with pleasing myths like the story of the Trojan prince Aeneas, according to myth the son of Venus, and his son, Julus, from whom Caesar traces his ancestry, it goes somewhat as follows:

About seven hundred years ago, a pack of bandits arrived in central Italy, led by two brothers named Romulus and Remus. They despoiled the nearby peoples of land and women and set up their own little bandit state. At some point, Romulus established a fine old Roman tradition by murdering his brother. Had it been the other way around, I suppose we might now be living in a city named Reme.

After a period of rule by kings, some of them Etruscan, our ancestors established the Republic. The pack of families who controlled everything called themselves patricians, and they owned all the land that was worth anything. Since they were nothing but wealthy farmers, they decreed that only wealthy farmers had any claim to honor and respectability. Money from any source save farming was tainted, since it was a kind of money they never got.

The lesser people were the plebeians, who got here a little too late to claim the better land, all that having gone to the first pack of bandits and passed on to their descendants. The plebeians had the virtue of numbers, and the patricians needed them if there was to be an army; and the rest of Roman history has been a struggle between the classes for power. These plebeians wanted to own land and be respectable, too; and some of them, my own family among them, managed the feat. It is a rule that good land is already claimed, so the only way to get some of it was to take it away from somebody else, and that was how we got started on the path to empire.

There was one exception to this wealth-from-land-equals-honor rule: Loot taken in war was also honorable. This consisted of anything the people you killed left lying about, plus the people themselves, if they were still breathing and capable of work. If you captured the wealthier ones, you could sell them back to their families. Crudely put, besides farming, the only honorable ways to make money were theft, slaving, and ransom.

Do not misunderstand me. Barbarians are usually far worse than we are and are mostly disgusting when they aren't being ridiculous. People who get enslaved generally bring it on themselves by losing wars or being stupid; and if they have any decent qualities at all, they can work themselves out of that state.

All my life I have enjoyed being an aristocrat, loaded with privileges and able to lord it over most of the population. It is just that, unlike Cato, I don't see any particular virtue inherent to the status of *nobilitas*. If my long life has taught me anything, it is that the only really vital quality to have is luck. Some have it and some do not, and it has nothing to do with character or inherited virtue. We can sacrifice and perform all the prescribed rituals to placate or buy off whatever god or goddess is in charge of whatever aspect of life;

but in the end, the only one that counts is Fortuna, and there is absolutely nothing we can do to influence her.

The maddening thing was that I had to agree with Cato, at least when it came to the problem and what should be done about it. I have often noticed that the most frustrating thing in life is, not when people disagree with you, but rather when they agree for the wrong reason. It looked as if Cato and I were to be allies on this thing, yet I detested the man, his bullheaded obstinacy, his vile, self-righteous brutality, his total lack of any sense of proportion, his complacent pride in his ancestry, and any number of other qualities and actions I found repugnant.

"First off," Cato said, "we must have names. With names we can bring charges before the court of the urban praetor. So far we have only Aemilius Scaurus and this contemptible contractor, Caninus. The former has already been in court a good deal of late, and the latter is little more than a glorified garbage hauler. We need more names, many names, and prominent ones. We'll attract little attention just prosecuting these two."

"I'm working on that," I told him, "but there may be problems."

"Eh? What sort of problems?"

"Well, if my past experience in this sort of investigation, which you know to be extensive, is anything to go by, people will soon be trying to kill me."

He scowled. "So what? You're a grown man. You should be able to take care of yourself. I myself have never shirked a fight, whether in foreign lands or right here in the Forum. If someone attacks you, kill him first. That's what I always do."

"Sage advice as always. Still, they may be more numerous than usual this time. They may succeed."

"Then I shall just have to go on without you. Rest assured, I shall pursue this matter until the last malefactor is brought to justice. There are still some fine old punishments for corruption on the books. I shall find them."

"I am sure you shall, Marcus Porcius, and knowing it is a great comfort to me."

"What need has any true Roman of comfort?" He really talked that way.

I walked away from him greatly relieved that I wouldn't have to talk to him again for a while. Disagreeable as the conference had been, I knew that he would work indefatigably on the case, and that he would put his clients to the same task, and that I might anticipate some progress soon. Awful as he was, Cato was a good man to have on your side.

In favor of Marcus Porcius Cato, I can say only this: He died splendidly, years later, in Utica.

Hermes and I made our belated way to the Temple of Ceres while I pondered my next move. When I saw the heap of old wood in the courtyard, a thought occurred to me.

"Hermes, go find the messengers assigned to the office. Send them out to locate Marcus Caninus and summon him here at once."

Hermes trotted off, and I consulted with my clients and petitioners for a while. While we talked, I made them all accompany me on a short walk down to the river. The water was ankle deep on the wharves, and a quick examination revealed that it was almost to the tops of the sewer outlets. Soon all would be backing up; and as jammed as the side drains were, the water could stand in the City for weeks after the river receded.

I dispatched clients to check on the lower-lying areas of the City and report on their preparations and ability to weather the coming flood.

In the last floods, I recalled, people had crowded into temples, basilicas, and porticoes, anywhere that they could find a roof. Most, however, had simply huddled miserably on the higher parts of the Campus Martius and on hillsides outside the walls of the City. Those floods had been accompanied by heavy rains, so sickness had been rampant and many people had died.

It occurred to me that we ought to have some sort of system to provide temporary relief in times of natural catastrophe. We had our old system of grain doles, but that was for times of siege, which had been rare in recent centuries. A warehouse or two holding tents or portable booths would make a great deal of difference. But who would pay for this and see to its maintenance? Oh, well, another problem to ponder.

In the afternoon, Marcus Caninus arrived, and he was not alone. The five men with him were tough-looking specimens of his own sort, and all of them were dressed in green tunics. This was the uniform of the followers of Plautius Hypsaeus, mob leader and candidate for next year's praetorship. Of course, I thought when I saw them, they might all work for the Green Racing Faction, or it might just be coincidence that they all wore green tunics that day. As I have said, I have little faith in the power of coincidence.

"You've summoned me, Aedile, so here I am," Caninus

said, his previous toadying servility replaced by insolence. "Now what do you want?" Clearly, my status had fallen in the two days since our last interview.

"You must remove all this timber," I said, waving a hand over the heap of rotten wood.

"I delivered it only yesterday morning," he said. "Where do you want it now?"

"First, I want to know why you switched the wood you took from the fallen *insula,* which was sound, although a bit green and then deliberately damaged, for this rotten stuff."

"Switched?" he said. "This is the wood I took from that basement, and anyone who says differently is a liar."

"Mind your tongue," I advised him. "You are speaking to a serving magistrate."

"Times aren't what they once were, Aedile. People don't look to you senators for leadership like they used to. An aedile doesn't have *imperium* anyway. You've got no lictors around you, and you don't have the special protections that a tribune of the plebs enjoys."

It sounded to me suspiciously as if someone had coached him on the niceties of the law concerning serving officials. Most citizens were woefully ignorant of these matters and assumed that anyone in office shared in the powers and immunities of the highest. The fact was, many of us were no more than State functionaries without special protection and privileges. Those trappings of the *imperium*-holding offices—the lictors and curule chairs and the purple borders on the togas—conferred far more than mere dignity. They set the officeholder aside as someone with extraordinary powers and to trifle with whom could cost your head. As a mere plebeian aedile, I had none of those things.

Behind Caninus, his green-clad thugs smirked. Such men always relish a leader's defiance of authority. I knew men like Caninus well from long, bitter experience. They are like the oversized curs that lead mongrel packs, and if you display the slightest weakness before them you are done for. I stepped up to him so that our faces were only inches apart and assumed the cold, imperious face for which Roman officials are famed all over the world. I was very good at this and practiced it often, in private.

"*Publicanus,*" I said, in my most withering tone, "it is only out of respect for the laws of the Republic that I tolerate your insolence. Display any more of it, and I will haul you before the urban praetor's court on a charge of *maiestas*. You are aware of that charge?" I had chosen my form of address deliberately. To most people, *publicanus* was a term of contempt and loathing, since the only *publicani* they were likely to encounter were the tax collectors, whom nobody loved.

His eyes flickered for a moment, his confidence beginning to slip before my arrogance. "I've heard the word. What of it?"

"It means gross insult to the majesty of the Roman people and their sacred State. The punishment is the same as that for treason."

"That is absurd! Just because I—"

"As an official of that State," I went on, not giving him a chance to collect his slow wits, "I embody the collective dignity of the Roman People! Lay so much as a hand on the lowliest quaestor, and you become an enemy of the State."

"Who is laying hands on anyone?" he blustered. "I spoke up for myself, that is all!"

I sneered as haughtily as Cato. "Insult of word or attitude is the same as personal violence. You are not in the midst of a mob now, Caninus, hurling anonymous abuse at your betters on the speaker's platform. You stand here alone, before witnesses. These are the sacred precincts of the Temple of Ceres, home of the plebeian aediles since the founding of the Republic. Do not compound your offense with sacrilege!"

This was purest bluster on my part. He could bend over, pull up his tunic, and expose his buttocks to the whole College of Aediles in perfect safety, to the best of my knowledge; and you could probably include the High Priestess of Ceres. But physical size and the toughness of a street brawler are no match for the *gravitas* of a highborn Roman official, raised from birth to sit in judgment and command legions. Facing down such a figure, backed by the power of the State, was a far cry from driving gangs of slaves.

"Now," I said, "be so good as to tell me why you substituted this timber for the wood you hauled from the ruins of the *insula*. And think carefully before you call me a liar."

He was cowed, but I couldn't be sure how long that would last. The men behind him looked sorely disappointed. His pique at losing face before his peers could easily overcome his ingrained subordination to authority.

He paused and thought, clearly an unaccustomed activity. "There is the wood. That is what I took from the *insula*. You have no evidence that says otherwise."

"So you are going to trade legal quibbles with me? Do you think you are qualified to do this? I've conducted many prosecutions, Caninus."

"And I've witnessed many trials, Aedile. I know that a mere accusation means little without evidence to back it up."

He had me there. I had no reliable witnesses to attest to what we'd found in the basement, just Hermes, and as a slave he could only testify under torture. Even if this is done in form alone, as by pouring water up the wretch's nose, it is a degrading business and nobody believes the slave anyway. If I told him what I had learned from Justus, the man would be dead by morning. I decided to hold the freedman in reserve.

"Marcus Caninus, it is clear to me that there is a criminal conspiracy here, a conspiracy to conceal evidence of fraudulent practices from investigation. If you do not reveal to me what you know about this matter, I will not hesitate to proceed against you and seek the most severe punishment."

He shifted uneasily, glancing in the direction of the men in green. He was beginning to regret that he had brought them along. "You'll be dealing with men far more important than I am, Aedile."

"Exactly. It is the custom of such men, when engaged in criminal conspiracy, to sacrifice the lowest-ranking man involved to save their own hides. That man would be you, Marcus Caninus."

His expression hardened. "Then I'm screwed by greater men. It wouldn't be the first time."

"You needn't suffer alone," I told him. "In fact, there is no need for you to face prosecution at all. I am not interested in bringing a mere *publicanus* to trial. Name to me the men who are engaged in this illegal traffic, which has cost the lives of a great many citizens, and be prepared to swear to this in court, and you will suffer no more than the forfeit of your public contract and a nominal fine."

"I am not an informer," he said, drawing himself up to his full, formidable height.

"Of course not," I said. "You are a loyal supporter of the Senate and People. Think about it. You know how to find me. Now, I give you leave to go."

Nonchalantly I turned and walked away, the muscles of my back tensed against a half-anticipated dagger thrust. Slowly I turned and saw him walking away with his hounds at heel. "Oh, Marcus Caninus?"

He turned, puzzled. "Aedile?"

"Don't forget to come back and haul away all this wood. The High Priestess is most insistent."

9

"THAT WAS WELL DONE," HERmes said, "but how long will it last? He'll collect his wits, see that his bullyboys think he's backed down from a weaker man, and come after you."

"But *were* they his men? He struck me as a busy man when I spoke with him two days ago. He has a business to manage. It's one that calls for a free use of the whip, and he may kill a slave or two on occasion as an example to the others; but holding a public contract like that, it must keep him active from dawn to sundown. When does such a man have time to lead thugs in the streets?"

In Rome, the activity of putting up new housing and demolishing old structures went on constantly. In later years, when Caesar enacted as permanent law the occasional legislation passed by tribunes of banning wheeled traffic from the streets during daylight hours, he specifically exempted carts carrying building materials or hauling away the rubble of demolition.

"I hadn't thought of that," Hermes admitted. "Those were Hypsaeus's men. Do you think they were sent along to keep an eye on Caninus, to make sure he didn't say the wrong thing?"

"That's as good a guess as any, but also to let me know that I now have enemies who don't hesitate to kill people who get in their way. The word must be out that I can't call on Milo for help in this particular matter."

We were hurrying through the streets in the direction of the Subura. I was heading home. It was yet early in the day, but I wanted to look at those documents I had demanded from the Tabularium. The streets were even more jammed than usual because the people who lived in the flood-prone parts of the City were moving to higher ground, along with such of their belongings as they could carry. These included pet dogs and birds, along with chickens and other household livestock, making the streets so noisy that Hermes and I were shouting at each other.

"You still have Caesar on your side," Hermes said.

"Caesar is far, far away," I said. "And if I get killed over a matter of politics and money, he'll be understanding about the whole situation. It will just mean that whoever is responsible will owe Caesar a big political favor to make up for it."

We came to a lane where all foot traffic was stopped by a group of men hoisting chests and other furniture onto the roof of an *insula*. Items that couldn't be carried were being moved to upper stories and roofs everywhere, but many things were too large to carry up the narrow stairways so they had to be lifted by ropes from the streets. Since few Roman streets were wide enough for two people to pass one another comfortably without turning sideways, the effects on traffic were predictably chaotic.

"What about your neighbors?" Hermes asked. "They've rallied to your aid before."

"Hermes, I get the distinct impression that you don't believe I am competent to handle this situation."

"I felt safer when the Germans held us prisoner."

At last the creaky bundle of household goods swayed aloft and we passed beneath it, feeling none too safe in the process. This same activity was going on in all the valleys between the hills, and once in a while you heard the snap of parting ropes, accompanied by the smash of shattering furniture along with occasional screams from someone who didn't step lively enough.

"Just let me get to my arms," I said, "and I will be ready to take on the whole pack of them!" The look Hermes cast at me in return for this boast was too eloquent to describe.

Eventually, we made it home. Even though the Subura lay primarily in the valley between the Quirinal and the Esquiline, it was well away from the river, and little of it was low enough to be liable to serious flooding. Even so, the streets were almost as chaotic as elsewhere. Jammed with people at the best of times, the load was doubled as those who lived near the river sought refuge with friends and relatives in the higher parts of the City, even if this just meant camping on the roof of a Subura slum.

The cacophony was made all the more colorful because

of the great variety of languages being shouted from all directions. Perhaps half of my neighbors were native citizens, speaking their own Suburan dialect of Latin. The rest were foreigners, either immigrants and resident aliens or recently freed slaves, all flocking to the Subura for the cheapest housing within the walls. There were near-black Numidians, Gauls with yellow mustaches and twisted neck rings, wigged Egyptians, Syrians with oiled ringlets, many Jews wearing pointed caps and striped coats, and the usual Greeks looking Greek. When excited, they all forgot their broken, outrageously accented Latin and reverted to the barking, beastly sounds of their native tongues.

Julia was in the colonnade surrounding the *impluvium*, apparently getting the household staff organized. Her eyes went wide when she saw me.

"You're home and the sun is still shining. Is anything wrong?"

"Father Tiber is about to throw one of his occasional rampages, and I may soon be attacked by armed men."

"If you aren't going to be attacked soon, perhaps you can suggest where we might put this."

She stood aside to show me what she had the slaves doing. They were prying boards away from a wooden crate, just under man height. Three boards had already been removed, and a litter of straw lay on the floor tiles, revealing a beautiful statue of polished white marble. The subject was Venus, or rather the Greek Aphrodite, about two-thirds life size.

"It's lovely," I said, my worries momentarily forgotten in the presence of such sublimity. The goddess was depicted nude except for her sandals, one of which she was fastening as she leaned on a smaller statue of Pan. It is one of the conventional poses of that particular goddess, and it takes a master sculptor to render it gracefully. This one had done the job perfectly. The white marble had been tinted so faintly that you had to look hard to make sure it was tinted at all. The result was the effect of genuine human flesh, but made of a substance as pure and insubstantial as the clouds. Her nipples, lips, and hair were gilded, a treatment that looks garish on most statues, but on this one the effect was breathtaking. I later determined that the underlying marble on those areas had first been stained dark, then the gold leaf had been lightly stippled on, rather than laid on in sheets.

"I've seen copies of this statue before," Julia said, "but none so fine as this."

"It isn't the work of a Roman shop," I agreed. We had long since looted Greece of its best art works, and there were never enough of them to satisfy the growing wealthy classes of the Empire. So there were many workshops turning out copies of the scarce originals. Some of these were comparable in quality to the originals, but most of them were quite inferior. Then I got over the wonder of the thing and thought of what it must have cost.

"Julia, have you bankrupted us buying this thing?"

"I didn't buy it," she said. "A team of men delivered it this morning. It's a good thing this district is full of metal workers. We had to borrow a pry bar just to get it open."

"But who sent it?" Even as I asked, I was relieved that Julia had taken the trouble to fetch a pry bar instead of employing one of her usual expedients, like using one of my swords.

"The deliverymen said they were hired by a man named

Farbus to deliver this from a warehouse near the Forum. My grandmother has a steward named Farbus. Perhaps this is a gift from her." She meant Aurelia, the mother of Julius Caesar. The old dragon disliked me, but she doted on Julia.

"I suppose it could be," I acknowledged. "Caesar left several buildings full of art works from when he was refurbishing the house of the *Pontifex Maximus* and the house of the Vestals. She knows how much entertaining we'll have to do when I stand for the praetorship, and she may want to dress up the house." It was like her to let me know how little she thought of my personal taste.

Julia dragged her attention away from the beautiful statue. "Are you serious about danger of attack?"

"I seldom joke about personal danger. I am going to double bar the gate and station a lookout on the roof."

"My, you *are* serious. Are you going to be here at the house for the duration?"

"I won't let some pack of thugs make me a prisoner in my own home. This is just to secure the noncombatants, you and the household staff. I have some work to do here; then I will go right back out again."

She rolled her eyes upward. "You are going to be a hero again. Spare me!"

I grabbed her and planted a kiss on her mouth. "I'm no hero. The streets are so confused right now that it will be easy to escape anyone who's after me. I've been doing this all my life, dear. Trust me."

"The last time I trusted you, you ended up with that German princess."

I winced. I had fondly hoped Julia wouldn't learn of

that, but no such luck. "We weren't married then. Besides, the woman was trying to kill me."

She shook her head in disgust. "The things men find attractive in barbarian women! Go, play with your weapons. I'll warn everyone not to open the doors to strangers."

I took refuge in my study, where Hermes already had my arms chest open and its contents laid out. The law against bearing arms within the *pomerium* was about to suffer some bending.

"You'd better begin by wearing this, for starters," Hermes said, holding up a sleeveless, waist-length vest of mail. It was one of twenty such defenses given to Caesar as a present from a Gallic chieftain, and Caesar in turn had passed some of them on to his favored officers. The Gauls invented mail, that ingenious armor of interlinked iron rings that is flexible as cloth and stronger than plates of bronze. My regular, legionary mail shirt was knee length, with short sleeves and shoulder straps that gave a double thickness on that vulnerable area, and it weighed more than thirty pounds. This vest was made of links one-fifth the size of those on legionary armor, and it weighed less than five pounds.

A hard-cast spear would pass right through it, but it was just the thing for stopping a dagger in the street. It would even resist the thrust of a short sword, if the attacker didn't get his full weight behind it. It shone with silver plating, which was as much practical as decorative. It needed no oiling and would not stain my clothes with rust and the inevitable grime that always adheres to iron armor.

"I don't know," I said doubtfully. "I've always avoided going around as if I were afraid of my fellow citizens."

"That's just who might want to kill you," he pointed out. "Be reasonable. Wear it under your tunic and nobody will know you have it on unless you get killed, and then what do you care who knows?"

"You've convinced me." I stripped, put on a thin tunic of the sort I usually wore for exercising, then slipped the steel vest over my head. It was exquisitely tailored so that it tapered at the waist and rested neatly atop my hip bones, feeling even lighter than it was. Then I put on my usual tunic, and the armor was invisible. I belted it with several turns of narrow leather straps, wound back and forth through heavy brass rings, charioteer-style. This gave me a secure place to tuck my sheathed dagger and my *caestus*, the spiked bronze knuckle bar worn by boxers, minus the elaborate strapping the boxers use.

"Do you want to pack a sword?" Hermes asked, holding out the light, wasp-waisted arena sword I sometimes carried in preference to the broad, heavy *gladius*.

"No, that would be too obvious. This is unobtrusive beneath a toga. A blind man wouldn't miss a sword. And find my oldest toga. It won't look dignified, but I won't miss it, either." A toga is nothing but an encumbrance to a fleeing man. If I should need to run, I would have to abandon it, and the formal garment I had worn in public since assuming office was far too expensive to throw away.

I picked up a five-foot, cylindrical case of leather. It contained a half-dozen light javelins. I tossed it to Hermes. "Here. Take this up to the roof and keep an eye on everyone who gets near the gate. If they look like they're going to try to break it down, skewer one or two of them."

He slung it over his shoulder by its carrying strap. "As

you yourself keep reminding me, I can be crucified for touching arms within the walls."

"I won't tell anyone if you won't. Besides, any slave can pick up arms to defend his master's house. Out on the street is another matter. Now get up there. Send word if anyone comes by, even if they look friendly."

I sat at my desk and began to go through the tablets and scrolls from the Tabularium. It was bureaucratic record keeping of the dullest sort, mostly the censors' copies of contracts let to various *publicani,* much of it for work that I had never known came under the purview of the office. There were, for instance, contractors who hauled off dead horses and oxen from the City's streets and squares. There were perfumers who paid handsomely just to sweep up the flower petals after a festival. The fullers were licensed to empty the public pisspots. I didn't even like to think what those people did to my togas with that stuff.

I glanced at a small scroll written in a fine hand and was about to set it aside when an unexpected name caught my eye. I was about to examine it more closely when Hermes appeared at the doorway.

"A pack of Milo's gang are at the gate," he reported.

For a moment, I felt a pang of betrayal. Surely Milo hadn't turned against me! "How many and what do they want?"

"Ten of them, but it looks like they've just cleared the way for Fausta."

"Oh. Well, back up to the roof then." He trotted off, and I set the little scroll aside for later examination.

In the atrium, I saw Milo's boys taking their ease, dressed in their new, white tunics. They were not bothering to disguise their occupation these days. Each man had his forearms wrapped in studded leather straps, all wore military-style boots, and each wore a skullcap of iron, bronze, or hardened leather. They carried five-foot oak staves in gnarled hands, and some of them wore spiked *caesti* as well. It looked as if Milo's men had shifted to wartime status, unless this was some special treatment Fausta had insisted upon. When she traveled the streets of Rome in her oversized sedan chair, it was like a warship cruising toward the enemy. It was get out of the way or be rammed.

I found Julia and Fausta by the pool, looking at the statue. Fausta was squatting unself-consciously, her gown hiked well up her long thighs.

"This is no copy," she reported. "It's an original, at least two hundred years old, from Aphrodisias." That Greek colony in Asia produces the finest sculpture currently made. "You can tell by the detail work. I've seen clever Greeks who can provide that polish, and the subtle gilding is something I've seen in high-quality copies, but look at this." Julia squatted to see what she was pointing at. "Look at Pan's scrotum. Every tiniest wrinkle is carefully carved in. Only a master includes such careful detail where nobody is likely to look." Trust Fausta to spot something like that.

"And her toenails aren't marble. They're alabaster, slotted into place." She stood. "Unless I miss my guess, this is the original *Aphrodite Fastening Her Sandal*, by Aristobulus the Second. As I recall, it was commissioned by one of the Seleucid monarchs, Antiochus Epiphanes or one of those."

"How did it end up here?" I asked. I wasn't accepting her evaluation all that easily. Fausta loved to show off and pretend that her knowledge of cultural matters was comprehensive. She might have made up the whole thing on the spot.

"Considering what part of the world it resided in, it may have ended up with old Mithridates, and Lucullus came home with most of his property. But for years the East has been our biggest source of Greek art since we conquered Greece itself. Gabinius could have plundered this or Pompey. It couldn't have been one of my father's acquisitions; he'd have kept it. But it could have been extorted by one of our governors or given as a bribe to a proconsul. Who knows? It might have been bought as an investment by a traveling businessman." A simple commercial transaction would be the last thing to occur to a daughter of Sulla.

"I must send word to Aurelia," Julia said. "She can probably explain this."

Fausta looked me over with a thousand years of patrician cynicism in her eyes. "Oh, I don't know. An aedile is in a position to acquire any number of trinkets like this."

I let this insult pass because it set off a tingle in the back of my mind, and I didn't want my dislike of the woman to distract me. She and Julia were close friends despite Fausta's contempt for me. But then, Julia detested Milo, my friend of many years. It all worked out.

"But where can we put this?" Julia said, straightening and brushing a few leaves from her hands.

"Don't move it an inch until you've studied it in several lights," Fausta advised. "Then place it where the most favorable light will strike it, but make sure it's under a roof so the finish won't be ruined. Something this exquisite was never intended for outdoor display." This made excellent sense.

"I don't think it should be in this house at all," Julia said. "We should take it to the country estate near Fidenae and build a little shrine for it, a round one in the Italian style with slender Ionic columns and a circle of poplars all around it." She turned to me. "If we do that this summer, the poplars will be well-grown by the time you inherit the estate."

"Sounds good to me," I said. "I'll talk to the old man about it; I'm sure he'll have no objection." But I already had reservations about this lovely work of art with its murky past. I was not at all sure that it had been sent to me as a friendly gesture.

I returned to my study, new suspicions boiling in my already overburdened mind. I have known men who allowed their minds to become so distracted by suspicion, seeing plots and conspiracies at every hand, that they became incapable of action. For the first time in my life, I felt myself approaching that paralytic stage. To calm my mind, I picked up the scroll I had abandoned and studied it carefully.

It was written in a clumsy hand by an official who clearly had performed this task himself rather than delegating it to a secretary. Young Roman men destined for public life are trained for public speaking, not how to write gracefully. We usually leave that to professionals. Still, I was able to forge my way through the report's ill-formed letters and awkward phrasing.

It was addressed to the censors Vatia Isauricus and Messala Niger, from the plebeian aedile Aulus Lucilius, a man completely unknown to me. The subject was the condition of the theater of Aemilius Scaurus. In bald, unsparing prose, it described the findings of his investigation: The all but new theater, beneath its unprecedented ornamentation, was built entirely of wood that was green, rotten, termite-chewed, or otherwise unfit for any sort of construction, much less for a structure in which a very large proportion of the citizenry would be seated, at peril of their lives, on festival days.

In considerable detail for so small a document, it went on to detail the bricks used as footing on the landward side of the theater, which were made of wretched clay, ill-fired, and easily crumbled in the hands of a strong man. He had sunk shafts in several locations and found nothing beneath except river mud, the whole weight of the theater resting upon either more of the inferior brick or, worse, on water-soaked timbers that were deteriorating by the day.

It was a thing of wonder, Lucilius concluded, that the structure had survived the Games celebrated by Scaurus in the year of its construction; and he went on to list the names of those he knew to be malefactors in this affair, with the recommendation that the results of his investigation be passed on to the urban praetor for prosecution. The names were: Marcus Aemilius Scaurus, builder; Lucius Folius, dealer in building materials; and—here my stomach sank while the hair on the back of my neck rose, a most disorienting phenomenon—Quintus Caecilius Metellus Pius Scipio Nasica, owner of the lumberyard and brickworks whence had come almost all of the structural components of the theater.

Appended to the bottom of the scroll was a note written by another hand: *"From M. Valerius Messala Niger. Censor to the urban praetor. This man is a notorious political enemy of Scaurus and Pompey. We can safely ignore this scurrilous rant."*

I slid the scroll aside and buried my face in my palms. My world was crumbling around me. My long-planned Games were to be held in a structure that was a death trap for the audience. If I were to expose this matter, which was my clear duty, I would bring a terrible disgrace upon my own family, just when they were arranging a political compromise that might save the City from chaos and the Empire from civil war.

This explained much, especially Scipio's sudden change of heart about prosecuting the fraudulent builders and my family's vehement objection. Scipio was a Caecilius Metellus by adoption, but among the great families, adoption was as firm as blood descent. He bore the name, and the name was everything. He had been adopted by the great Metellus Pius, *Pontifex Maximus* before Caesar and a man revered for that most primal of Roman virtues, *pietas*.

When the wharfmaster Ogulnius had spoken of Folius's barges transporting building materials from sources downriver, it had never occurred to me that my family could be involved because we owned no land in that direction. I had forgotten that the Scipios held extensive lands between Rome and Ostia.

There was nothing to be gained by lamenting this unwelcome turn. What I needed, as usual, was information.

Julia and Fausta were still admiring the statue. They had the crate and padding completely cleared away, and the slaves were levering it about so that the two women could examine how the light fell upon it from different directions.

"Do either of you know of a senator named Aulus Lucilius? He was plebeian aedile a couple of years ago, while I was still in Gaul."

"The name seems familiar," Julia said. Then, to Fausta, "Wasn't there some sort of scandal?"

"Isn't there always? Yes, the man's dead. He was murdered in a *lupanar* down by the wharves, one of the really low dives that the bargemen frequent. You know, I've always wanted to see the inside of one of those places. Decius, could you arrange it? You aediles are in charge of the whorehouses, I understand."

"Was he still aedile when he was killed?" I asked, ignoring the rest.

"Let's see," she pondered, "it was after the first of the year, I recall, so he must have just stepped down from office. There's usually a much bigger fuss when an officeholder is killed. Gossip had it that he was discovered in a crib with his throat cut, and the girl fled." She put a finger to her chin. "At least I'd assumed it was a girl. Now that I think of it, it might have been a boy. That sort of thing is becoming more and more popular even in fashionable circles."

"Did he leave a family behind?" I asked.

"Why do you need to know about him?" Julia demanded.

"It might mean something with regard to an investigation I am working on," I said stiffly. I didn't want Fausta thinking too hard about this. She might talk about it later among Milo's friends, and then it would be all over the City before I was ready.

"His wife was a sister of Curio's," Fausta said. "The house they lived in was hers, and last I heard she still lived there and hasn't remarried. It's not far from here, up on the Esquiline across from that old Temple of Hercules—the one with the statue of the infant Hercules strangling the serpents, by Myron."

I knew the one she meant. "I'll be back later," I said to Julia.

"Wait!" she called, catching up with me in the atrium. "Where are you going? You said yourself the streets are very dangerous for you now."

"They are, but I must question someone." I started to walk around her, but her outstretched arm stopped me.

"Not so fast. You are an official, not some low-level flunky! Send one of your clients; that is what they're for. You have dozens of capable men who yearn to earn your gratitude, so use them!"

"Some things I must do myself, dear. Have no fear, I'm perfectly safe. I'll take Hermes along with me." I went into my study and tucked my weapons away out of sight.

"Perfectly safe?" she said. "Is that why you're wearing that ratty old toga?"

"It will be dark before long. It's easy to ruin a good toga stumbling around in filthy alleys in the dark." I kissed her and then pushed past, bellowing for Hermes.

"At least take some of Fausta's thugs with you!" she called, but I was already out the door, with Hermes close on my heels.

"Where to now?" he asked. He carried a two-foot stick of olive wood, capped at both ends with bronze and banded with that metal at intervals along its length. It was perfectly legal, and he could perform fearful damage with it.

"We're going to pay a visit to a widow," I informed him.

The streets were still chaotic and got no less so as we trudged up the slope of the Esquiline. There were many fine houses on its upper slopes, and people seeking escape from the coming flood were milling about everywhere, trying to find wealthy patrons to take them in or good spots in the occasional public gardens.

As it happened, I knew the widow's brother, Curio. He was one of the more scandalous members of the young nobility, a great friend of Antony's and renowned throughout society for his loose living, his extravagant debts, and his many love affairs. Needless to say, he was great company, and I had always found him a most congenial carousing companion. His father had disowned him, and he spent much of his time cadging meals and accommodations from friends and had put the arm on me more than once. Curious to say, he was also an energetic and effective senator and had recently become an adherent of Caesar. Rumor had it that Caesar had cleared all of Curio's debts.

The house of the late Aulus Lucilius was not hard to find. Situated directly across the street from the dilapidated old Temple of Hercules, its gate was wide open and a small crowd filled its atrium and courtyard. It seemed that a good many clients or poor relations from the lower parts of the City were imposing upon the widow for accommodations wherein to wait out the flood.

I left Hermes in the atrium and found the lady herself in the courtyard, assigning places to the petitioners and discussing their rationing with her steward. She was doing this very efficiently, and I got the feeling she had done it before, many times. I stepped up to her and waited until she glanced my way.

"Have I the privilege of addressing the widow of the aedile Aulus Lucilius?" I asked.

The steward looked at me disdainfully, giving undue attention to my shabby toga. "I can imagine what a privilege it must be for you," the man said.

"Now, Priam, none of that," the woman chided gently. "This is a senator, and he has the look of one of my brother's friends, so we shouldn't be too hard on him. If you are looking for a dry place to sit out the next few days, I may be able to find a corner of my roof for you, although the larder is already strained."

"Most generous and I thank you," I said, having heard far worse in my disreputable life. "As it occurs, I have a roof to shelter me. I am the plebeian aedile Decius Caecilius Metellus."

Her eyes widened. They were very attractive eyes. "You're a serving official? I would think you were in mourning, but you look as if you shaved this morning."

"Service of the Senate and People have reduced me to a beggar," I said. "I am sorry to bother you at so busy a time. And as it happens, I am a friend of your brother's."

Her mouth bent almost into a smile. "Well, that last is no recommendation. What sort of business could an aedile have with me?"

"I must ask you some questions concerning your late husband," I told her.

The smile died before it could blossom. "Official interest after all this time? I find that peculiar. I certainly could get no action, or even interest, when he was murdered."

"I am sorry. I was with the legions when it happened. Recently I have been looking into some serious violations of the law. I suspect Aulus Lucilius was investigating the same thing, and this is what brought about his murder."

"Priam, see to these people. We can take in no more than three or four more adults, then close the gate. I will be in the green room, conferring with the Aedile Metellus."

"It is most generous of you to give shelter to so many of your clients," I commended her, as I followed her through her crowded courtyard.

"Obligations are not to be ignored," she said, "and the condition of the City is a disgrace. People are helpless when a natural disaster strikes."

"I could not agree more." She led me into a small room painted pale green, its walls decorated with twining vines painted in a darker shade of the same color. Besides two chairs and a small table between them, it had a desk and a large wall case holding dozens of scrolls.

The woman beckoned to a serving girl. "Thisbe, bring wine and—"

"No," I said, holding up a hand. "It would be criminal of me to impose on your stores just now."

She nodded. "That is thoughtful. How may I help you?"

I took out the little scroll and handed it to her. "Read this."

She took it and her face turned pale upon seeing her dead husband's handwriting. She read it through and put it on the table.

"I remember that investigation. It is one of a good many he conducted that year. He said to me many times that the theater of Aemilius Scaurus was the greatest hazard to public safety since Catilina's arsonists, and that Scaurus was a thief with aspirations to mass murder."

"What about the censor's appended comments? Was your husband a political enemy of Scaurus and Pompey?"

"He was an enemy of anyone who flagrantly endangered the public good for private profit, and Scaurus certainly qualified on that account. I understand the Sardinians have good cause to think so, too. As for Pompey, that remark makes no sense. He usually voted on Pompey's side in the Senate."

"Did he mention any specific threats from builders or dealers in building materials?"

Her lovely eyes darkened. "A number of them. It followed the usual pattern of such things: first excuses, then offers of bribes, then veiled threats, then open threats of violence. My husband was a proud man. Everyone assumed that he would jump at a chance to enrich himself since his office was so costly."

"You don't have to tell *me* about that."

"I suppose not. Anyway, he was contemplating years of penury, but he would countenance no corrupt offers. He even tried to bring charges against those who tried to suborn him."

"That is not easy to do," I told her. "Of all the magistrates of my acquaintance, only Cato has made such charges stick."

She nodded sadly. "So we found it to be. In any case, he grew disgusted with the censors, the consuls, and his fellow aediles. He decided to go directly to the Plebeian Assembly. He was sure that at least two or three of the tribunes would be willing to demand reform legislation and special courts to prosecute the builders."

"Then he had greater faith in those demagogues than I have," I said. "What happened?"

"He never got the chance. The night before he was to

address the College of Tribunes in the Circus Flaminius he was murdered." She said this dry-eyed, as a Roman noblewoman should, but a lifetime of dealing with people of my own class had taught me the little signals of body and facial expression, the tones and cadences of speech that serve us to express those feelings we think it unfitting to display before strangers. This woman still grieved for her husband, and she raged at his murderer.

"And"—I began, wondering how to put this delicately—"might you be able to tell me how he came to be—"

"Murdered in a whorehouse?" she said forthrightly. "As you are no doubt aware, regulation of those establishments falls under the purview of the plebeian aediles."

"People never fail to remind me of the fact," I acknowledged.

She managed another, even fainter, smile. "Aulus complained of the same thing. Well, this had nothing to do with his duties. He had just stepped down from office anyway, and he was hoping that the new year's crop of tribunes would take up his cause before the bribery could take hold."

I made sympathetic noises. I found it hard to believe that the man had spent so many years in politics without understanding that most officials get their biggest bribes *before* they actually take office. Doubtless he had been putting a rosy interpretation on the matter for his wife's sake. He must have been growing quite discouraged by that time.

"In any case," she went on, "on that evening, while he was preparing his presentation to the Tribunate, a messenger arrived. My husband received him and a short time later told me that he had to go out and confer with a man who was to present him with important evidence, evidence conclusive to his case. I urged him to take some slaves for an escort because it would soon be dark. He said that he would hire a torchbearer to see him home; that it was possible it might be dawn before he returned in any case. That was the last time I saw him."

"Did he tell you who this person might be?"

"No, only that this was important, and the matter would brook no waiting."

This was frustrating, but I knew that I was amazingly fortunate to have learned this much from her. Most Roman officials tell their wives absolutely nothing about their business. The usual explanation is that it is unfitting for a woman to take an interest in such things, that breeding children and conducting a household are their only proper concerns. The truth is that they seldom trust their wives, and for good reason. One of the reasons for Caesar's great success was that he conducted continuous affairs with the wives of his rivals and was thus always able to anticipate their husbands' maneuvers against him and take preemptive action.

"And what was the, ah, the *establishment* in which he was found?"

She lowered her eyelids in token of distaste. "It is called the Labyrinth."

I couldn't stop myself in time. "He was found in *that* place?"

She looked severely pained. "I was given to understand that it is rather notorious."

"Scarcely the word for it," I muttered, trying to retrieve my aplomb. Hastily, I said, "Did he by any chance leave behind the address he was preparing for the tribunes?"

"Some pages of notes only. It was his custom to organize

his thoughts in this way, then to deliver his oration, and afterward, with his secretary, to write down the speech and publish it."

This was a standard practice among Roman lawyers of the time. Cicero made a minor literary form of it. Instead of speaking from a prepared text (and there were lawyers of the old school who thought it unfitting even to use notes), the speaker orated from his rough notes, fine-tuned his presentation as he gauged audience reaction, and then published the speech in its corrected and polished form. Often as not, the published form differed noticeably from the speech itself.

"Might I have a look at his notes?"

She rose and went to the desk with its honeycomb of scrolls. After a bit of searching, she unrolled a scroll and took from it a few sheets that had been stuck into it for safekeeping. These she handed to me. At a glance I spotted a few familiar names among some verbiage that told me he planned to make his oration in the florid Asiatic style, then going out of fashion but still practiced. This was going to take some work.

"Might I take these with me?" I asked her. "I will return them as soon as possible. I know you want to preserve your husband's papers for your sons."

"I have no sons," she said, standing, this interview at an end. "If you can bring his murderers to justice, you may burn his whole library on their funeral pyres for all I care."

She saw me to the door through the crowd of refuge seekers, and I took a hasty leave. It was almost dark as Hermes and I found ourselves on the thronged street outside.

"Back home?" Hermes said.

"Not yet." He put on an exaggerated look of fatigue so

I told him, "You're going to like our next visit."

"Where are we going?"

"To a whorehouse."

His face split in a broad grin. "It's about time!"

10

IT WAS TIME FOR ANOTHER long walk; and while the hour was late and the time of year dismal, it might as well have been Saturnalia. The push to high ground was in full force, but there was no panic. It takes a great deal to panic Romans, and a mere flood was not among the things that upset them greatly. Even an approaching enemy only makes them a little nervous. A big fire or an earthquake will unnerve them completely, but little else. They do riot from time to time out of anger. At least they used to, before the First Citizen made things so tame.

But this time there was an odd, almost festive atmosphere to the dislocated populace. Whatever damage and devastation the event might portend, it was a break in routine, and such a break puts most people in a giddy mood. Men knew they would not have to go to their work tomorrow, if they had any. Their wives knew that they would not have to make the long trudge to the fountain for water, then carry the heavy jar up the steep stairs of the *insula*. Children knew that there would be no schoolmaster to face in the morning.

Perhaps there would be no home to return to afterward, but that was a worry for later on. For now they were doing something different, seeing friends and relatives they hadn't seen in a while, maybe spending a few days in a garden or on a rooftop with strangers. There would be gambling and storytelling to pass the time. Perhaps the men would be drafted into work gangs to stave off damage or clear rubble. It would be something different in their otherwise dull lives.

The best thing about a flood was that, unlike a fire or an earthquake, it killed few people outright. It was easy to get out of the way of rising water. Mortality would come later, from exposure and disease and, I greatly feared, contaminated water. Those clogged, backed-up drains, now overflowing, would spread filth throughout the City. Anyone who has ever endured a siege knows that filth and pollution breed disease. This may be because, as some believe, evil spirits inhabit foul-smelling things or because uncleanliness angers the gods or for some reason entirely unrelated to the supernatural world; but it is irrefutable. *It is well that these people are enjoying themselves,* I thought, *because many of them are going to die in the weeks and months to come.*

The crowd thinned as we crossed the Forum. This, as I have mentioned, was once a swampy area, and already I saw murky, brown water bubbling from the street drains and a foul odor suffused the splendid place. Idly, I wondered what had become of old Charon and his boat. Doubtless, I thought, he had a refuge. He must have endured many floods in his long years below the City.

The Forum Boarium and the area near the Circus Maximus were getting decidedly damp, and I was glad to climb the embankment and walk out onto the Sublician Bridge, which would remain well above the waterline throughout the flood. The bridge was lined with gawkers, observing and commenting importantly upon the progress of Father Tiber's rampage.

There was something unreal about the scene, and it wasn't just the incongruously festive attitude of the citizens. I decided that it was the juxtaposition of the rising river with the clear sky and the unseasonable warmth. We always associate floods with heavy rain. It was hard to believe that this was all the result of a wind from Africa and melting snow in mountains far away.

"If we cross the river," Hermes said apprehensively, "we may not be able to get back to the City for days."

"Nevertheless," I assured him, "the Labyrinth is in the Trans-Tiber and that is where we must go. Don't worry. The bridge will stay above water. If the river goes over the artificial embankment, it will settle in the low places. It may be deep in spots, but there will be little current. Look." I pointed to the embankment, where already men were dragging small boats and barges cobbled together from scrap wood. "The river fishermen and other enterprising souls are already preparing to make some money ferrying people through the flooded areas. We may have to get home by boat, but we will get home."

While I spoke these reassuring words, I was studying

the huge theater of Aemilius Scaurus, just a short distance upriver of the bridge. The water was well up the support works we had seen being set in place that morning, which now seemed so long ago. Thought of that time span made my stomach growl, reminding me that we had eaten nothing since pausing at the tavern after our visit to the lumberyard of Justus.

"Come along," I said to Hermes, "enough sightseeing. We have important official business to see to."

"In a whorehouse?" he asked.

"As it happens, yes."

The Trans-Tiber area lay outside the walls and therefore outside the City proper, but the authority of the aediles extended to the first milestone on each of the roads leading away from Rome, and those were well out into farmland. Compared to the vast sprawl of cities like Alexandria and Antioch, Rome was a rather compact city, although disagreeably crowded.

As we walked, I informed Hermes of what I had learned at the widow's house. "Why are you smiling?" I snapped.

"Well, I was right this morning! The theater really is made of bad timber and by the same people who built that *insula!*"

"You might take less satisfaction in the knowledge. Now I'm caught between two millstones. My Games could end in unprecedented catastrophe, or my family could disown me. It's hard to choose."

"Too bad we can't torch the place," he said.

"You *would* think of a criminal answer to this. Not only is arson the most heinous crime on the law tables, but that place would make a bigger, hotter fire than the Circus Maximus. Half the City would burn down."

"I was just speculating idly," he said, the scheming little rogue.

The relatively new Trans-Tiber district was a lively place. Over the centuries, successive censors and aediles had tried to expel from the City those elements seen to be parasitic or corrupting. These were the actors and gladiators, the whores, mountebanks, fortune tellers, and purveyors of foreign cults, in short, all the most interesting and entertaining people.

The result of these purification efforts was to make the Trans-Tiber the most raffish district of Rome, where the entertainment facilities were concentrated. It was also where most of the rivermen lived, or at least stayed, while they were in Rome. It lacked the concentration of wealth, power, and politics that was to be found clustered around the Forum, and it had no important temples or other sacred sites, but the inhabitants did not seem to miss these things. It was less crowded as well as more lively.

Best of all for my purposes that evening, most of it lay on higher ground than the eastern bank, and it did not suffer from the problem of jammed sewers and drains.

Of all the *lupanaria* in Rome, within or without the walls, the Labyrinth was the most famed. It was the largest, had the most harlots, offered the widest variety of entertainments and perversions (depending upon your interpretation of that word, of course), and enjoyed the greatest and most varied clientele. People came from all over the world to see the place. There was nothing in Alexandria, Antioch, or, for all I know, India or Babylon to match it. If whorehouses were temples, the Labyrinth would be the Temple of Jupiter Optimus Maximus.

It sat in the center of a sizable square, surrounded by fruit trees planted in enormous ornamental tubs instead of the clutter of monuments that crowded every public space in the City within the walls. It was four stories high and painted a glaring scarlet. Most of the buildings nearby were small taverns and inns catering to the rivermen's trade, as well as to foreign visitors who wanted to escape the high prices and general squalor of the opposite bank.

The sign that let you know you had found the right place was infamous throughout the world. It was named the Labyrinth for the maze beneath the palace of Minos, and the sign was a statue depicting the most notorious queen of that palace, the insatiable Pasiphae. That queen, you will recall, was caused by Poseidon to conceive an inappropriate passion for an exceptionally beautiful bull, which her husband, Minos, had refused to sacrifice to the god. Pasiphae sought the aid of Daedalus in consummating this difficult lust, which he accomplished by building a lifelike wooden cow and concealing the queen therein. The bull was deceived, the queen was presumably satisfied, and the result was the birth of the bull-headed Minotaur.

The statue depicted this bizarre coupling, but the artificial cow was represented symbolically by a pair of horns bound to the queen's brow and cleft hooves covering her hands and feet. Otherwise, the voluptuous queen was depicted as nude, and the bull was more than merely realistic. Both figures were life sized and rendered in the most exacting detail. This day had turned into an extended art lesson.

"Come in, dears, come in!" cooed a woman in a blonde wig and a flame-colored gown. In the subdued light, it took me a second look to realize that she was actually a man. "The Labyrinth features something for everyone!" as this person demonstrated amply. We joined the group of people of both sexes passing within. Nobody here was worrying about any trifling flood.

We passed through a tunnel lined with niches. In each niche burned candles, illuminating small statues of couples and groups engaged in ecstatic copulation. Above each niche was painted the name of its particular variation, in Latin and Greek. Thus you could make a selection and name your pleasure when you negotiated with the management of this uninhibited place of business.

From the tunnel, we emerged into a vast courtyard filled with tables, overlooked by the galleries of the three upper stories. There was constant traffic between the courtyard and the upper floors, with whores of both sexes leading their customers, also of both sexes although predominantly male, to the rooms conveniently provided by the management.

Everywhere, torches burned in sconces, lamps stood on stands, and candles burned by the hundreds. Here was one place where candles, rare elsewhere in Rome, were used in abundance. By their light, I could see that the decor, like the statue outside, conformed, after a fashion, to the myth of Theseus and the Minotaur. The wall paintings illustrated the doings within the original Labyrinth. The legend relates that the Athenians each year had to pay as tribute seven youths and seven maidens to be given to the Minotaur. The legend is not specific concerning what use the Minotaur made of these youths and maidens, but the paintings left no doubt.

The Minotaur, though manlike in form, inherited more than just his father's head.

"How may we entertain you?" The questioner was a young whore wearing a beautiful smile and little else.

"If we are to have the strength to go on," I said, "we'll have to eat. Then we can see about stronger entertainment."

"This way." We followed her twinkling, white buttocks to a small table in a corner. As we made our way, I scanned the somewhat loud but generally orderly crowd. Aside from the professionals, the clientele included more than just the rivermen and visiting foreigners. I saw a few of my fellow senators there as well, none of them taking any pains to conceal their identities.

I took a seat at the table indicated, and without needing to be told, Hermes pulled up a stool behind me. Since I was there in my official capacity, there was no question of the two of us sitting together as we had at lunch that afternoon. There is an unspoken but understood protocol in these matters. Immediately, slaves set food and wine on the table.

"Be so good as to send the owner to me," I told the whore.

She looked me over doubtfully. "And who might I say is making this request? It's most unusual." She spoke like a native of Cyprus. It is more musical than most foreign accents.

"The Plebeian Aedile Metellus," I said. Her winglike false eyebrows went up a bit, but she did not challenge me. Perhaps, I thought, the dingy old toga hadn't been such a good idea, after all.

The food and wine were uniformly excellent. There were shellfish in garlic sauce, bread baked with fennel seed, cheeses and dried fruits, most of the foods being the ones believed to stimulate the carnal appetites. For once I went easy on the wine, which was Cossian.

I was pushing the dishes aside, when I saw a woman coming across the courtyard toward me. She paused from time to time to speak with the customers seated all around, smiling, caressing a shoulder here, a bald head there, clearly the madame making sure all her guests are happy and well looked after. Crossing that distance, passing seated people, I understood how tall she was only when she was a few paces from my table.

Andromeda, the famous proprietress of the Labyrinth, was taller than all but the very tallest men in Rome, a good six inches taller than I, and I was not considered short. Adding to her already imposing height was an amazing wig made from the hair of several different German and Gallic women, golden, flaxen, and red locks mixed together and piled high. She did not wear the *peplos* of a respectable woman, but rather the feminized toga Roman law requires prostitutes to wear when in public. Unlike the plain, citizen's toga, hers was a brilliant aquamarine with a Greek fret embroidered on the hem in gold thread. Her many jewels were worth a good-sized country estate.

She stopped at my table, placed the back of one hand in the palm of the other, and bowed gracefully. "Aedile, you do us an unexpected honor."

"I am here on a matter of official business," I said. "Please be seated." She folded her long form into a chair, leaned forward, and patted me. I thought she was being flirtatious, then her fingers dug in at my waist. She withdrew the hand and sat back, wearing a serious expression.

"You came ready for a fight," she said. "The *ludus* is three streets away. This is a place for joy, for abandoning everyday cares. Yet you come here with weapons in your belt and armor under your tunic and a toga cast off by your poorest freedman."

I fingered the worn wool. "Oh, come now, it's not that bad. I'll not prevaricate. The times are dangerous, and, like every public personage these days, I have enemies. I may have to fight, and I may have to run."

She nodded. "That is understandable. But I'll have no disorder in my establishment." She inclined her head toward an alcove in the painted wall. There were several such and in each stood a huge man with a heavy cudgel thonged to his wide, nail-studded belt. They were gladiators from the nearby *ludus,* earning extra money as bouncers. "I insist on good behavior; and at the first sign of trouble, I throw the troublemaker out, whether sailor or senator. My girls are clean, my wine is unadulterated, and I keep plenty of water and sand handy in case of fire, more than the law requires. I pay all my fees on time, and if your fellow officeholders think I should give them a little more, I don't argue." Her look was defiant, but she had the wrong idea about why I was there.

"From what I hear, things aren't always peaceful here."

This took her aback. "But I just said—oh, there was a murder here awhile back, but it was just one murder in the six years I've been in business. Other than that, no more than an occasional bloody nose or black eye, maybe a cracked pate if one of my boys has to get rough, nothing worse."

"Many a senatorial mansion cannot boast of so clean a

record," I told her, "but it is that very murder I have come to discuss. An aedile named—"

She held up a hand for silence. "No! A private citizen named Aulus Lucilius was found dead here. If he had previously been an aedile, that means nothing once he was out of office, you know that perfectly well."

"I grant your point. Anyway, I want to hear about the circumstances surrounding that gentleman's death. Be so good as to enlighten me."

"But the urban praetor's man questioned me about that long ago," Andromeda protested. "Why don't you just read his report?"

"I don't trust other people's reports," I told her. "They don't ask the right questions in the first place, and then they make mistakes when they record the results. After that, often as not, the report gets misfiled or lost or destroyed altogether, so why don't you just tell me what happened?"

She smiled and blinked her gilded eyelids. "Your business is far more disorderly than mine, Aedile. Well then, on the night this happened, Lucilius arrived awhile after sunset. It was dark and the lamps were lit, just like now. He had his toga pulled over his head, but I recognized him from the year before, when he'd inspected twice."

"Had he ever been here as a customer?"

"Not to my knowledge, but look around you. We have a hundred customers on a slow night, a thousand or more during the big festivals. I try to give them all personal attention, but that's futile. The ones I know by sight are the regulars."

"I see. Go on, please."

"Well, a girl named Galatea met him at the door. She

led him to a table over in that corner," she pointed to one opposite from where we sat. "There was already a man seated there, wearing a cloak with the hood pulled over his head."

"Do your customers usually hide their identities like that with togas and cloaks? I would think that would arouse your suspicions."

"Hardly. Remember, this was between the nones and the ides of December. Everyone was pretty well wrapped up, that being one of the colder winters of recent memory. I remember Galatea was wearing a wool gown. The girls don't go around naked until spring, normally. They've only left their clothes off these last few nights because of this African wind that's made it so warm."

"All right. So the girl Galatea conducted Lucilius to the table of the cloaked man. What then?"

On a stage in the center of the courtyard, beneath an enormous candelabra in the shape of the Hydra with multiple candles atop each of its heads, a troupe of Iberian dancers appeared like a vision and began to perform the famous dances of Gades to the frantic music of flutes and the rhythm of the little, wooden clappers they held in their palms. These women, like most of the inhabitants of Gades, were of mixed Greek-Phoenician ancestry and had all the most salacious qualities of those nations.

The girls of the dancing families were raised from birth to perform in public, and their dances were the most lubricious imaginable. Actually, they also performed sacred dances with perfect decorum, but not in the Labyrinth, needless to say. Each woman was not only a dancer, but an acrobat and contortionist, a combination I have always liked.

"Aedile, are you listening?" Andromeda waved her fingers before my eyes.

"Eh? Of course. Just got distracted a bit, that's all."

She laughed. "They're pretty distracting, all right. That's the troupe of Eschmoun, the oldest of all the Gadean dance troupes. They're on their way to dance at the Great Dionysia in Athens, and then to the court of Ptolemy before they return to Iberia. That beauty on the top of the pile is Yeroshabel, said to be the finest dancer in the world."

"I can believe it," I said, my throat gone oddly dry. I took a hefty slug of wine to wet it. I considered myself to be more worldly than most, and I had seen Gadean dancers before; but these women were doing the most shockingly orgiastic things I had ever beheld. The strangest thing was that it was all in pantomime, but with none of the broad, farcical gestures you see when Italians practice that art. The women's faces remained as serene as those of sculptured Muses, their movements had swanlike grace, and nothing was really happening if you looked closely enough (I did). They simply left you with the impression that you had seen something only gods should look upon without being struck blind.

When the performance ended, I jumped to my feet and applauded as vociferously as the rest. Even the most hardened whores were struck with admiration, and I instructed Hermes to go and toss some coins onto the stage. He complied eagerly, before they could get away.

I resumed my seat. "Now, where were we?"

"Would you like to meet Yeroshabel? I can arrange it."

"Alas, duty forbids, not to mention my wife."

"Most men don't," she said.

"Don't what?" I was still slightly befuddled by the spectacle. I know it wasn't the wine. "Mention their wives, you mean? I suppose not. Well, mine is Caesar's niece, and she shares many of his qualities."

She whistled. "I'd be careful around a woman like that, too. Caesar has been among my patrons, too. One of the best, in fact."

"I can believe that," I assured her, now thoroughly relaxed in this woman's company. It was her profession to be agreeable, I suppose.

"Actually, he usually came here when he was entertaining important foreigners. In sizable parties most often. He saw to their entertainment, but his own feats weren't quite up to his reputation, if you know what I mean."

"Oh, I suppose his inroads among senatorial wives left him with little energy." Somehow, I felt I should come to his defense.

"I think little excites him except that which increases his power. He doesn't care a bit about food, wine, or comfort, you know, despite his reputation as a rake."

"I know that better than most," I said ruefully. "I've campaigned with him in Gaul."

"It's the same with women or boys. He'll go through the motions of being congenial, but I think he's always planning his next election or campaign."

"You judge men shrewdly, Andromeda." I, too, was always on the lookout for contacts who could be of use to me. It struck me that this woman was uniquely placed to ferret out useful information about important men, both residents and visitors. Some have held that such information would be unworthy of the dignity of a Roman official. I'd never thought that way.

"How long would I last if I didn't?" She seemed to be thinking along the same lines as I. Well, we were both at the peak of our professions. "A man like you, on your way up, needs to know such things. You understand, I have to be discreet about certain of my patrons, the regulars and the ones in a position to do me real harm."

"But you can always use a friend and protector, can't you?"

"I can never have too many of those. But I am a professional woman, accustomed to charging for my services."

"Understood. I am never reluctant to pay for good value. But the matter we were discussing comes under the heading of an official investigation."

She sighed. "Just so you don't get in the habit of expecting free information. Anyway, those two men talked for a while. At one point they started to argue, and a bouncer went over and rapped on their table with his stick. They quieted down, and that was the end of it."

"Send the bouncer to me," I said. "He might have overheard something."

She thought for a moment. "You're out of luck. It was Astyanax, and he was killed at the funeral games for Terentius Lucanus in Capua four months ago."

"Why did it have to be a clumsy swordsman?" I groused. "Oh, well, no help for it."

"A short time after that the man in the hooded cloak got up and left."

"He left?"

"Went right out through the front door. So Lucilius went upstairs with Galatea—"

"Wait a moment. Was Galatea with them the whole time?"

She thought about that. "No. She led Lucilius to the cloaked man's table, then she went off. She went back to the table either just before the cloaked one left or just after. I wasn't keeping a close eye on all this, you know. I had plenty of other patrons to attend to, even at that time of year."

"All right. She went upstairs with Lucilius. Did she murder him?"

Andromeda shrugged her white shoulders. "I wouldn't know. I wasn't up there with them. Late in the evening there was a commotion. Another of the girls was taking a customer upstairs and she rapped on the door, didn't get any answer, and went on in. She started screaming, and I ran up there. Lucilius was on the floor, alone and dying from a stab wound."

"Where was Galatea?"

"Nowhere to be found, then or later."

"And you didn't see her go?"

"This isn't a prison. It's not hard to leave. She could have just wrapped up in a *palla* and gone out."

"In most *lupanaria,*" I said, "the girls are kept locked up when they aren't on duty, and the door is guarded."

She snorted contempt. "And you've seen what frightened, beaten, washed-out drudges they are, haven't you? My customers come here for enjoyment and congenial companionship, and I provide it. They pay more here than anywhere else, but the girls and boys are skilled, good-looking, and willing. There's something wrong with men who go to a prison for sex."

"You'll get no argument from me there. So he was still alive when you found him?"

"Not by much, but breathing. I sent for the physician and he did what he could, but it was too late. The man babbled a little, nothing I could understand, then he croaked."

"Who was the physician?"

"The one from the *ludus,* Asklepiodes."

"If you sent for him, Lucilius lasted more than a few minutes."

"I didn't have to send far for Asklepiodes," she said. "He was right down here in the courtyard, like he is most nights."

"Asklepiodes is a regular?" I asked, astonished.

"He ought to be. He's the only man in Rome who gets his entertainment here for free. We have an arrangement. A place like this needs a physician's attention regularly."

So Asklepiodes had a special arrangement with Andromeda? Well, well. "Is he here tonight?"

"He was here earlier. I'll find him for you if he's still around." She raised a hand to the back of her wig and a man appeared at her side. Apparently she had a system of secret signals. The man was well built, heavily bearded, and wearing a woman's dress. "Find the Greek doctor. Send him here," she said. The odd person disappeared.

"What did you do once he'd died?" I asked.

"As I said, I recognized him, so I sent a boy to find his house and tell his family, or whoever was there, but he just wandered around lost all night. Have you ever tried to find an unfamiliar house in the dark? Anyway, there wasn't much to be done before daylight. After that the Libitinarii arrived, and then the praetor's man to get my story."

A moment later, Asklepiodes arrived, beaming. He bowed to Andromeda. "Beauteous hostess," then to me, "distinguished Aedile, how may I be of service?" The order in which he ranked our relative importance did not escape me.

"Sit down, old friend," I said. "We were just discussing a murder."

"You rarely talk about anything else," he said.

"You two know each other, I see," Andromeda said.

"For a long time," I told her. "I can see that he hasn't been bragging of our friendship to raise his stock around here."

"In this neighborhood, my intimacy with great champions of the arena gains me more esteem than the friendship of any number of senators." He was perfectly unabashed. "Are you still investigating the killings you were looking into yesterday?"

"He's looking into the death of that ex-aedile," Andromeda informed him.

"As it occurs, I think that man's death and the killing of Lucius Folius and his wife may be—"

"Folius!" Andromeda spat on the colorful tiles. "The day he and that sow died ought to be commemorated as a holiday, with sacrifices and rejoicing!"

"You knew Folius?" I asked, startled.

"Ha! Who didn't?" She laughed without mirth. "When he moved up to Rome from whatever town must have kicked him out—"

"Bovillae, I understand," I said.

"Bovillae, then. A happy town without that couple. Anyway, when he got here with all his money and his taste for blood and pain, he started working his way through all the *lupanaria* in Rome, starting with mine."

"Rumor has it," I said, "that you cater to every imaginable taste."

"Not *every* one of them," she insisted. "Think about it: If you rented horses, would you rent one to a man who'd beat it and run it until it collapsed and return it to you half dead?"

"Those girls and boys last year," Asklepiodes asked, "Folius was the one?"

"Him and the woman both," she said, nodding. "Thought they could buy me off with a few coins and come back for more of the same. I told them I'd leave orders with my men to knock them on the head and dump them in the river if they ever came back. I couldn't keep a single girl here unchained if I let them be treated like that. I don't mind a little playacting, no harm in that, and I have people specially trained for it. Those two wanted the real thing."

"I saw how their household slaves were treated," I admitted. "There really should be provision in Roman law to prevent such things."

"I heard later that they found places to cater to them," she went on grimly. "Slaves die all the time. Nobody looks into it."

It occurred to me that I was looking into the very timely deaths of two people who might have been among Rome's most illustrious mass murderers. They were merely careful about whom they killed, never doing away with anyone of rank. It was rare for rich *equites* to make themselves so repugnant to so many persons in so brief a time. Everybody from Proconsul Antonius Hybrida to madame Andromeda, yet their neighbors barely knew who they were!

"I want to see the room where Lucilius was killed," I said.

"Whatever for?" she asked.

"You never know what such a place will tell you," I answered.

"My friend has created his own branch of philosophy," Asklepiodes assured her, "or perhaps a form of necromancy. Sometimes it is as if the spirits of the slain speak to him."

Andromeda rubbed an ivory ring she wore on her forefinger and kissed it. "I want no dealings with the dead here, but I'll show you the room." She rose to her full, amazing height, and I followed her, with Asklepiodes at my side and Hermes padding along behind. I decided I'd better count my money when we got home. The boy might have slipped off with one of the girls while we conversed.

The stairways that connected the upper galleries were arranged in pairs. Those nearest the courtyard were for upward traffic, those next to the wall for descending. It was most orderly, almost like a theater. Some of the rooms we passed were illuminated, others were dark. From within came sounds of music and cries of passion and sounds that defied interpretation. It might have been amusing to pause and try to interpret some of these noises as an intellectual exercise, but duty called.

Andromeda led us to a door and rapped on it. There was no sound from within, so she pushed open the door. Light poured out, its source a floor lamp that supported four wicks. The room was no larger than necessary for the activities inside. Its furnishings, beside the lamp, were a small table holding a basin, pitcher, and washing materials; a bronze brazier that held no coals that evening; and a rather commodious couch with ample cushions and a backrest.

"The larger rooms are on the ground floor," Andromeda said. "Some of them are for groups and have special equipment. Nothing fancy here."

I walked over to the room's single window. Its frame was of fragrant cedar, a luxurious touch. The inner shutter was likewise cedar, carved in an intricate fret to admit light and air. The solid, outer shutter was of painted pine. I opened both shutters and looked out. It was a straight drop to the paved square below. I could see no convenient place in the room for attaching a rope. The killer or killers must have left by the door.

"Are you certain this is the room?" I asked. "Except for those on the ground floor, they must be much alike."

Andromeda indicated the door, which was painted red and bore a stylized design of a lyre. "Most of the girls and slave staff can't read, so I don't use numbers. I use a different color door on each of the three upper floors: blue for the second, yellow for the third, and red on this one. Each door has a symbol for one of the gods that everyone knows: lightning for Jupiter, a moon for Venus, a spear for Mars, a serpent staff for Mercury, and so forth. I tell a slave, 'Go up to Yellow Hercules,' he knows to go to the third floor and find the door with the club on it." She rapped the door with a knuckle. "Lucilius was killed in Red Apollo; I'm not likely to forget it."

"A very logical system," I commended. I studied the brazier. "Did this hold a fire that evening?"

"Certainly. I've said it was cold. But you saw the fire buckets standing outside the doors. I always—"

"Please," I said, gesturing for silence, "I've told you I'm not here enforcing the fire regulations. Your precautions are exemplary. Asklepiodes, how did you find the victim?"

"Breathing his last. He had been stabbed beneath the ribs on the left side, consistent with a right-handed assailant. As near as I could discern by candlelight, the weapon had been a straight, double-edged dagger. The wound was approximately five inches long, slightly curved as the blade followed the contour of the rib cage. Viscera, also lacerated, protruded from the wound. It was certain death for any man."

"But not immediate," I commented.

"No, a man may linger for days with such a wound, depending upon which internal blood vessels have been severed. I saw immediately that his bleeding was severe. His toga was soaked—"

"He was still wearing his toga?"

"Yes, he was fully dressed."

I took another look at the door, swung it on its hinges. It was set almost in the center of the wall, with about three feet of space on each side of it. This room had no window opening onto the balcony outside. I decided that the room had told me all that it was going to.

"Let's go," I said. As we descended into the courtyard, I asked, "Do you remember any other distinguished persons being here that night?"

Andromeda shook her head. "The killing pretty much drove everything else from my mind."

"And you?" I asked Asklepiodes.

"I had been entertaining some friends from the Museum

in Alexandria. They were on a visit to Rome, staying at the Egyptian Embassy. I am sure if there had been any Romans of distinction present, I would have pointed them out to my colleagues."

"So much for that, then. Andromeda, please describe Galatea."

"A pretty girl, but then all of mine are. About sixteen, dark hair, brown eyes. She'd only been here for a couple of days. She wasn't from Rome, but she wasn't from very far away either, to judge by her accent. A small town girl. I get a lot of those."

"Were there any other disappearances at that time?"

"What do you mean?" Andromeda asked.

"Was there any other member of your staff here that night that you never saw again afterward?"

She looked at Asklepiodes. "What's your friend getting at?"

He smiled happily. "Just bear with him. It often makes sense after a while. Like Socrates, he comes at the truth by asking questions rather than making pronouncements."

"As you will. Now that I think of it, there was a bouncer I'd hired about the time I took Galatea on. He said his name was Antaeus and that he was from the south and had come up to Rome to fight in the big Games. He was a huge brute, like most of them, and wore a heavy beard, the way citizens hardly ever do."

"And he disappeared after the murder as well?"

"Right. This is always part-time work for the funeral fighters. The only reason I noticed he'd gone was when he didn't show up to collect a few night's wages. I never connected it with the killing, though. These boys usually work during the day as bullies for one of the gang leaders, so they end up dead or laid up with wounds pretty often and I don't take much notice."

By this time, we were at the courtyard entrance to the tunnel. "Andromeda, you have been of great assistance to me in this matter, and I hope to see more of you in the future."

She smiled fetchingly, something she did well, since she did it for a living. "Aedile, you will always be welcome in the Labyrinth whether in or out of office."

She left and Asklepiodes started to go, but I placed a hand on his shoulder. "Just another moment of your time, my friend."

"Assuredly, as much of it as you wish."

We began to stroll through the tunnel, Hermes close behind us. "There are a couple of matters I thought our hostess had no need to hear. She mentioned that Lucilius babbled something she couldn't understand. Could you make anything out?"

"I cannot be certain. He seemed to be in the delirium that often precedes death and not in his best voice. It sounded to me like he was saying 'filthy dog, filthy dog.' His teeth were tightly gritted, but that much was clear."

"Are you certain he was using the masculine form?" I asked, thinking that the man might have been calling the treacherous whore a bitch.

"Yes, the word was masculine."

"And the wound you describe: Not only did the dagger have to penetrate a heavy woolen toga and a layer or two of clothing beneath that, but it was dragged upward several inches. That takes a strong man."

"Yes, I suppose it would," he agreed, nodding.

"And it didn't occur to you to point this out at the time?" I asked, exasperated. "A whore can easily murder a man, but first she gets him out of his clothes, relaxed and unsuspecting. Then she can stick a tiny knife into his jugular or slip a stiletto into his heart, and he'll die practically without noticing it!"

"Yes, that makes sense. But, my old friend, I was summoned to give the man what aid I could, which was very little indeed. I was never questioned by an investigator." This, to Asklepiodes, took care of everything.

I sighed. Sometimes I wondered whether I was the only man in the world who reasoned in the fashion I did. "And you've done well, if somewhat belatedly. Thank you. I thank you."

"Always happy to be of assistance to Senate and People," he assured me, and went off to rejoin his companion for the night, probably some painted, pretty boy. He was, after all, a Greek.

"I hope you've kept your ears open through all this," I said to Hermes. He was purchasing a bundle of small torches from a vendor.

"Yes, though those dancers strained my eyes." He ignited a torch at a wall sconce and preceded me back toward the bridge. "The whore Galatea sounds like she might have been that poor, whipped girl we saw at the *insula*."

"My own thought. Andromeda said her accent sounded local but not Roman. Bovillae is only about thirty miles down the Via Appia. People there talk almost like Romans. And the bouncer, Antaeus—"

"The big slave. He was hiding behind the door. There

was plenty of space there and no window in the wall on the courtyard side where someone might see what was going on inside."

"I've taught you well, Hermes!" I commended him. Sometimes the boy was almost worth what he ate, drank, and stole. "Lucilius must have been attacked and stabbed as soon as the door was shut. Then the big slave and the girl would have left the room separately, after an interval. With all the comings and goings in a place like that, who would notice?"

"That's why they went to work there a few days before the killing!" Hermes said, getting excited. "They needed to be there long enough so nobody would notice them, and they needed to pick a good room to carry it out. They settled on one way on the top floor, with plenty of room behind the door and no window in the front wall! The big man went up there earlier; so if anyone knocked, he'd yell that the room was occupied."

"You're learning to think like a criminal, Hermes, but I suppose it must come naturally to you. Now I am wondering who the man in the hooded cloak might have been and why Lucilius went up to that room with Galatea."

"The man in the hood was probably Folius," Hermes said. "The girl and the big slave were his property. And as for going upstairs with Galatea, I know why I'd have been going up there with her."

"No doubt. But you shouldn't always jump at the easiest answer. There are too many people involved in this."

"What, then?"

"I was thinking about Lucilius's dying words." Ahead of us I could see the torches burning along the parapets of the Sublician Bridge. Beneath them people were still watching the ominous rise of the river.

"You mean 'filthy dog?' What—oh, I see what you mean."

The boy still had much to learn. It had just occurred to him what had occurred to me the moment Asklepiodes had said it. The Greek physician, whose ear for Latin was not as perfect as he liked to think, had heard the gritted, dying words of Lucilius incorrectly.

He hadn't been saying *canis*. He had been saying Caninus.

11

"Wait," I said as Hermes was about to set his foot on the bridge.

He turned. "What?"

"Go upriver. We're going to cross at the Cestian Bridge."

"We're going to the Island?"

"Well, I suppose we could jump into the river instead, but ordinarily if you cross the Cestian, you end up at the Island." The long, puzzling, fatiguing day had reduced me to second-rate sarcasm.

"Whatever you say." He turned left and preceded me along the embankment, which on this side of the river was well above the waterline. As Ogulnius had told me, the current was far slower and less destructive here on the inner curve of the river bend than on the opposite bank. I do not know why this should be, but perhaps it is rather like the way the hub of a chariot seems to be turning rather slowly, while the rim, which is still part of the same wheel, is turning furiously. I decided I would have to ask a philosopher about this sometime.

Whatever the reason, the water that flowed by below us was almost tranquil, while that in the center of the stream had grown turbulent. Light from the moon and the torches on the bridges revealed a good deal of wrack from the flooding upstream. I saw no full-grown trees, but there was a fair amount of brush and what appeared to be drowned animals. Once, we saw a straw hut, such as shepherds use, float by, bottom up, like some bizarre boat.

You would have expected a great deal of noise to accompany such a spectacle, but that was not the case. Father Tiber worked to accomplish his mysterious purpose rather quietly. There was a mild, pleasant murmur of rushing water at the points of the breakwaters that protected the upstream sides of the bridges and an occasional scrape as a floating log struck a bridge or embankment; otherwise, it was almost as quiet as a normal night.

It took us only a few minutes to walk the distance between the Sublician and Aemilian bridges, the whole way passing sightseers and fishermen who were still dragging their boats to safety. Ordinarily, the bulk of the population went to bed as soon as it was dark, but not on this night.

Past the Aemilian, the river took a sharp turn leftward, to the west. Here the two branches of the Tiber rejoined after splitting around the Island. It was a somewhat longer walk to the Cestian Bridge, which joined the Island to the west bank as the new Fabrician joined it to the eastern one. This stretch was lonelier, with little but open fields to our left, since that area had yet to be developed. Farmers still kept market gardens there.

The Island devoted to the God of Healing rode like an oversized ship in the middle of the flood, and that is not just a fanciful simile. The gigantic retaining walls and breakwaters at the ends of its elliptical length were constructed in the shape of a galley, with the prow facing upstream. With the Tiber now foaming over its huge, marble ram, it gave the incredible impression of speeding away from us.

The uncanny sight seemed to fill Hermes with superstitious dread. "Should we go over there?"

"It's just an illusion," I assured him, a little unsettled myself. "That island's not going anywhere. It was right in that spot before Romulus showed up, without all the fancy stonework, of course. If it were really moving, it would be tugging at the bridges, wouldn't it?" I slapped a parapet, almost as much to reassure myself as him. "See? Perfectly solid. Now, come on."

"I didn't really think it was moving," he muttered under his breath.

As we climbed the steps of the temple, I admired the fires blazing in the new, bronze braziers before the doors. I could tell from the brightness of the flames and the thin smoke that they were burning high-quality wood. Even as we passed by, an elderly slave tossed a split log into one of them, sending a column of glittering sparks skyward.

Inside the temple, the statue of the benign god Aesculapius stood vigil over a small crowd of sufferers. Most of them lay on pallets spread on the floor, although a few wealthy patients had brought proper beds with them and were attended by slaves. Others, unable to sleep, sat on their blankets, hunched into knots of abject misery. All these unfortunates would sleep before the god in hope that he would send them dreams indicating a cure for their ailments. The priests were expected to be expert in interpreting these dreams.

I found the high priest, Gavius, in consultation with some of the others before the statue. All wore their full vestments, as if for a nighttime ceremony. Aesculapius was a god associated with both the upper world through his father, Apollo, and with the lower through his tutelary serpent, so he was accorded both daytime and nighttime services and both white and black animals were sacrificed to him, usually cocks. All over the walls were hung models, usually clay, of hands, feet, eyes, and various other members and organs. These were dedicated to the god in thanks for cures to the represented parts. Every few years all this clutter had to be cleared out, and the offerings were cast into a special, sanctified pit.

"Aedile!" Gavius said, when he saw me. "We hardly expected to see you here at this hour." He was a very dignified old man, whose obscure but patrician family had supplied priests for the temple since its founding. Even before Aesculapius arrived in Italy, they had been priests of an earlier healing god. "We were just consulting about what measures to take should the river rise high enough to swamp the Island."

"Has that ever happened before?" I asked him.

"No, but who are we to tell Father Tiber how high he may rise?"

"That is very true."

He shook his head sadly. "Many of us feel that we are

overdue for a chastening from the gods, with so much sacrilege and uncleanness in the City. And what god is closer to Rome than Tiberinus? He was ancient when Romulus reared the first walls here. The other gods have many worshippers throughout Italy and the world. Father Tiber is ours alone."

"A very pertinent point," I said. "Actually, I am here to speak with the slave-priest Harmodias. Could you have him summoned?"

"I would be most happy to." He beckoned for an acolyte and whispered something in his ear. The boy dashed off on silent, bare feet. "Might I inquire what this concerns?"

"I left a slave here in his care. The man was a survivor of the *insula* collapse three nights ago."

"Oh, yes, I heard of the matter. The unfortunate fellow died and was taken away, I understand."

"Exactly. There are some circumstances of his death I need to know about."

It seemed that we had a little wait, and something the dutiful old priest had said was beginning to blossom in my mind. "Revered Gavius, you spoke of the ritual pollution of the City a moment ago."

"Oh, yes, a most serious matter."

"I agree, and I think something needs to be done about it. If I were to go to the Senate and propose that a special court be held to prosecute those responsible for this terrible state of affairs, would you and the other high priests and *flamines* be willing to back me on this?"

"I think it is a splendid idea. Now, the *Pontifex Maximus* is away from Rome—"

"I think Julius Caesar, my uncle by marriage," throwing

that in for effect, "will approve. I'll send a messenger to him at first light."

"Then as soon as the condition of the City permits, I will call for a meeting of the priesthoods to discuss this matter. It is customary to convene such a meeting following a disaster anyway, since we must know how we have offended the gods."

"Venerable Gavius, my report will detail exactly how we have offended Father Tiber."

The boy returned, and Gavius bent low while the acolyte whispered in his ear. Everyone spoke quietly in this temple. The old man straightened. "This is strange. I am told that Harmodias went out to the fields on the west bank to find some healing herbs he required. He has not been seen since."

"When was this?"

"Yesterday afternoon."

"That is most odd," I said, thinking that it was not odd in the least. He had fled right after I'd spoken with him, afraid to be exposed for his part in the killing of the slave. I took my leave of the old man and went out through the broad front doors.

For a while I stood on the fine porch at the top of the steps. There were times when I found it difficult to believe in the gods, when they seemed like the childish creation of frightened peasants, trying desperately to control forces they did not understand. There were other times when the gods seemed very close. The river in this condition made them seem very close indeed.

I wondered what the gods wanted of us, and whether they were really pleased with the bribes we offered them: all those bulls and boars, the rams and horses and birds, the occasional dog. Did they really find this pleasing, or was it just blood and feathers and smoke?

Each May, the Vestals cast twenty-four straw mannikins off the Sublician Bridge as an offering to Tiberinus, imploring him not to flood. Once, those had been human sacrifices. *Maybe,* I thought, *we should go back to human sacrifice.* I could think of several candidates to go into the first batch of twenty-four.

A sudden noise shook me from my reverie. The old slave had tossed another log into one of the bronze baskets. Again the plume of sparks rushed skyward.

"Why are you burning so much expensive wood, old man?" Hermes asked him. "There's hardly anyone here to see it."

"The man who restored the temple and donated these fine braziers here paid to have first-rate firewood burned in them all night for five years."

"That's extravagant," I commented. "Is this to honor the god? Was the man granted a cure here?"

The old slave gave me a gap-toothed smile. It was the utterly cynical smile of the true Roman. "If you ask me, the rich bugger just wants to make sure everyone can read his name no matter what time it is."

He jerked a thumb upward and the two of us raised our gazes. On the broad, low-peaked triangle of the pediment, surrounded by ornamental carving and smaller inscriptions, beautifully illuminated by the flames was a name. It was spelled out in huge letters, as is the right of a man who has restored a public building:

M. VAL. MESSALA.

This explained a few things. Messala, the great benefactor of the temple, would have had the run of the place. No difficulty then to suborn as many low-level priests as he needed to carry out a murder in the temple and dispose of the body afterward.

We paused on the Island side of the Fabrician Bridge.

"What was that business about a special court?" Hermes wanted to know.

"If I can't get them before a praetor's court, if the corruption runs too deep to prosecute them successfully before a jury, then I'll denounce them before a religious court. The charges are as binding as they are in any civil matter, and the punishments are far worse, no slap-on-the-wrist fines or temporary banishments. Cato's beloved ancestors set down some genuinely barbarous sentences for offenses that could anger the gods against the whole Roman people.

"This flood is going to be truly disastrous, and the Assemblies are sure to demand blood to pay for their suffering."

"That's going to call for some crowd-pleasing speeches," Hermes said doubtfully. "Caesar is good at that sort of thing. So is Clodius. It's not your style."

"Cato was a popular tribune of the people, and he is a demagogue to match the best of them. He'll support me. He loves this sort of thing."

Hermes nodded, lighting another torch with the dying flickers of the last. "It could work. There's one thing you've got to do first, though."

"What is that?"

"Live long enough to pull it off."

"There is that little problem," I allowed.

"Maybe we shouldn't try to return to your house tonight.

They'll be out to kill you for sure, now. You have been asking too many questions about too many important people. There's no way to keep that quiet in a city like Rome. Their best place to ambush you is in the street leading to your door."

He spoke with some authority. We had fought our way through more than one such ambush on that street. "You may be right," I acknowledged. "Let's see what it looks like on the other end of this bridge; then perhaps I can find a friend I can cadge a night's lodging from, somebody I don't owe too much money to."

"That narrows the list," he said, and I could hear the smirk in his voice.

"Watch your mouth. I've been allowing you too much familiarity lately. It's time I shortened your leash." He made no smart reply, so I decided he was learning.

The top of the embankment on the eastern side of the river was still dry; but a few steps down its landward side, the water started. Either the river had overflowed its banks farther upstream, perhaps in the Campus Martius, and then flowed down here, or, as I judged more likely, all the sewers had backed up and water was surging up through the drains.

"Needing a ride, neighbors?" The speaker was a boatman who was poling his little craft toward us. From the prow of his boat thrust a long pole with a torch burning on its end, identifying the man as a night fisherman. Ordinarily, he would be out on the river at this hour, where the torch would lure fish near the surface to be caught by his cast net.

"Yes, but we don't know exactly where we are going," I told him. "What's still above water?"

"The whole Forum Boarium is awash," he said. "So is the Valley of Murcia," this being the old name of the depression in which lay the Circus Maximus. "The Forum was wet, but not much higher than your ankles, just awhile ago. Might be deeper now." The area near the Forum was densely populated, though not as densely as the Subura, where I lived.

I looked up to our left, where the Capitol rose in splendor, crowned by the great Temple of Jupiter. Uphill and to our right was the Temple of Ceres on the lower slope of the Aventine Hill, where I had what was termed, sarcastically, my headquarters as aedile. I pointed toward it.

"We could go up there. I have a right to use the place at any hour. The slaves will find couches for us. They hold feasts there, so there must be some sort of furniture."

"Probably no food, though, or any other comforts," Hermes said. "You have friends over there on the Palatine." He nodded toward the hill that rose to the east above the Circus Maximus. "It's not so far."

"The problem is," I said quietly, "I don't know who my friends are anymore."

I negotiated with the boatman until we agreed on his fare, and we boarded the boat.

It was a strange, dreamlike experience drifting slowly southward in this place where I had walked all my life. We passed silent buildings, and the water was alive with the rats flushed from their cellars. We passed other boats and barges as people were ferried to and fro. The boatmen called out to each other, using the peculiar jargon of their trade. The moon was bright, spreading a silvery light over the strange scene. It might have been almost pleasant, except for one thing.

"What a stench!" Hermes said, gagging. Owing to some

trick of the still air, the smell had been nearly unnoticeable from atop the embankment; but here, just a few feet from its surface, the foul reek was all but visible, making my eyes water. I had been right. It was the sewers backing up, flushing years of neglected corruption right back into the City.

"It's ripe," the boatman agreed. Neither the smell nor the situation seemed to upset him. "I wish there was money in rat fishing. I'd get my nets out and be a rich man by sunup. It's certain that there's no fishing to be done on the river this night or for a good many nights to come." He shook a couple of rats off his pole to emphasize his point. When he pushed it back in, I could see that the water was no more than knee-deep, but it might as well have been deeper than Oceanus, as far as I was concerned. There was no way I would ever wade through *that* water.

We poled across the Forum Boarium, now as bereft of occupants as it had been before the Aborigines came to Italy. We drifted past the towering chariot gate end of the Circus, and I decided that some work would be called for before I could hold my races there. The condition of the track would have to be horrendous after this.

Eventually, we nosed ashore at the base of the Aventine. Even before Hermes and I could disembark, a couple rushed down the gentle slope, calling for the boatman to wait. He was in for a busy, profitable night even without any money to be had from rat fishing.

"Take us to the Palatine at once, good man!" said a haughty female, and somewhat familiar, voice. I went impolitely close and stooped, squinting, toward the patrician features beneath the shawl that covered the woman's head. The light of the boat's torch and the much smaller one carried by Hermes revealed an unmistakable face, which glared at me like a Gorgon.

"Why, revered Lady Cornelia! I scarcely expected to see you here so late."

"Why are you here, Aedile Metellus?" she spat out. "No doubt out carousing late as usual, with the City in a state of emergency!"

"The whole City is my concern, and I never rest in the service of Senate and People. I was about to pay a visit to the temple, and who should I find but the lady second in esteem only to the wife of the *Flamen Dialis* and the *Virgo Maxima,* accompanied by one of her eunuchs." But there was no chance I would have mistaken the blocky, shaven head of her companion with its furious face. "Why, excuse me, Marcus Porcius, I thought you were one of the temple drones! Well met, indeed! You are just the man I need to talk to."

"Metellus," Cato said, or rather growled, "if you have any ambitions to live until sunrise, you'd better take care!" Cornelia put a hand on his arm, and he quieted like an unruly dog who calms at its master's touch. This was a night for revelations.

"Decius Caecilius," Cornelia said, in an entirely new voice, "how may I help you?"

"Oh, as it happens, I can't go home tonight, and I'm sure all my friends are putting up clients from the lower parts of the City, so I thought I'd just go to the office of the plebeian aediles and curl up in a corner."

"By no means," she said. "Just tell the slaves to take you to the guest quarters. They are quite well appointed. Tell the slaves that they must render you every service or risk my severe displeasure."

"Why, that is most kind of you, my lady. And Cato, I need to confer with you at first light tomorrow."

"Why should I—"

"It's about that matter we discussed earlier today."

His eyes narrowed. "You've learned something, eh?"

"A great deal. You will like this. And there may be some violent action very soon."

He jerked his blocky head in an emphatic nod. "I'll be here if I have to swim!"

"You haven't been out on that water yet. Don't make any promises you can't keep."

I helped Cornelia aboard. "Decius," she whispered, "you have the reputation of a man who can keep his own counsel. They say that is why Caesar trusts you with important matters. May I also rely on your discretion?"

I placed a hand over my heart. "To the grave, beauteous Cornelia."

The boatman poled them away toward the Palatine, and I laughed as Hermes and I strolled up toward the lovely temple. "Cato and Cornelia! Who would have imagined it? The most reptilian man in the Senate, and the most fearsome dragon this side of Caesar's mother! Cato has a human weakness after all!"

"It's not his only weakness," Hermes said. "He drinks too much; everyone knows that."

"That is not a weakness," I pointed out, "it is a mark of character. Well, I don't think it makes me like him any more, but perhaps it makes me detest him just a little bit less." I held my thumb and forefinger a trifling distance apart to show him just how little that was. We climbed the temple steps. "We're in luck, Hermes! I had no idea the Temple of Ceres even *had* guest quarters!"

As it turned out, the temple had very fine guest quarters indeed; and when I'd rousted the slaves from their rest and threatened them with Cornelia's wrath, they led us there and saw to our comfort.

"Oh, yes sir!" twittered the head eunuch as he proudly displayed the suite that lay behind the splendid nave. "We often entertain the high priestesses and chamberlains of the great temples in Greece and Magna Graecia, where Ceres is worshipped as Demeter."

I studied the sumptuous rooms. "Kept this all to themselves, eh? While we poor aediles sweated away in tiny little offices downstairs! Well, no more of that! Bring us whatever food you have handy and some decent wine. No! Make that the best!"

The half man bowed obsequiously. "At once, Aedile!"

Within minutes we were tearing into some of the best cold food to be had in Rome that night. We had dined earlier that evening, but we ate like starving men anyway. A soldier knows that he has to fill up when he has the chance because the next meal may be days away and plenty of fighting to be had in the meantime. I had a strong feeling that things were going to be moving very fast, very soon, and I had better be fortified for it.

I took the time to wonder if what we were eating was the remains of a dinner prepared for the incongruous couple and almost choked on my wine at the thought.

Soon I was replete, and Hermes looked like a calf

stunned by the slaughterman's hammer, reeling where he sat. The hour was late, but I did not feel ready to sleep on the heavily cushioned couch.

"Come, Hermes," I said, rising. "Let's get a little air before we turn in."

"If you say so," he said, rising. We walked out through the nave, past the statue of the stately, seated goddess. A single slave tended the lamps that burned before the goddess and along the walls, all the rest of the staff having gone back to their beds. We walked out onto the porch and looked out over the City. The sight was breathtaking in the bright moonlight, with water glimmering where ordinarily there would be only murky gloom. On the hills, there burned far more torches than usual, where people had gathered in open places and on rooftops. Looking to the west, the river seemed impossibly wide.

"You think you can get out of this?" Hermes asked as we sat on the top step. He set a pitcher and a pair of cups between us.

"I have to," I told him. "It's not only desirable to stay alive, but I have to get this business out of the way quickly. I have far too much work to do, and this is absorbing all of my attention. As soon as it's light in the morning, I want you to dash to the house with a message for Julia."

"I'm sure she must be worried about you."

"Yes, yes, but this is urgent. I want that statue boxed up and out of the City immediately. She'll have to hire a cart and get it sent to the country estate. It'll have to be hidden there until all this blows over."

"Hidden?" he said. "The Venus? Why?"

"Because it's a bribe."

"And a handsome one, too. What were you bribed to do?"

"Nothing, Idiot! I've never taken a bribe in my life! No large ones, anyway. Not for anything important, at any rate."

He looked into the bottom of his cup. "The wine must be making me slow. What are you talking about?"

"I should have seen it immediately, but this business of the *insula* has kept me too distracted. Look, Hermes, I've taught you how officeholding works: I can't be sued or charged with a crime while I hold office, right?"

"I understand that much."

"But the minute I step down, I can be charged. It's practically customary. A political opponent, personal enemy, or young lawyer will accuse you of something, and you'll have to defend yourself. The charges are usually bribery or extortion, but it can be anything. When Caesar was starting out, he charged old Rubirius with a murder committed twenty-five years before!" I held out my cup, and Hermes refilled it. "The important thing is, the charge can be completely false. It all depends on how clever and forceful the lawyers are. Evidence is secondary.

"But consider this: Suddenly, I am in possession of a great masterpiece, an original Venus by whatever-his-name-is. This is a treasure I could never afford by myself, even throwing in Julia's dowry. Where did this thing come from? I would bet on Messala or Scaurus. They're both rich, and they've governed provinces where such items are to be squeezed from the locals."

"Why a statue?" Hermes wanted to know. "Why not money?"

"Money is easy to hide; it can be explained away; it's anonymous. But you saw the fuss Julia and Fausta—no, you were on the roof, weren't you? Well, they were cooing over the thing as if it were a team of first-rank chariot horses. Whoever sent it knew that we'd be showing it off to everyone we know. If it weren't for this flood, Julia would already be inviting everyone who counts for anything in Rome to a big party so they could all gawk at it! I'll be charged with selling out my office, and it will look credible. I know I'd have trouble explaining it."

"Maybe we should just smash it up and hide the pieces," Hermes suggested.

"No, Julia would never forgive me. Besides, it's too valuable. We'll just send it out to the country estate, hide it in a goatherd's hut, or something."

"You're going to keep it?"

"Of course I'm going to keep it! Do you think I'm a fool? In two or three years, we can take it out and put it in the shrine Julia wants to build for it. All this will have been long forgotten; there will be new scandals and crimes to divert everyone. There's no dishonor in accepting a bribe that didn't buy anything."

"Is that in the law tables?"

"I think so. I'll look it up. Now get to bed. I want my writing materials ready at first light; I have a letter to write to Caesar. And find out which of the aedilician messengers is the best rider."

He got to his feet. "I'll get it done. You'd better get some sleep, too. If tomorrow is going to be as long and exciting as the last few, you'll need rest."

"I will be in shortly," I told him. He nodded and went

back into the temple. He really was maturing well and showed a lot of promise for a conniving young thief.

I needed a little time to myself to get my thoughts in order. He was right when he said that I faced a full day on the morrow. I had made light of it, but I fully expected that at least one attempt would be made on my life, perhaps several, and any of them might be successful.

It seemed to me that never before had I been called upon to deal with a problem that arose so suddenly, involved a business of which I was so ignorant and persons with whom I had not the slightest acquaintance. I was used to having my life threatened over politics or wealth or women. Never had I expected to be fighting for my life on account of lumber. Yet this seemingly trivial matter had caused the deaths of hundreds of Romans as surely as if they had been slaughtered by a foreign army. I was a plebeian aedile, and it was my job to see that justice was done and there was no avoiding it.

Satisfied, I got up and followed Hermes back into the temple. Ceres didn't look as if she cared about my problems, but she wasn't really a Roman goddess anyway. I might have appealed to Juno or Minerva, but Ceres was from Greece.

I slept very well in her guest chamber.

12

EVEN BEFORE THE SUN ROSE, the morning was one of furious activity.

I was somewhat surprised to see the other aediles arrive in the early gray light, accompanied by their slaves and their crowds of clients. It transpired that almost all parts of Rome were readily accessible if you didn't mind taking a circuitous route or using a boat. As they gathered, I was sitting at a table outside the temple, scribbling away on my message to Caesar by the light of several lamps I had dragged outside.

Since I was writing to Caesar in his capacity as *Pontifex Maximus,* arbiter of all matters concerning Roman religious practice, and since I intended for this letter to be read by the Senate and the various priestly colleges, I wrote in a far more formal style than I usually employed. I found it no easy task to remember all those obscure cases and tenses that had been drilled into me as a boy, many of them leftovers from archaic Latin and never used except in religious matters and in certain types of poetry.

When I finished what seemed to me a creditable document, I handed it to my staff of secretaries and ordered them to make copies of it until I ordered them to stop. They had arrived only minutes before, still yawning and scratching.

"Jupiter protect us!" wailed a voice in the dimness. "Metellus is toiling by lamplight! Surely this is an omen sent by the gods!" This was the occasion of much raucous laughter. The speaker was Marcus Aemilius Lepidus, the curule aedile. He walked up to my desk, followed by his own pack of flunkies.

"Why, Lepidus, I hardly recognized you without your fat backside planted in your folding chair."

"No markets today," he said, beaming. "I decided to come lend a hand to you poor, sweating drudges. Surely you were expecting me."

"Why?"

"Didn't a Senate messenger call on you last night?"

"I've been here all night."

"Decius! This devotion to duty is astounding! Anyway, the *interrex* has summoned an emergency meeting of the Senate to be held in the Temple of Jupiter tonight before sundown. All the aediles are to assess the condition of the City and submit a report."

"Fine idea," I said, "but you can just about see it all from here." I was thinking that a Senate meeting was just what I wanted.

"Odd sort of flood, isn't it?" Lepidus said. The growing

light was making the spectacle visible. "All that water just sitting there, more like a lake than a rampaging river. I've seen floods that tore whole buildings from their foundations. I don't think this one is going to be so bad. Maybe the water will just recede and there will just be some mopping and bailing to do."

"This flood," I told him, "has turned the entire lower part of Rome into a vast chamber pot. And it's going to stay right there until Helios dries it up."

"Is that true? Well, my house is right on top of the Quirinal, well away from it all."

"Lepidus, civic virtue like yours is what made Rome the greatest power in the world."

"Here comes Cato," he said, ignoring me. "This should be fun. What do you think he's here for?"

"He's here to confer with me," I told him.

Again I received a stare of round-eyed wonder. "Cato conferring with you? Truly, this is a day for miracles! Let it not be an omen!" He accompanied this old formula against evil with an elaborate traditional hand gesture. There was more laughter from his stooges.

Cato had indeed arrived, and he was not alone. He had at least twenty men with him, most of them young *equites* or junior senators. I recognized few of them by sight for they were not members of the set with whom I socialized most. They were all stern-faced men with close-cropped or shaven scalps. *Ancestor worshippers to a man,* I thought; *stoics and defenders of old Roman virtue.* Their sour faces were scarred and graced with gaps where teeth had been knocked out, and their knuckles were swollen and broken. These were men who trained hard on the Campus Martius and brawled hard in the streets. I might not invite them to my parties, but they were just the sort of men I wanted at my back that day.

Cato shouldered Lepidus aside. "Hail, Aedile!" he shouted. Lepidus and his lackeys strolled off, smirking and tapping their temples to indicate what they thought of Cato's soundness of mind.

"I have to get this message off right away, Cato. Give me your opinion." Baldly, I told him of the condition of the sewers and how I was going to use their horrid state to convene a religious court.

"Unsanctified corpses in the sewers! Infamous!" Cato yelled. "No wonder the gods have forsaken us!" Then, in a quieter voice, "So you are going to prosecute them for sacrilege if you can't get them for corruption? That is most ingenious, Decius Caecilius."

"I have my moments. What do you think of this letter?" I handed him a copy, and he began to mumble, reading the words to himself. He had gotten no more than halfway through it before he threw it down. "You moron! Did you learn absolutely nothing from your teachers of style and composition?"

"Better men than you have praised my prose style!" I said, offended.

"This is not some trivial, chatty missive full of gossip and politics! This is a document touching sacerdotal matters to be read by the *Pontifex Maximus!* You'd better let me show you how this is done." He slapped the table with a calloused palm, producing a sound like a snapping board. Cato practiced hard with sword, shield, and spear almost every day. "Attend me!" he bellowed to the scribes. "Set this down exactly as I dictate, or I'll have the hides off your backs!" They jumped at the noise, grabbed fresh sheets, dipped their reed pens, and watched him with rapt, worshipful attention. They never behaved that way with me.

In a slow, sonorous voice, Cato began to translate my letter into the old-fashioned Latin he adored, using forms that had been ancient in the days of Numa Pompilius, the rolling vowels and clanging consonants sounding like a battle hymn. The crowd gathered around the temple silenced to hear the performance, even the ones who didn't know what it was about and scarcely understood the archaic words. It was almost worth getting up early to hear, and he received a handsome round of applause when he had finished.

We quickly scanned the copies for mistakes; then I sealed the best of them into a copper message tube and handed it to the horse messenger, bidding him ride like the wind for Caesar's winter camp in Gaul, where I judged Caesar and his army would be for at least another ten days, if I knew Gaulish weather. With luck, decent road conditions, and good, grain-fed horses, he could be back with Caesar's reply in eight days. Caesar's system of relay stations was incredibly quick and efficient. This was not so that he could keep in contact with the Senate, which he despised and ignored, but so that he could trumpet the news of his latest victories in the Forum.

We then dispatched foot messengers with copies to the heads of the various priestly colleges, to the tribune of the people, and one to the *interrex*. I would have given much to see Scipio's face when he read it.

"Now you must read this. It was among the records I took from the Tabularium two days ago. I only found it late yesterday afternoon, and I've discovered quite a bit since then. Do you remember an aedile named Lucilius?"

He took the rolled up papyrus. "Quite well. I thought the man very promising, the sort of conscientious official we rarely see any more. He disappointed me, though. Died quite squalidly." He began to read loudly, but his voice lowered as consternation replaced his usual expression. He handed it back. "All right. Tell me about this."

Then Cato sat by me, and we began some serious plotting. I gave him a quick account of my findings of the past few days. He said nothing while I spoke, but I could tell by his various nods and snarls at events and names that he was paying attention and had deep feelings about at least some of it.

"It may not have been such a good idea to send Metellus Scipio a copy of the letter," he said, when I was finished. "Not only is he implicated in this, but he is *interrex*. The powers of that office are not entirely clear. They are certainly not those of a dictator, he has no *imperium*, and he can't command armies and won't go out to govern a province; but in civil matters he is in a better position than any pair of consuls. He has no colleague to obstruct him, and some authorities maintain that an *interrex* can even override a tribunician veto. He might take action against you."

"I don't believe he will."

"Don't count on family loyalty," Cato warned. "He is a Metellus by adoption, not by birth."

"I'm perfectly aware of that. I think he will comply for three reasons: First, he is prouder of his heritage as a Scipio than of his adoption as a Caecilian—"

"That is perfectly understandable," Cato said.

"—and everyone expects a Scipio to act as a savior of

the Republic. Second, he will be stepping down soon anyway and isn't likely to abuse the powers of the office at this late date. Third, I don't think he was directly involved anyway."

"I am glad to hear it, but why don't you think he's one of the conspirators? Lucilius seemed to think he was."

"The morning after the *insula* collapsed, Scipio came to observe; and at that time he was eager for me to bring charges against the builders. He even saw it as a good case for his son to make his reputation as a lawyer. It was only the next day, after Messala had been at him, that he came to try and discourage me. I suspect that he was unaware that inferior materials bought at his estate downriver were being used illegally here in Rome. It's going to be an embarrassment, but he has an out. He can produce some conniving steward who was selling the goods and salting away the profits and have the man publicly executed."

"That could make a good midday entertainment at your Games," Cato pointed out.

"I hadn't thought of that. Maybe we could get rid of all the criminals that way: build a big, fake *insula* in the arena, one with no walls, so they can be seen. Have it collapse and crush them all to death. Pure poetic justice. The audience would love it."

"That has possibilities. Wouldn't they die too quickly, though? They deserve something lingering."

"I'm not as traditional as you are, Cato. Just find the guilty parties, try them, condemn them, and execute them, that's how I do things. Besides, we need to arrest them before we can dole out punishments, so let's stick to that. We must move very quickly if we're to bag them. I want you to grab the freedman, Justus, and hide him in your own house. He's by far our best witness, and I'm only hoping that he hasn't been killed already. He may not like testifying against his patron, but he'll do it to save himself from execution."

"It will be done." Cato beckoned a pair of his high-born brawlers forward, and I told them how to find the salvage yard.

"It should be above water," I told them, "and he will almost certainly be there because people will be buying wood to build barges or shore up endangered buildings. If not, he almost certainly lives nearby. Find him and arrest him on my authority. He already knows I want his testimony."

"Take him to my house," Cato told them, "and sit by him with swords in your hands until I relieve you. Don't let him get away, and don't allow anyone near him." They saluted and ran off.

"I want the Trans-Tiber and points west combed for the slave-priest Harmodias. He can identify the killers of the big slave I entrusted to his care, and he can tie Messala to that deed."

Cato snorted. "You know Messala kept his own hands clean."

"If I can implicate enough of his friends and slaves and freedmen, he will have a large task weaseling out of it. But you've named the biggest task: getting verdicts against the aristocratic likes of Valerius Messala Niger and Aemilius Scaurus."

"Scaurus!" Cato said scornfully. "When I was praetor two years ago, he was tried in my court for gross corruption in his administration of Sardinia. Acquitted, of course, because he bribed the jury, but there was no question as to his guilt. He extorted money far in excess of the required taxes;

he accepted bribes for all of his judgments in court; he executed wealthy men just to lay his hands on fine art works they owned! I remember one fellow in particular that Scaurus charged with treason and executed summarily just because he owned a famous statue of Venus tying up her—"

"Actually," I said, wanting to interrupt this particular train of thought, "since he's already been acquitted of those deeds, I think we should concentrate on his death trap of a theater."

"And that's another thing!" Cato said, just working himself up to the proper pitch of righteous indignation. "That theater is a disgrace to Rome!" He pointed toward the huge structure, which was clearly visible from where we stood. "In the first place, theaters should never have been allowed in Rome! They are impious, degenerate, foreign institutions and they weaken and corrupt the youth of Rome. Even if they must be built for a particular set of Games, they are supposed to be torn down immediately afterward. Yet there sits the theater of Aemilius Scaurus, years after its construction, and all so that the greedy villain can rent it out for filthy profit!" He was in full-powered rant now.

"In the year of my praetorship, I protested that abomination to the censors—"

"One of whom was Valerius Messala," I pointed out.

"Yes, you are right." He wiped a hand down his face. "The gods will make a desolation of Rome, and we deserve it."

"Let's get back to making our case if you don't mind," I said. "It looks like there shouldn't be much of a problem crossing the river if you use the embankment south of the Sublician, then cross there. A team of men on horseback and foot should be able to find Harmodias. Like everyone else, he may be expecting everything to stop for the duration of the flood."

"I'll see to it." That was the good thing about Cato. He got things done and didn't waste time with a lot of frivolous objections. He saved his pigheadedness for public debate.

"Our toughest enemy to beat will be Messala. He's rich; he's influential; he's Pompey's close supporter. The testimony of men as lowly as Justus and Harmodias won't mean much against such a man, but as censor he was to have assigned *publicani* to scour the drains and sewers. This he did not do, and I am going to charge him with sacrilege for it."

"Excellent."

"Last time I saw Caninus," I said, "which was right here, he was with a pack of Plautius Hypsaeus's men. Hypsaeus was praetor the same year you were, wasn't he?"

"No, the year before. He was praetor of the foreigners, and never in the City. Out taking bribes from barbarians, no doubt. He's thick as thieves with Scaurus."

"Even thicker," I said. "I got these from Lucilius's widow. Look at them." I handed him the notes the woman had given me. He frowned and muttered as he plowed his way through the verbiage and crude handwriting.

"Asiatic style. I detest it. Well, the oration itself might have proved competent, but this list of names will be invaluable. I see our friend Hypsaeus right here. I never knew he owned a brickworks, but it shouldn't surprise me. How many senators these days make their money decently, from their crops and rents?"

I sighed. "Alas, too few. Hypsaeus is protected by his gang, but we can get him. He's out of office, and his hirelings will desert him when we put the pressure on. The rest of the names are mainly builders, public contractors, and so forth, low-level people who can be dealt with easily."

"Your friend Milo will be happy," Cato commented. "Not only is his name not on the list, but Hypsaeus is his rival for next year's consulship."

I gazed upward. "I fear they are both to be disappointed."

"What?" He shot a suspicious glance at me. "What do you mean? Do you know something?"

"Let's just say I have a premonition about who is going to be consul next year."

"You Metelli think you are the secret masters of Rome," he growled.

"Let's get down to business," I said. "The sun is already up. If we move fast, we can have a case to cast before the assembled Senate this evening. There will be an uproar, but with this flood they'll be terrified of how the populace will react when it's found that there would be only minor damage if not for senatorial neglect."

"They'll be in a mood to toss some of their colleagues to the wolves," he agreed.

"The tribunes will all be there. I want you to talk to them. Get them to convene a meeting of the Plebeian Assembly. I want you to harangue the Assembly and get them to vote me the power to levy all the labor, resources, and money I need to thoroughly cleanse every inch of the drainage system. And I want it paid for out of the public treasury. And I want a permanent commission appointed for the purpose of disaster relief, with resources to supply temporary shelter and rationing for displaced persons." Suddenly my mind was buzzing with ideas. "One of the priestly colleges or brotherhoods could be given that job. Politicians and magistrates come and go yearly, but the priesthoods last forever."

"I will do it." He was looking at me with an expression I'd never expected to see on his face: respect. "Decius Caecilius, you are going to have the most eventful aedileship in recent memory, if you can survive it." He wheeled and strode away, barking orders at his followers like a general preparing for battle. In a way, that was what he was doing.

For a few minutes the other aediles crowded around me, wanting to know what was going on. Suddenly and unexpectedly, it seemed that they were looking to me for leadership. I didn't waste the opportunity. I snatched a piece of papyrus from a scribe and scrawled a crude map of my beloved, beautiful, awful old City. This I divided into sections, giving each aedile one to subdivide among his helpers. I saw Acilius standing by with his men and ordered him to provide a detailed report on the condition of every cloaca, tributary sewer, and drain hole in the City and have it ready by afternoon.

The State freedman smiled and gestured to one of his slaves. The man withdrew from his satchel a thick scroll, which Acilius presented to me. "What do you think I have been doing these last two years?"

"You see?" I cried, loud as Cato. "Somebody here has been doing his duty! I charge you all to go and do the same! Meet me on the terrace before the Temple of Jupiter one hour before sundown and have your reports ready!"

"At once, Aedile!" they chorussed, dashing off to do something useful, instead of fretting endlessly over actors and chariot races and public banquets.

I stood there for a while, savoring the moment. I felt better than a general with six victorious legions out killing barbarians.

A few minutes later, Hermes arrived, puffing and sweating like an Olympic runner.

"We got it boxed up," he panted, when he had breath. "Old Burrus is escorting it out to the country estate, says he'll see it stowed away, and nobody will get a look at it."

He sat down, and while he caught his breath, I told him about the statue's provenance. "It was Scaurus's safety precaution," I said. "He wanted to make me look like one crook accusing another. It could have worked, too."

"Tell me something," Hermes said. "Why did they kill Folius and his wife? They were all together in it, weren't they? Living in each other's money chests, doing the trade in trashy building materials, all of them making each other richer than they were already—who turned on Folius and why? It's where all this started, as far as we're concerned, with that *insula* coming down and us finding the two of them under it all. They were doing so well. How did they fall out?"

The temple slaves were bringing out breakfast unasked. They laid out bread and honey and sliced fruit on the table, along with watered wine. I sat and gestured to Hermes to sit with me.

"That is a very astute question." Somehow I knew that this was the right time to broach the most delicate subject that lay between us. "Hermes, someday soon I will grant you your freedom. Instead of master and slave, we will be patron and client. You will have every right and privilege of citizenship except that of holding office."

He covered his astonishment by gulping some wine and

smearing a cake with honey. "I always expected that, someday."

"These last few days you have pleased me greatly. I intend to keep you close to me in future years as I rise in office. If you will live up to the promise you have shown lately, you can look forward to becoming one of the great men of the Republic."

Now he was truly embarrassed. "I never—I mean, I—"

"You know Tiro, who was once Cicero's slave and is now a freedman. Senators and foreign kings court him. That could be you. Anyway, I tell you this by way of warning. Keep this up, but conduct yourself prudently. Too many men use their servile origin as an excuse to be worthless. Watch, listen, think, and act wisely. You may have a distinguished future ahead of you."

I watched him hard. He swallowed, fumbled with his cup, but said nothing. I nodded with satisfaction. "You are silent. Yet another good sign. Very well, we will say no more about this for a while, but I want you to bear this firmly in mind."

"I am not likely to forget it," he said.

"You asked about Folius and his wife. That we may never know for certain, but I have been thinking about it. You remember how I have taught you to anticipate your enemy by trying to think like him?" Hermes nodded. "It works as well in this sort of investigation. I found myself pondering this: Suppose I were a criminal conspirator and I had found a useful tool, say, a man from Bovillae, perhaps a neighbor who had great ambition and no scruples, whose career I could push to my own great profit? And suppose further that I brought this unscrupulous man to Rome and set him up in one of my profitable enterprises? Then suppose I found that, after a mutually profitable partnership, this man showed himself to be a madman, a murderer capable not only of embarrassing me, but of destroying our whole, beautiful business?"

"You'd want to get rid of him," Hermes said. "You mean the habit the Folii had of torturing and killing slaves? That might be a little rich for aristocrats, but it's legal."

"To our shame, yes. But I think it was getting beyond that. Andromeda gave us a hint. Folius and his wife were getting entirely out of control in their love of blood and pain."

I sat back and scratched my unshaven chin. The old scar was itching abominably, the way it usually did when I hadn't shaved for a while. "There is something wrong with such people. Most of us have a natural desire to witness combat and strife, and our customs provide the circus and the arena where these things may be displayed in an orderly, lawful fashion, where the blood that is shed is that of malefactors and the volunteers who wish to fight for their own satisfaction or profit or glory."

I shook my head. "But that is not enough for certain people. These must torment innocent, powerless people. And such persons are never satisfied but must progress from atrocity to atrocity. I think that the Folii had degenerated to the point that they were about to do something irrevocably unforgivable. They had outlived their usefulness. Either Scaurus or Messala decided they had to go."

"But take down a whole *insula* and more than two hundred people?" Hermes said. "Why? It's not as if killing two people is that hard to accomplish!"

"That is something I intend to learn before the day is

out," I told him. Then for a while we went over plans for the evening meeting. I was ready to set off for a tour of the flooded areas when a messenger came running down the slope of the Aventine behind the temple.

"Aedile Metellus?" the man asked, halting before the table.

"You've found me." I took the message he handed me and read quickly. After a formal greeting the message was brief:

We must discuss the condition of my theater, which I am now inspecting for damage from this flood. Please come at once. This need not detain you long, but I must speak with you. Below was appended the name: M. Aemilius Scaurus.

"What happened to his trip to Bovillae? Wasn't he concerned about his fig trees?"

"It was grape vines," I said, handing a tip to the messenger, who saluted and trotted off. "Either he went there and returned at a gallop, or he never went at all."

"Whichever it is, he's a fool to think you'd step into so transparent a trap." He chuckled, but I said nothing. Hermes looked at me with growing alarm. "He *is* a fool to think that, isn't he?"

"Under ordinary circumstances he would be, but I am feeling rather foolish just now."

"Wait a moment! Just a short time ago you were lecturing me like a Greek schoolmaster about virtues such as prudence, discretion, and so forth. You do remember that, don't you?"

"Those," I told him, "are the desirable qualities of a man of humble station who would rise in the world and earn the esteem of his fellow citizens. I, on the other hand, was born an aristocrat. I don't have to behave that way. Look at young Marcus Antonius. He's a very capable soldier from a noble family, so he is destined to be a great man despite the fact that he's an irresponsible fool and a bit of a maniac. That wouldn't work for you."

"But have you no regard for your own life?"

"A reasonable regard. But we live in times that reward boldness that borders upon the foolhardy. I think I'll go see what's on Scaurus's mind."

Hermes knew better than to argue. "Let's get some reinforcements first." He looked out over the river. "The bridge is still passable. I can run over to the Trans-Tiber and go to the *ludus*. Statilius will be happy to rent you five or six of his boys for the day. I can be back with them in an hour or less."

"That would be no good," I told him. "I don't want a standoff. Not only would he not attack me, he wouldn't admit anything either. I need all the evidence I can get if I am going to convict a man like Aemilius Scaurus." I glanced toward the angle of the sun. The morning was warming nicely. "Well, at least we will have a fine day for a little boat trip on a backed-up sewer. Let's go see if we can catch a ride."

13

OUR CRAFT THIS TIME WAS A flat-bottomed barge that nosed in at the base of the Aventine. Before boarding, we waited for two or three passengers to step off. One of them, coincidentally enough, was the high priestess of Ceres.

"Revered Cornelia!" I said, helping her step ashore dry-shod. "Is there to be a sacrifice this morning?"

"No, Aedile, it is just that my house is full of clients from the lower City and is dreadfully crowded. I have decided to move into the guest suite of the temple for now. I trust you enjoyed a restful night." She smiled prettily.

"I cannot praise the accommodations highly enough."

"You seem extraordinarily cheerful on so dismal a day," she said.

"There are days when the service of Senate and People

is even more satisfying than others. Today is one of them," I assured her.

"I suppose it must be so. Please feel free to call upon the hospitality of the temple at any time, Aedile."

"Rest assured I shall, revered lady."

Hermes and I stepped aboard and greeted the other passengers, mostly people who preferred a boat ride to walking long distances to avoid the water. Some were priests who had morning sacrifices to perform.

"Where to, sir?" asked a bargeman. There were two of them poling the clumsy craft in the stern, while another stood in the bow with his pole ready to fend us away from walls and push away floating wreckage.

"The theater," I said, pointing to the hulking building.

"The whole lower part's flooded, sir," the man told me.

"I am a plebeian aedile, and I am assessing flood damage," I said. "Just drop me off there."

There were a number of craft plying the streets and plazas and squares that morning. With the bright sunlight and still air, it might almost have been pleasant, like boating on the Bay of Baiae, had it not been for the appalling stench that permeated everything. If anything, it was even stronger than the night before. Here and there I saw chains of bubbles coming to the surface and bursting, spreading an ever fouler smell. Queasily, I realized that these were the gases of decomposition coming up through the street drains.

The barge made a couple of stops to discharge passengers, then we were nearing the theater. The towering facade, with its triple rows of arches, each bearing a sizable statue, dwarfed everything nearby, looming like a palace of the gods set down among mortals to remind them of their insignificance.

The bargeman steered his craft right into the main entrance, going in perhaps twice the length of the barge before scraping bottom. I wasn't looking forward to stepping into that water, but I told myself that here, so near the river, perhaps it was clean. At least the little tunnel was relatively free of the overpowering stench, so I could always hope.

I took off my sandals and handed them to Hermes to stuff into his satchel, then gave him my toga to roll up. Then I gritted my teeth and stepped off the bow of the barge. The cold water came to somewhat less than midway between my ankles and knees.

"I can't wait for you, Aedile," said the bargeman. "I have these other passengers to deliver. Do you want us to return?"

"I don't know how long I'll be here," I told him. "I'll flag someone down from an upper floor when I need a boat."

Hermes jumped in without raising too much of a splash, and we watched the bargemen work their craft back out of the passageway, using their poles to push themselves away from the walls. There was something decidedly odd about the sight, and it wasn't just the incongruity of a boat in a theater. The symmetrical decoration of the walls revealed that the water was higher on one side than the other.

Hermes had noticed as well. "The water looks like it's tilted."

"It isn't the water," I told him. "The building isn't sitting level. I should have expected it. We know what it's built of. Come along."

We sloshed along through the muddy water, alert for swimming rats, of which I saw a few. Something leapt and splashed in the water.

"What was that?" Hermes asked, startled.

"I don't know, but I hope it was a fish." No sooner did I say these hopeful words than the building emitted a huge, creaking groan that seemed to go on for minutes. "Don't be alarmed," I said to Hermes, thoroughly alarmed myself, "you've been in the Circus just after the sun comes up. The heat makes the wood complain."

We came out into the gigantic half bowl of the auditorium and gazed around. Overhead the sky was brilliantly blue, the tall masts stood as always, and the seats looked ready to receive the audience. Above the stage, the *scaena* towered three stories, all ornamental architecture, gilded pilasters, artificial wreaths draping the balconies, and everything bright with new paint.

Below the seats and the stage, though, was nothing but water. I wondered if I was seeing another trick of the light because this water, instead of being brown like the water outside, was a dark red color, like drying blood.

"Let it not be an omen!" I said, using the old formula Lepidus had spoken a few hours earlier.

"What makes it look like that?" Hermes asked. "Is it the paint they were using?"

"I don't think so." I stepped out into the orchestra where the senators would sit during a performance, stooped and scooped up a handful of mud. It was like damp, red sand, full of larger flakes and irregular chunks, all of the red color.

"What is it?" Hermes asked. He carried my toga rolled

up over one shoulder, his metal-shod stick held at its balance point in one hand.

"It's dissolved brick," I told him. "After sitting here for several years deteriorating, this flood was all it took to turn the foundation of this building into mud." There was another, even longer and louder groan, and the whole theater seemed to shudder.

"Aedile Metellus!" A portly man came waddling from the false architecture of the *scaena* onto the stage area. "How good of you to come!" He walked to one end of the stage and descended the three or four steps to the orchestra without hesitation. "Quite a mess, eh? Well, at last we meet." He sloshed straight up to me and grasped both my hands in his. Hermes stood ready, his eyes scanning the nearby corridors. Scaurus appeared to be about forty, with a heavy thatch of hair gone white already. His cheeks were fat, and they wrinkled deeply as he beamed. Above the cheeks, his eyes were as steely as Caesar's.

"Yes, I have been wishing to speak with you, Aemilius Scaurus," I said. "I—"

"Please, Aedile, we have little time for pleasantries, I fear to say. Come with me for just a moment; I have something to show you." He turned and walked into the corridor through which we had followed the actor-playwright Syrus only the morning before. I followed the fat back before me, one hand on the hilt of my dagger, while Hermes followed after me, walking backward most of the way to keep an eye on the entrance we had just used.

We came out onto the balcony area that overlooked the river, and my stomach took a turn as I saw that we stood on what appeared to be a sinking ship. The river had risen right up to the level of the floor on which we stood. Back on the City side of the theater the water was still; but here, in the most acute curve of the river bend, Father Tiber was turbulent, and the balcony vibrated like a plucked lyre string. It was very nearly as upsetting a sight and situation as I had ever experienced.

Scaurus turned, smiled, and leaned easily upon the railing. "You see, Aedile? I fear that holding your Games here will be out of the question. I am going to have to condemn this building and pull it down, as so many old-fashioned senators have demanded I do anyway. A pity, it was the finest Rome has ever seen. No help for it now, though, don't you agree?"

So he was going to make it a test of nerve, leaning there as if he were standing by the pool in his own house, trusting his patrician aplomb to overwhelm my plebeian effrontery. Well, I had been in tight spots he had never dreamed of. None quite like this one, though.

"Now," he went on, "of course I shall refund the money you paid out to rent the theater for the year, and I agree I really should pay you a little extra for your inconvenience." He pretended to count on his fingers, then looked upward as if he were adding up figures in his head. "Shall we say, ten times what you paid?"

"Good try, Scaurus," I told him, "but we're a little past the bribery stage now. And the statue was a clever move, but it won't work, either."

"Isn't it exquisite?" he said, a salacious note slurring his words, like a man describing his favorite sexual practice. "I have many more of them, and you may have your pick. I agree, art is so much more dignified than mere money."

"Forget it, Scaurus," I said, my words almost drowned out by another groan from the tortured building. I turned slightly and saw that the Sublician Bridge was packed with people now; and upriver, a little farther away, I could see a similar crowd on the Aemilian. Father Tiber was giving them a real spectacle today.

"Don't play the virtuous servant of the people with me, Metellus!" Scaurus snapped, dropping the jovial act. "You *need* what I have to offer! I know what your office is costing you! I will cover all your debts if you will simply cooperate with me. Many of your friends are not too proud to ask the same favor from Pompey or Crassus or Caesar."

"That isn't what I want, Scaurus," I said.

"Then what *do* you want?" he cried, honestly exasperated and mystified.

"I want your head mounted on a pole on the *rostra* next to the head of Valerius Messala Niger. The rest of your gang can be hanged or crucified or given to the bulls and bears for all I care, but a pair of patricians like you and Messala deserve to have your heads exposed in the Forum for the public to ridicule." For a man of his family, such a fate was infinitely worse than any manner of death, no matter how painful.

"For what?" he asked. "For violating some antiquated laws? For violating some building codes? Half the Senate does worse by far!"

"Half the Senate aren't involved in putting up *insulae* that collapse and kill hundreds of people at once."

"I was not responsible for the collapse of the house of Folius!" he said. "The filthy rogue may have cut some corners in building it, but he intended to *live* in it, you idiot! Do you think he'd build a house just so that it would fall down on his head?"

As near as I could read him, he meant it. "Even if that's true, there have been a dozen others in the last three or four years, with more than two thousand dead. I'll tie your name to every one of them and prove Messala's connivance as well."

"Well, then," he said, recovering his equanimity, "that's something for a jury to decide, isn't it? I've had juries find in my favor before; it isn't difficult."

The building gave another groan and lurch. "You're forgetting the murder of Lucilius."

He shrugged. "Senators are murdered all the time. These are rough days, Metellus, you know that. The man was knifed in a whorehouse. He didn't even die brawling with his enemies in the Forum. Anyone who could testify about his death is dead now, anyway."

"You admit you knew about the big slave and the girl, Galatea?"

He shook his head, chuckling. "Metellus, you know perfectly well that I am admitting nothing at all. I know that the swine and his sow died in the collapse of their house. I sold the brute to Folius three or four years ago. The bitch wanted a bodyguard and Antaeus was a wrestler from one of my estates in Bruttium. I think the girl was from their town house in Bovillae. About a month ago the wrestler came to me and begged me to buy him and the girl. I had no use for him so I sent him away, and that is the last I saw of him. So you see, whatever happened was the doing of Lucius Folius."

I was beginning to see what had happened in that *in-*

sula. It was a bit of a disappointment, but I still had plenty of evidence against Scaurus.

"No matter. You and Messala can try to throw all the guilt on Folius, who was nothing more than a middleman for the two of you; but everyone will know the truth whatever verdict the jury returns. At the very least, you'll be expelled from the Senate, stripped of your patrician status, all your wealth forfeit to the treasury, and, best of all, every poor man in Rome will be longing to kill you on sight. Even if you run, you'll end your days in poverty in some wretched barbarian town wishing you'd died when you had the chance."

He sighed. "You are quite sure that we can't come to an agreement then?"

"Forget it," I said, turning. "Best to be out of here anyway. I don't want to die in another of your death-trap buildings."

"I am afraid that will be unavoidable," he said. At that, the men who had been waiting on the balcony above us came scrambling down the steps, knives in their hands.

Well, it wasn't as if I hadn't been expecting it. We stood between two of the stairways and they had us neatly boxed in, two men to each stair. I already had my dagger in one fist and my *caestus* on the other, and I'd decided to kill Scaurus before dealing with the others. I'd shown him all the forbearance I was going to that day.

He hadn't been expecting me to move so quickly, and he let out a squawk, jumping back as I lunged, moving very fast for a bulky man. I would have had him then, but the building gave a sickening lurch and I stumbled sideways, only scoring a long scratch on his chest and shoulder. He twisted away and ran past the two men behind him. They had to pause to let him by, and this gave me a moment to recover my guard.

Hermes was already dealing with the first man on his side. Because the passage was narrow, they could only attack one at a time, a piece of luck we really didn't deserve. The man had a long, straight dagger, and he came in low. Hermes slung my old toga off his shoulder and it unfurled, enwrapping him like the net of a *retiarius*. He stepped in and his stick lanced out like a shortened trident and the muffled man folded around it, the wind blasting from his lungs. Hermes grasped the man around the waist and straightened, sending him flying over his shoulder to hit the river with a great splash. It was done as prettily as any fight you are likely to see in the arena, but I shouldn't have let it distract me.

The first one bulled in like a street brawler, and my punch, instead of smashing his jaw, just ripped his cheek open to the bone. He screeched and wrapped one arm around me, jamming his knife into my rib cage. I didn't bother to block, but instead brought my own dagger up under his chin. It was like getting kicked hard in the side, but the mail shirt I wore beneath my tunic held. His chin, on the other hand, didn't even slow my blade down. It went in to the hilt, piercing his brain, and he was dead before he hit the floor.

Behind me I heard a blade ring against Hermes's stick and knew that the boy was dueling with a more skillful opponent this time; but I had no attention to spare, for Marcus Caninus was almost on top of me and I was still trying to drag my dagger free of his friend, who seemed reluctant to let it go.

I let the hilt go and brought up my bronze-plated knuckles to knock aside Caninus's first short, vicious jab. He had seen what had happened to his accomplice's stab and didn't bother to go for my body. He was trying for my neck as if he wanted to behead me. His weapon was a large *sica* with a blade curved like a boar's tusk, and it looked eminently suitable for the task. With his other hand, he grabbed my right shoulder in a grip like a blacksmith's tongs.

I went for his knife wrist with my free hand while I tried to knee him in the crotch, but he was an old brawler and too canny to fall for that one. He turned and caught my knee with his own thigh. I got him in the ribs with the *caestus,* and he grunted as one or two of them broke; but I lacked the distance and the firm stance for a full-strength punch. I had his wrist in my right hand, but that blade was getting closer all the time. I hit his ribs again, but by now he was pressing me against the railing so hard that the blow had no power. The face above me looked as if it were carved from oak, cruel and unfeeling as a crocodile's.

I heard the unmistakable sound of smashing bone, and I hoped it was Hermes dispatching another opponent rather than the other way around. I certainly wasn't doing well where I was. I stomped on one of Caninus's feet, and this brought a groan of pain; but I was barefoot so the damage wrought was minimal. I knew I could feed him weak body blows all day, and I didn't have all day. I fell back and let my grip weaken. The knife came up for the kill, his elbow rose, and with what strength I had left, I brought my *caestus* up into his armpit, trying for that spot which, if struck correctly, paralyzes the arm, sometimes the whole side, and can even render a man unconscious. Of course, placement is everything. If I missed by an inch, I would die in the next second.

His eyes bugged out, and he screamed. The wide blade fell from his numbed fingers, and I wrestled him to the railing. He was too heavy for me to lift, but a moment later another pair of hands were assisting me and Marcus Caninus made the biggest splash yet. Hermes and I were about to congratulate each other when the floor shuddered and something gave way beneath us.

Horrified, gripping the railing for support, we saw the support work that Manius Florus and his crew had planted there the day before disengage, torn away by the rushing flood, the big timbers shooting to the surface like sporting porpoises. The people lining the Sublician Bridge shouted with astonishment. They didn't get to see a thing like this every day. I wondered whether they had been following the fight, or if we were just a trivial part of the spectacle that was Rome in a disaster.

We almost fell as the whole side of the theater began to sag.

"Let's go!" Hermes shouted. "It's beginning to break up!"

"No," I said. "There's still one to go!" I placed a foot against the face of the man I'd stabbed, grasped my hilt, and yanked the blade free. "Get out of here. I'll attend to this and be with you shortly."

I lurched for the crazily leaning steps and half-dragged myself up by the handrail. The theater seemed to be in continuous motion now. I wondered if Scaurus had gotten clean away, but I doubted it. A fight always seems to last much longer than it really does. The whole little battle had taken no more than a couple of minutes. I came up on the second-floor gallery but saw no one. A flutter of clothing caught my eye, and I saw a foot disappear from the next staircase as someone made it to the gallery above. I followed.

On the third-floor gallery, I caught up with him. Scaurus was leaning against a wall, a hand clasped to his brow, which was bleeding freely. During one of the theater's lurches, he had struck his head on something, slowing him enough for me to catch up to him.

"Marcus Aemilius Scaurus," I called, "come with me to the praetor!" His eyes widened with disbelief at hearing the old formula for arrest.

"Why didn't those fools kill you? There were four of them! And what business have you arresting anyone? We have to be away from here! We can sort out the legalities at another time."

"Sorry, it has to be now," I said, lurching along toward him, my feet trying to slide out from under me on the slanting floorboards. "You leave here only as my prisoner, and now I have yet another capital charge to lay against you, plotting the murder of a Roman official in the course of his—"

At that moment the theater gave its biggest lurch of all, and it began to slide. I dropped my dagger and wrapped my arms around a wooden pillar to keep from falling as there began a sickening, indescribable sense of unnatural motion, accompanied by the greatest cacophony of noises that had ever assaulted my ears. It was a blend of screaming, rending wood, pops, smashes and snaps, grindings, and, above all, a tremendous roar of rushing, hurling water.

The sliding seemed to go on forever; then it metamorphosed into a sort of whirling, rocking, leaping motion, and I saw the opposite bank of the river rising and falling as if in an earthquake. Then I realized what had happened:

The theater wasn't collapsing, it was *floating!*

Before my amazed eyes the scene began to turn and the Sublician Bridge moved slowly into view from my left. It was almost as if I were at the still center of things, and the world was moving around me. The people on the bridge were applauding in openmouthed joy, leaping into the air and cheering, as if this whole spectacle had been put on just for them.

Next to me I saw a pair of hands emerging from a hole in the floor. It was Hermes, dragging himself up the last of the stairs. He clawed his way along the floor and hauled himself up beside me.

"See what you've done!" he cried. "We could have got away!"

"Where is Scaurus?"

"Who cares! In a few seconds, we're going to smash into the bridge; and if we're going to live, we'll need to be better acrobats than those Greek women last night!"

"They were Spanish!" I saw that he was right. Slowly and majestically, the theater of Marcus Aemilius Scaurus was bearing down on the bridge like a ship about to ram. The people on the bridge were waking up to the fact and scrambling off it at both ends. But everyone on the embankments and the nearby rooftops was cheering and shouting as if the Greens were about to score the upset of the year in the Circus.

"Let's get up on the railing," Hermes advised, "but hug this pillar until the last moment."

It seemed like a good idea, so the two of us stood barefoot on the rail while the bridge drew closer. I was sure we were going too fast and we would be hurled off the railing to our messy deaths, but I had forgotten about the breakwaters that protected the bridge supports. They were submerged, and when the underwater part of the theater struck them, its forward motion slowed, and through the soles of my feet I could feel the timbers of the building part like bones splintering in a numbed limb.

A moment before the face of the theater hit the bridge proper I shouted, "Now!" We hurled ourselves off the railing and landed on the bridge, ten feet below us, plowing into a few citizens who were still trying to push their way off the bridge through the panicked crowd. Stars flashed before my face as I was knocked almost unconscious.

But I had no leisure for oblivion, knowing what was coming. I located Hermes and hauled him to his feet. "Come on!" I bawled. "We have to be away from here!" He shook his head for a while, glanced toward the theater building, and wasted no more time. We forced our way through the crowd fleeing the bridge. Hermes drew his stick from beneath his belt and I still had my *caestus* on my left hand. These helped.

When we were atop the bridge abutment, we paused and looked back. The theater was jammed against the bridge, and it was folding up. Between the power of Father Tiber and the immovable massiveness of the old stone bridge, it was like a bird's nest being crushed between the hands of a giant. The siding split and peeled away as huge beams shot out, piled against each other, crowding and flying as the immense building flattened, pieces of it rising, almost toppling over onto the bridge, all of it accompanied by a noise audible for miles.

Then, just as it seemed that the bridge had to give way or the no longer recognizable theater fall on top of it, the shattered hulk began to sag, falling back into the water as floating timbers shot out from beneath the arches on the downriver side. The river was shredding the building and washing it out beneath the bridge.

Slowly, as the wreckage subsided beneath the bridge rail, we walked back out onto the Sublician. By the time I reached the middle, the theater, so vast and imposing just minutes before, was a pile of miscellaneous wood, getting smaller by the second as its pieces washed away. Suddenly, in the whirling eddies below me, surrounded by splintered timbers, a white, terrified face stared up at me. Then I saw Marcus Aemilius Scaurus disappear into Father Tiber as the fragments of his folly closed over his head.

All around me I heard the crowd chanting something over and over, again as if they were watching a chariot race or a fight between champions. I raised my eyes to the eastern bank, which looked like a jawbone with a tooth knocked out of it. Gradually, I understood what the people were shouting: "Ti-ber! Ti-ber! Ti-ber!" Yes, first and forever champion, Father Tiber was victorious once more.

JULIA FOUND ME AT THE TEMPORARY aedile's headquarters I had established on the terrace before the Temple of Jupiter Optimus Maximus. I had been hearing the reports of my fellow officeholders even while Asklepiodes bandaged my many small wounds. Cato had Justus under guard, his searchers had a good lead on Harmodias and expected to bring him in soon, and he had men watching the dwellings of all the rest of the men on Lucilius's list. Not the least of my satisfactions was that I would be clearing a good man's name.

Julia had brought my best toga and a barber to shave me. I had already managed to wash up a bit in a horse trough.

"Why must you do these things, dear?" she asked, as Hermes helped her make me presentable. She threw her arms around me, and I protested.

"You know how our peers frown on public displays of affection," I said.

She smiled. "Yes, old Cato will fall down in an apoplectic fit."

"Well, in that case—" I grabbed her and planted a very sound kiss, to the horrified astonishment of half the Senate.

"The strangest thing," I said, as she tried combing my hair in different styles, "is that with all the crime and fraud and greed these loathsome men perpetrated, it was the love of a slave that brought them all down."

This brought her up short. "What do you mean?"

"Love and despair," I said. "It was the slave who called himself Antaeus. When we found him, he could scarcely speak. He finally said something like, 'Gala—Gala,' and then 'accursed.' He was trying to speak the name of that poor girl, Galatea. He loved her, it seems. One of these men, Scaurus or Messala or Folius or all three, put the two of them up to the murder of Lucilius; and after that she was kept like a prisoner in the house of Folius. She must have tried to run because she was wearing a runaway's collar when we saw her body.

"Antaeus tried to get Scaurus to buy the two of them out of that house, but he wouldn't. The girl became the latest toy in that couple's games. So the slave decided to murder them and disguise it as an *insula* collapse. He drilled holes in the support beams, and plugged them with candles in case someone should come into the cellar before he was finished. Maybe Messala promised the man his freedom if he would get rid of the Folii. They were an embarrassment to everyone. Or maybe he did it on his own. He may have planned to carry the girl off as the building collapsed behind them.

"But that night they let their games go a little too far, and the girl died under their whips. Antaeus decided to finish it. First he broke their necks, which as a wrestler he knew how to do efficiently, on the off chance that they might survive. Then he just kept drilling until it was over. He must have been very surprised to learn that he was alive."

"How horrible!" she said, grimacing. Then, more practically, "Is this going to alienate you from your family?"

"I don't know, and I don't care greatly. Their plan for Pompey will go through with or without Messala. If some of them turn out to be entangled in this, too bad. They've never been reluctant to use me to their advantage; I'm not going to let affection get in my way."

Just then Cato approached and saluted the pair of us. "We have them, Decius Caecilius. We'll bag the lot of them. Valerius Messala will be tough; it will take some time, but we will bring him down, too. Unfortunate that Scaurus won't stand trial, but that was the finest manifestation of divine will in my lifetime."

"Yes," I said, standing as senators began to drift into the temple, "Father Tiber is the one god we see every day. We neglect him at out peril." The setting sun gleamed from a cluster of white buildings out on the Campus Martius. I draped an arm around my wife's shoulders. "Julia, it looks as if it will have to be Pompey's Theater for my plays after all."

Cato scowled first at my unseemly display, and then at the theater out there on Campus Martius. "And that's another thing: That building is an abomination! Pompey stooped to every shameless subterfuge to build a permanent theater in Rome! Oh, I grant you that he built it outside the walls and put a temple on top of it, but still—"

That was Cato for you, a deeply tiresome man. He died splendidly, though. There are times that I wish I had died with him all those years ago in Utica.

These are the events of four days in the year 701 of the City of Rome, during the *Interregnum* of Quintus Caecilius Metellus Pius Scipio Nasica.

GLOSSARY

(Definitions apply to the year 701 of the Republic.)

Arms Like everything else in Roman society, weapons were strictly regulated by class. The straight, double-edged sword and dagger of the legions were classed as "honorable."

The *gladius* was a short, broad, double-edged sword borne by Roman soldiers. It was designed primarily for stabbing.

The *caestus* was a boxing glove, made of leather straps and reinforced by hands, plates, or spikes of bronze. The curved, single-edged sword or knife called a *sica* was "infamous." *Sicas* were used in the arena by Thracian gladiators and were carried by street thugs. One ancient writer says that its curved shape made it convenient to carry sheathed beneath the armpit, showing that gangsters and shoulder holsters go back a long way.

Carrying of arms within the *pomerium* (the ancient city boundary marked out by Romulus) was forbidden, but the law was ignored in troubled times. Slaves were forbidden to carry weapons within the City, but those used as bodyguards could carry staves or clubs. When street fighting or assassinations were common, even senators went heavily armed and even Cicero wore armor beneath his toga from time to time.

Shields were not common in the City except as gladiatorial equipment. The large shield *(scutum)* of the legions was unwieldy in Rome's narrow streets but bodyguards might carry the small shield *(parma)* of the light-armed auxiliary troops. These came in handy when the opposition took to throwing rocks and roof tiles.

Balnea Roman bathhouses were public and were favored meeting places for all classes. Customs differed with time and locale. In some places there were separate bathhouses for men and women. Pompeii had a bathhouse with a dividing wall between the men's and women's sides. At some times women used the baths in the mornings, men in the afternoon. At others, mixed bathing was permitted. The *balnea* of the republican era were far more modest than the tremendous structures of the later Empire, but some imposing facilities were built during the last years of the Republic.

Basilica A meeting place of merchants and for the administration of justice.

Campus Martius A field outside the old city wall, formerly the assembly area and drill field for the army, named after its altar to Mars. It was where the popular assemblies met during the days of the Republic.

Cerialia The annual festival in honor of the goddess Ceres, the Greek Demeter, who was imported to Rome in accordance with an interpretation of the Sybilline Books.

Circus The Roman racecourse and the stadium that enclosed it. The original, and always the largest, was the Circus Maximus. A later, smaller circus, the Circus Flaminius, lay outside the walls on the Campus Martius.

Cloaca Maxima The chief sewer of Rome. Built when Rome had kings, it was at first a mere channel dug to drain the swampy Forum Romanum. Later it was lined with stone, then roofed over with massive stonework. It was a sewer until the nineteenth century and drains the underground springs of the Forum to this day.

Curia The meetinghouse of the Senate, located in the Forum, also applied to a meeting place in general. Hence Curia Hostilia, Curia Pompey, and Curia Julia. By tradition they were prominently located with position to the sky to observe omens.

Cursus Honorum "Course of Honor": The ladder of office ascended by Romans in public life. The *cursus* offices were quaestor, praetor, and consul. Technically, the office of aedile was not part of the *cursus honorum*, but by the late Republic it was futile to stand for praetor without having served as aedile. The other public offices not on the *cursus* were censor and dictator.

Curule A curule office conferred magisterial dignity. Those holding it were privileged to sit in a curule chair—a folding camp chair that became a symbol of Roman officials sitting in judgment.

Equestrian *Eques* (pl. *equites*) literally meant "horseman." In the early days of the military muster soldiers supplied all their own equipment. Every five years the censors made a property assessment of all citizens and each man served according to his ability to pay for arms, equipment, rations, etc. Those above a certain minimum assessment became *equites* because they could afford to supply and feed their own horses and were assigned to the cavalry. By the late Republic, it was purely a property class. Almost all senators were *equites* by property assessment, but the Dictator Sulla made senators a separate class. After his day, the *equites* were the wealthy merchants, moneylenders, and tax farmers of Rome. Collectively, they were an enormously powerful group, equal to the senators in all except prestige and control of foreign policy.

Families and Names Roman citizens usually had three names. The given name (praenomen) was individual, but there were only about eighteen of them: Marcus, Lucius, etc. Certain praenomens were used only in a single family: Appius was used only by the Claudians, Mamercus only by the Aemilians, and so forth. Only males had praenomens. Daughters were given the feminine form of the father's name: Aemilia for Aemilius, Julia for Julius, Valeria for Valerius, etc.

Next came the nomen. This was the name of the clan *(gens)*. All members of a *gens* traced their descent from a common ancestor, whose name they bore: Julius, Furius, Licinius, Junius, Tullius, to name a few. Patrician names always ended in *ius*. Plebeian names often had different endings.

The stirps was a subfamily of a *gens*. The cognomen gave the name of the stirps, i.e., Caius Julius Caesar. Caius of the stirps; Caesar of *gens* Julia.

Then came the name of the family branch (cognomen). This name was frequently anatomical: Naso (nose), Ahenobarbus (bronzebeard), Sulla (splotchy), Niger (dark), Rufus (red), Caesar (curly), and many others. Some families did not use cognomens. Mark Antony was just Marcus Antonius, no cognomen.

Other names were honorifics conferred by the Senate for outstanding service or virtue: Germanicus (conqueror of the Germans), Africanus (conqueror of the Africans), Pius (extraordinary filial piety).

Freed slaves became citizens and took the family name of their master. Thus the vast majority of Romans named, for instance, Cornelius would not be patricians of that name, but the descendants of that family's freed slaves. There was no stigma attached to slave ancestry.

Adoption was frequent among noble families. An adopted son took the name of his adoptive father and added the genetive form of his former nomen. Thus when Caius Julius Caesar adopted his great-nephew Caius Octavius, the latter became Caius Julius Caesar Octavianus.

All these names were used for formal purposes such as official documents and monuments. In practice, nearly every Roman went by a nickname, usually descriptive and rarely complimentary. Usually it was the Latin equivalent of Gimpy, Humpy, Lefty, Squint-Eye, Big Ears, Baldy, or something of the sort. Romans were merciless when it came to physical peculiarities.

Fasces A bundle of rods bound around with an ax projecting from the middle. They symbolized a Roman magistrate's power of corporal and capital punishment and were carried by the lictors who accompanied the curule magistrates, the *Flamen Dialis,* and the proconsuls and propraetors who governed provinces.

First Citizen In Latin: *Princeps.* Originally the most prestigious senator, permitted to speak first on all important issues and set the order of debate. Augustus, the first emperor, usurped the title in perpetuity. Decius detests him so much that he will not use either his name (by the time of the writing it was Caius Julius Caesar) or the honorific Augustus, voted by the toadying Senate. Instead he will refer to him only as the First Citizen. Princeps is the origin of the modern word "prince."

Flamines see priesthoods.

Forum An open meeting and market area. The premier forum was the Forum Romanum, located on the low ground surrounded by the Capitoline, Palatine, and Caelian Hills. It was surrounded by the most important temples and public buildings. Roman citizens spent much of their day there. The courts met outdoors in the Forum when the weather was good. When it was paved and devoted solely to public business, the Forum Romanum's market functions were transferred to the Forum Boarium, the Cattle Market near the Circus Maximus. Small shops and stalls remained along the northern and southern peripheries, however.

Freedman A manumitted slave. Formal emancipation conferred full rights of citizenship except for the right to hold office. Informal emancipation conferred freedom without voting rights. In the second or at least third generation, a freedman's descendants became full citizens.

Games/Ludi Public religious festivals put on by the state. There were a number of long-established *ludi,* the earliest being the Roman Games *(ludi Romani)* in honor of Jupiter Optimus Maximus and held in September. The *ludi Megalenses* were held in April, as were the *ludi Cereri* in honor of Ceres, the grain goddess and the *ludi Floriae* in honor of Flora, the goddess of flowers. The *ludi Apollinares* were celebrated in July. In October were celebrated the *ludi Capitolini* and the final games of the year were the Plebeian Games *(ludi Plebeii)* in November. Games usually ran for several days except for the Capitoline Games, which ran for a single day. Games featured theatrical performances, processions, sacrifices, public banquets, and chariot races. They did not feature gladiatorial combats. The gladiator games, called *munera,* were put on by individuals as funeral rites.

Imperium The ancient power of kings to summon and lead armies, to order and forbid and to inflict corporal and capital punishment. Under the Republic, the *imperium* was divided among the consuls and praetors, but they were subject to appeal and intervention by the tribunes in their civil decisions and were answerable for their acts after leaving office. Only a dictator had unlimited *imperium.*

Insula Literally, "island." A detached house or block of flats let out to poor families.

Interrex When both consuls died in office or were unable to assume office, the Senate appointed an *interrex* (lit. "king-between") to preside over the Senate. He had limited consular powers.

Janitor A slave-doorkeeper, so called for Janus, god of gateways.

Latifundia A large, slave-worked plantation.

Libitinarii Rome's undertakers. Their name comes from Venus Libitina, Venus in her aspect as death-goddess. Like many other Roman customs associated with the underworld, the funeral rites had many Etruscan practices and trappings.

Lictor Bodyguards, usually freedmen, who accompanied magistrates and the *Flamen Dialis,* bearing the *fasces.* They summoned assemblies, attended public sacrifices, and carried out sentences of punishment.

Ludus (pl. ludi) The official public games, races, theatricals, etc. Also training schools for gladiators, although the gladiatorial exhibitions were not *ludi.*

Lupanar (lit. "wolf's den") A Roman brothel. They were quite legal, but regulated by law, under the supervision of the aediles.

Munera Special Games, not part of the official calendar, at which gladiators were exhibited. They were originally funeral games and were always dedicated to the dead.

Necropolis An area of graves and tombs along the road outside the city.

Offices A tribune of the people was a representative of the plebeians with power to introduce laws and to veto actions of the Senate. Only plebeians could hold the office, which carried no *imperium.* Military tribunes were elected from among the young men of senatorial or equestrian rank to be assistants to generals. Usually it was the first step of a man's political career.

A Roman embarked on a political career had to rise through a regular chain of offices. The lowest elective office was quaestor: bookkeeper and paymaster for the Treasury, the Grain Office, and the provincial governors. These men did the scut work of the Empire.

Next were the aediles. They were more or less city managers who saw to the upkeep of public buildings, streets, sewers, markets, and the like. There were two types: the plebeian aediles and the curule aediles. The curule aediles could sit in judgment on civil cases involving markets and currency, while the plebeian aediles could only levy fines. Otherwise, their duties were the same. They also put on the public games. The government allowance for these things was laughably small, so they had to pay for them out of their own pockets. It was a horrendously expensive office but it gained the holder popularity like no other, especially if his games were spectacular. Only a popular aedile could hope for election to higher office.

Third was praetor, an office with real power. Praetors were judges, but they could command armies and after a year in office they could go out to govern provinces, where real wealth could be won, earned, or stolen. In the late Republic, there were eight praetors. Senior was the *praetor urbanus,* who heard civil cases between citizens of Rome. The *praetor peregrinus* (praetor of the foreigners) heard cases involving foreigners. The others presided over criminal courts. After leaving office, the ex-praetors became propraetors and went to govern propraetorian provinces with full *imperium.*

The highest office was consul, supreme office of power during the Roman Republic. Two were elected each year. For one year they fulfilled the political role of royal authority, bringing all other magistrates into the service of the people and the City of Rome. The office carried full *imperium.* On the expiration of his year in office, the ex-consul was usually assigned a district outside Rome to rule as proconsul. As proconsul, he had the same insignia and the same number of lictors. His power was absolute within his province. The most important commands always went to proconsuls.

Censors were elected every five years. It was the capstone to a political career, but it did not carry *imperium* and there was no foreign command afterward. Censors conducted the census, purged the Senate of unworthy members, and doled out the public contracts. They could forbid certain religious practices or luxuries deemed bad for public morals or generally "un-Roman." There were two censors, and each could overrule the other. They were usually elected from among the ex-consuls.

Under the Sullan Constitution, the quaestorship was the minimum requirement for membership in the Senate. The majority of senators had held that office and never held another. Membership in the Senate was for life unless expelled by the censors.

No Roman official could be prosecuted while in office, but he could be after he stepped down. Malfeasance in office was one of the most common court charges.

The most extraordinary office was dictator. In times of emergency, the Senate could instruct the consuls to appoint a dictator, who could wield absolute power for six months. Unlike all other officials, a dictator was unaccountable: He could not be prosecuted for his acts in office. The last true dictator was appointed in the third century B.C. The dictatorships of Sulla and Julius Caesar were unconstitutional.

Palla A cloak, a cover.

Patrician The noble class of Rome.

Plebeian All citizens not of patrician status; the lower classes, also called "plebs."

Pomerium The ancient boundary of Rome, marked out by Romulus with his plow. Though by the late Republic Rome had spread far beyond this boundary, it was retained and nothing could be built upon it. The dead could not be buried within the *pomerium*, nor could citizens bear arms within it.

Pontifical College The pontifexes were a college of priests not of a specific god (see Priesthoods) but whose task was to advise the Senate on matters of religion. The chief of the college was the *Pontifex Maximus,* who ruled on all matters of religious practice and had charge of the calendar. Julius Caesar was elected *Pontifex Maximus*, and Augustus made it an office held permanently by the emperors. The title is currently held by the Pope.

Popular Assemblies There were three: the Centuriate Assembly *(comitia centuriata)* and the two tribal assemblies: *comitia tributa* and *consilium plebis, q.v.*

Praetor of the Foreigners Praetor Peregrinus, the annually elected magistrate in charge of cases involving noncitizens.

Priesthoods In Rome, the priesthoods were offices of state. There were two major classes: *pontifexes* and *flamines. Pontifexes* were members of the highest priestly college of Rome. They had superintendence over all sacred observances, state and private, and over the calendar. Head of their college was the *Pontifex Maximus,* a title held to this day by the Pope. The *flamines* were the high priests of the state gods: the *Flamen Martialis* for Mars, the *Flamen Quirinalis* for the deified Romulus, and, highest of all, the *Flamen Dialis*, high priest of Jupiter. The *Flamen Dialis* celebrated the Ides of each month and could not take part in politics, although he could attend meetings of the Senate, attended by a single lictor. Each had charge of the daily sacrifices, wore distinctive headgear, and was surrounded by many ritual taboos.

Another very ancient priesthood was the *Rex Sacrorum*, "King of Sacrifices." This priest had to be a patrician and had to observe even more taboos than the *Flamen Dialis*. This position was so onerous that it became difficult to find a patrician willing to take it.

Technically, *pontifexes* and *flamines* did not take part in public business except to solemnize oaths and treaties, give the god's stamp of approval to declarations of war, etc. But since they were all senators anyway, the ban had little meaning. Julius Caesar was *Pontifex Maximus* while he was out conquering Gaul, even though the *Pontifex Maximus* wasn't supposed to look upon human blood.

Publicanus One who bid on public contracts.

Puticuli Pits outside of Rome for the burial of the indigent. Those who could afford it had their graves and tombs along the roads outside the city in the Necropolis.

Rostra (sing. rostrum) A monument in the Forum commemorating the sea battle of Antium in 338 B.C., decorated with the rams, *rostra,* of enemy ships. Its base was used as an orator's platform.

Senate Rome's chief deliberative body. It consisted of three hundred to six hundred men, all of whom had won elective office at least once. It was a leading element in the emergence of the Republic, but later suffered degradation at the hands of Sulla.

SPQR Senatus Populusque Romanus The Senate and the People of Rome. The formula embodying the sovereignty of Rome. It was used on official correspondence, documents, and public works.

Tabularium The state archives, located in a sprawling building on the lower slope of the Capitoline Hill, containing centuries' worth of public documents. Private documents, such as wills, were kept in the various temples.

Tarpeian Rock A cliff beneath the Capitol from which traitors were hurled. It was named for the Roman maiden Tarpeia who, according to legend, betrayed the Capitol to the Sabines.

Temple of Ceres The temple of the Asian/Greek goddess of the harvest located on a slope of the Aventine. The aediles had their headquarters in this temple.

Temple of Saturn The state Treasury was located in a crypt beneath this temple. It was also the repository for military standards.

Temple of Vesta Site of the sacred fire tended by the vestal virgins and dedicated to the goddess of the hearth. Documents, especially wills, were deposited there for safekeeping.

Toga The outer robe of the Roman citizen. It was white for the upper class, darker for the poor and for people in mourning. The *toga praetexta,* bordered with a purple stripe, was worn by curule magistrates, by state priests when performing their functions, and by boys prior to manhood. The *toga picta,* purple and embroidered with golden stars, was worn by a general when celebrating a triumph, also by a magistrate when giving public games.

Trans-Tiber A newer district on the left or western bank of the Tiber. It lay beyond the old city walls.

Tribunate The period of office of a tribune of the people.

Triclinium A dining room.

Triumph A ceremony in which a victorious general was rendered semi-divine honors for a day. It began with a magnificent procession displaying the loot and captives of the campaign and culminated with a banquet for the Senate in the Temple of Jupiter. Every general wanted to triumph and it was a tremendous boost for a political career.

Triumvir (lit. "one of three men") A member of a triumvirate: a board of three men, most famously the governing junta consisting of Octavian (later Augustus), Mark Antony, and Lepidus.

Virgo Maxima The head of the College of Vestals and the most revered and prestigious woman in Rome.